THE FINAL YEN

A Novel

R. SEBASTIAN BENNETT

MILFORD
HOUSE

Milford House Press

Mechanicsburg, Pennsylvania

MILFORD HOUSE
an imprint of Sunbury Press, Inc.
Mechanicsburg, PA USA

FIRST MILFORD HOUSE PRESS EDITION: September 2021

Set in Garamond. Interior design by Chris Fenwick | Cover by **Chris Fenwick** | Edited by Chris Fenwick.

Publisher's Cataloging-in-Publication Data
Names: Bennett, R. Sebastian, author.
Title: The Final Yen / R. Sebastian Bennett.
Description: Revised trade paperback edition. | Mechanicsburg, Pennsylvania: Milford House Press, 2021.
Summary: It is 1989, the height of Japanese economic power, and a young American businessman in Tokyo is facing a prison sentence for a crime he did not commit.
Identifiers: ISBN 978-1-62006-870-0 (softcover).
Subjects: BISAC: FICTION / Political | FICTION / World Literature / Japan | FICTION / Historical

Continue the Enlightenment!

ACKNOWLEDGMENTS

I would like to thank Fabian Skibinski, Edward Roybal, James Hill, and Tim Siemers for their comments on the manuscript; Chris Fenwick and Lawrence Knorr at Sunbury Press, and Literary Agent Maryann Karinch of The Rudy Agency for all of their assistance; and thank my parents—for their endless support of all things creative.

Selections from this manuscript have been published, in a slightly different form, in the following magazines: "Grace Under Pressure" in *The Tulane Review*, "Honorable Crab" in *Indiana Review*, "Jewel Beetle" (excerpts) in *The Connecticut Review* and *The Bombay Review* (India), "N-10" in *The Heartland Review*, "Persistence" in *The Galway Review* (Ireland) and *Art Mag*, "Salaryman" in *Pennsylvania Literary Journal*, "Sprats" in *The Brooklyn Review*, "The Cherry Tree" in *The Nassau Review*, "Entrance to Paradise" in *The Worcester Review*, and "Thoughts from the Heart" (excerpt) in *The Southwestern Review*.

Furuike ya
kawazu tobikomu
mizu no oto

The old pond
A frog jumps in—
Water sounds

BASHŌ

CONTENTS

I. THE WATER TRADE

TOKYO, JAPAN 1989

With a screech of brakes, the taxi swerved to the side of the street and stopped. I stepped off the curb and reached to open the back door, but it swung open automatically with a hydraulic hiss. After a year in Tokyo, I still hadn't gotten used to those taxi doors. Once I had almost broken a door when I tried to yank it shut before the metal control arm at the top slid into a narrow black cylinder. This time, I pulled back my hand and pretended I was just buttoning the cuff of my shirt. Mr. Ono and Mr. Ishikawa probably wouldn't notice my mistake anyway. They were too drunk.

Ishikawa, stout for a Japanese, grunted as he slid into the taxi. Then Ono waited for me to get in. I hated sitting in the middle of the back seat. I was easily car sick and claustrophobic—but I didn't say anything. Not tonight.

The three of us had just spent the last hour gorging in Ono's *Restaurant Karina*. We ate a sizzling hot plate of *shabu shabu*, sautéed meat and seafood (I could still feel my burnt tongue), and we drank three bottles of a special brackish wine which seemed to be Ono's favorite, at least for his guests. There was no charge for all of this. We were celebrating the year-long, full-color advertising contract with my company that Ono had signed earlier in the day. Ishikawa wasn't involved in the contract. He was just a friend of Ono's who happened to be at the restaurant and was invited out for the celebration. Of course, he accepted, with a pudgy smile of thanks.

"*Shinjuku ni-chome.*" Ono waved his hand like a field general and directed the driver toward the *Sakari Ba,* the pleasure quarter. I knew that we were going to a hostess club, but I wasn't sure which one. The Shinjuku district had hundreds of them, maybe thousands, lining the streets or secluded in tall buildings and announced by an aged seductress. Ono surely knew where to go. He had promised to take us only to the clubs with the prettiest girls.

I pressed my feet against the floor to steady myself as the taxi stopped abruptly next to a one-story building. Out front stood a bright neon sign, at least eight feet high, with a picture of a naked blonde girl surrounded by colored stars. Glowing pink neon tubes ran in and out of her body.

I followed Ono down a wooden staircase and into a bar below street level. It was dimly lit. Small couches and glass tables were set up along the walls. Red-faced Japanese businessmen and scantily-clad Asian hostesses sat together like nesting lovebirds. Some of the men had draped their arms around the girls and weren't at all shy about where to rest their hands. Soft music played over the sound system, just slightly louder than the clink of glasses and whinnies of laughter. This was the *mizu shobai,* the water trade, where drinks flowed freely. I was the only foreigner in the club.

One of the girls trotted over to us. "Ah, Ono-san! How are you?" *"Genki! Genki!"* Ono smiled.

Six other girls flocked over and waited patiently while Ono selected the two best-looking girls and shooed the others away, making clucking noises like a farmer choosing hens. He didn't want to pay for them all.

A waitress came to the table. In a firm voice to show how confident I was—a man used to nightly hostess bars—I ordered Scotch. The waitress must have known Ono's order and somehow determined Ishikawa's, because they weren't asked. But all Japanese businessmen drank Scotch, just like they all used chopsticks to eat their sticky rice. Ono leaned forward. "It is good business to drink together," he said.

"Hai." Ishikawa patted his stomach.

I nodded and made an appropriate grunt.

"We are all Tokyo businessmen, and we need to drink." Ono's words were a little slurred, but I understood his real point. He was trying to minimize our differences, to group us all together in a set like dominoes. In a way, it was touching.

Ono hiccupped and kept talking. "We are typical Japanese businessmen, Ishikawa-san and I." He waved his fingers to show the connection. "Are you typical American?"

I answered honestly. "No, not really. I have some different—"

Ono clenched his teeth. He didn't like this answer.

"However, in certain ways, I <u>am</u> a typical American." I gave a firm-jawed, earnest look.

Ono nodded approvingly.

With their heads held high like runway models, more girls filed past our table. Ono selected an additional girl, soft and glowing in an emerald green dress. She slid in next to me, and I could feel the heat of her body. I could smell her clean, musky scent.

"Good evening," she said, with long-lashed, deer-eyed blinks. "My name is Hana." Only a little accent. She had probably practiced the phrase thousands of times in front of a mirror. "*Hana*" meant "flower," but I hadn't heard the word used as a first name before. Was it her real name?

I glanced at the other women. Ono had his arm around his hostess in a happy squeeze. Ishikawa's girl was whispering in his ear. I was glad that my hostess, Hana, with her pretty almond-shaped eyes and smooth skin, her luscious thighs, and tight dress, was the best-looking of the three. At least I thought so. But Western views of beauty were not always the same as those of the Japanese. Maybe Ono knew what I would like in a woman and had chosen Hana especially for me.

The waitress tip-toed back to our table and gently set down our drinks. There was a pitcher of water, a gold bucket of ice, a bottle of *Suntory Olde* Japanese whiskey, and three smoked glasses which sat in circular indentations on a tray, surrounded by etchings of birds and swords.

Hana grasped a pair of tongs and reached to take some ice cubes out of the bucket. Leaning over so her body was draped across me, she placed a few ice cubes into my glass. Then, resting a tiny beautifully manicured hand on my knee for balance, she poured in some Scotch. When she reached for the water, I shook my head. "Straight," I said.

Obediently, she set the water pitcher back down on the table.

I guzzled down the drink.

Her eyes widened. "You are a strong man," she said, rubbing my leg. She slid closer to me. Her body was so pliant and fiery that I shivered.

"Maybe," I said. But I knew that Japanese Scotch was pretty mild to begin with and had a syrupy taste which only got worse when you watered it down. Hana poured more whiskey into my glass. Her massaging hand seemed to have moved slightly further up my thigh.

"You must be very important to come here with Ono-san," she continued.

"Does he come here often?"

Hana smiled knowingly. "Sometimes . . ." She lifted my glass and patted the circle of condensation beneath it with a napkin. "You are very intelligent," she said, without changing her expression. But so far, I had said barely anything to the girl. She had no way of knowing if I was intelligent or not. Perhaps she had made a telepathic assessment.

Ono turned to me, but I couldn't see his eyes. His hair was much longer than the usual Japanese style, and it fell over his forehead. "Do you like Hana-san?" he asked.

"Yes."

"Which part of her do you like?" Ono had a lewd grin.

I gave a good accommodating laugh. Ishikawa wasn't talking, but he looked happy as a well-fed baby, content and sleepy after suckling. His left hand had ventured under his hostess' bottom. She squirmed back and forth in her seat. Then she lit his cigarette.

Another waitress came over, carrying a tray with a tall glass of beer and a small white sake cup beside it. She placed the glass on the table, lay two chopsticks in parallel across the top, and gently positioned the sake cup balanced on the chopsticks. Ono began to count loudly, "ICHI, NI, SAN." Then he slammed his fist on the table and shouted, "**SAKE BOMB**!" The sake cup fell into the beer—which splashed onto both Ono and the waitress. She clapped her hands and smiled widely. Then she dashed away.

Ono signaled to the bartender and urgently ordered more whiskey, even though our bottle was still half full. That was okay. He would be paying.

Hana massaged my lap. "You are very nice looking. Very strong," she whispered. I could feel her warm breath in my ear. "And you are handsome, like *Tah-mu Cruisu* in *Toppu Gun*."

"Yeah," I said, a little embarrassed. The hostesses were paid to entertain men and pour their drinks. To stroke their egos and make them feel clever and virile. As customers, we were literally *paying for compliments*. Or, more precisely, Ono was paying for compliments for the three of us. It was getting tedious. I wondered if there was a back room for more intimate relations with the hostesses. I decided to check. "Where is the restroom?" I asked, and Hana pointed.

In the back of the lounge area, there was a hall and closet, but no place for *special* relations with the girls, at least none that I could find. I did locate the bathroom, though. It stank of urine, and the floor was suspiciously wet. Soon after I entered, the door banged open, and a putty-faced Japanese man holding his stomach staggered in. He rushed past me into the toilet stall, let out a loud groan and a mule's belch, and released a stream of vomit. It smelled very bad. I held my breath and exited quickly.

In the rear corner of the lounge, a door was half-open, and a pale light fought its way out. I could see into a tiny office space where a balding Japanese man was counting out stacks of yen and sorting bills. His hair was permed into curls. He caught my gaze and glowered at me. He was almost certainly *yakuza*, a gangster type known to control the hostess bars and the *mizu shobai*. Even though I was in the company of Japanese, the management would surely prefer that no foreigners—no *gai-jin*—were there at all.

Back at the table, Hana smiled at me and touched my shoulder. "I am sorry. I must go to another table now," she said. "I will come back." With a little moan, trailing one hand behind her, she slid off the couch.

I felt a moment of loss, but that was silly. I knew the system. Hostesses were rotated among the tables at regular intervals, like carpet samples at an interior decorating luncheon. Customers were charged both by the time each girl spent at their table and by the number of different girls who visited them. Each girl who sat down could easily add 10,000 yen, about eighty dollars, to the bill. The evening might run over a thousand bucks if we stayed for a while and kept ordering drinks.

Ono waved his hand like a sheik with a thousand women in his harem. "Don't worry," he said. "I will get you a better girl." Then he shouted something at the waitress and turned back to his own hostess, who had a pretty enough face and a perfect figure but wore so much white base make-up that she seemed almost to be made of wood.

Smiling like a mischievous little boy, Ono touched his girl's neck in two-fingered prod. Then he let his hand slide down to her chest. "I am all hot," he teased and stroked back the girl's hair, exposing her ear to make sure she heard. "Do you like *number six* relations?" Sex was supposed to give such a wonderful feeling that it took, not five, but six senses to appreciate.

The girl wrinkled her nose and mouth in feigned disgust. "*Iyarashii,*" she said. Then she slapped him ever-so-lightly on the arm and made a soft grumbling noise. She didn't mean it. She was just teasing back in the childish way so characteristic of Japanese girls.

Another hostess slipped in beside me. She wasn't as pretty as Hana but had more of a buxom, wanton look. Her perfume was stronger too. Then Hana came back and had to sit on the edge of the couch because there wasn't much room. This position gave her ample opportunity to display her legs.

"Ah, Hana-san is back," said Ono. "She likes ice. It is cold when she is hot." He bit the tip of his tongue softly, insinuatingly. Hana gave a faint dimple of a smile. Ono stared at me. "Would you like to play the ice with Hana-san, where she is hot?"

I wasn't sure—was Ono just toying with words? Suggesting a possible rendezvous with Hana? I dodged the question, *"Toki-doki sore wa ii deshoo . . ."* Sometimes that's good . . .

Ono leaned back in his chair and seemed satisfied. Perhaps he had been testing my eagerness, pushing me to admit my lust, which could then be fulfilled or denied as he pleased. But I had parried the question. Maybe this also was what Ono had been testing, to see just how adroit I was at such games.

Ono glanced at his watch. "It is time to go," he said urgently. "Are you ready to drink more?"

Again, I had the feeling I was being tested. This time, to see if I was a man of character who would stick by his friends in drinking—to see if I was a worthy business partner. I held up my glass. *"Ippai yarimashoo!"* I said. "Let's do a full glass!"

"Hai! Hai!" Yes! affirmed Ishikawa, sobering his face to show fortitude. This was *hashigonomi,* ladder-drinking. We would move from bar to bar, jumping from rung to rung.

Ono held out his glass for a toast. *"Kampai!"* A dazed smile was frozen on his face.

"Ono-san, are you drunk?" I asked.

Ono shook his head rapidly as if the possibility were nonexistent. "No, I do never get drunk," he said. But his face was very red, and his eyes were glazed. This was the way he had looked at all of our business meetings, so maybe he was telling the truth. Suddenly, he peered at me without blinking. "Are you ready for sex?" he asked.

"Ikimashoo! Let's go!" said Ishikawa, drooling a little.

"*Hai.*" I nodded. I was ready—a bit tipsy but not inebriated. I hadn't drunk as much as Ono and probably weighed seventy pounds more.

We walked toward the door. Just as I had expected, Ono was a frequent customer. No money changed hands, no bill was presented, and nothing was signed. Everything was very discreet. The evening would simply be put on Ono's tab.

Just then—heels clicking, dress shimmering—Hana ran after us. "Excuse me!" She touched my shoulder and handed me a purple card. "I want you to see me," she said in her falsetto voice. For a moment, I gazed into her eyes. Then she trotted away.

On the card, Hana had written her name next to the address of the club. What did she mean? Was she looking for a foreign man? I had to remind myself that bar girls liked clients to ask for them by name. Then they were paid more. I slipped the card into my pocket. Falling for a bar hostess was a sucker's game.

I climbed up the stairs and walked into the street. The fresh air felt good on my face. I took a deep breath. Ono was still inside the bar. He was probably giving the girls one last fondle. A taxi drove up and darted next to me. The driver turned toward me, frowned when he realized that I was a foreigner, and sped off. I had learned to hide my Western features, to keep my face turned away from the street when I actually wanted to hail a taxi. By the time I got in the cab, it would be too late for the driver to refuse. Well, in two more weeks, I would be back in California, away from all this. I would just try and enjoy my final days in Tokyo.

The bar door slammed shut. I turned around to see Ono on the sidewalk, swaying on unsteady legs as he walked. His head and torso gyrated in opposite directions. He grinned, rubbed his cheek, stuck out his tongue—and lost his balance, knocking over the big neon sign at the top of the stairs. It fell over and crashed down onto the sidewalk with a huge spray of sparks and an electric hiss.

Ono grunted and laughed. Wisps of smoke and an acrid smell of burnt wiring rose from the broken sign. Shards of glass and broken neon tubes covered the sidewalk. A small fire erupted on the pavement where a red-hot electrical connection had come into contact with some paper trash. Quickly, I jogged over and stomped out the flame.

Ono just stood there with a dazed grin on his face. Then the balding *yakuza* manager stalked up the stairs. He saw the shattered sign, stood dead still for a moment, glared at me, and immediately began to shout. "**YOU BROKE IT! YOU BROKE SIGN!**"

It was interesting how automatically I was accused. The manager could not have seen who caused the damage. He was underground in his office, and there were no windows. But immediately, the *gai-*

jin was blamed.

"It wasn't me," I said. "I was out in the street, and I heard it fall. Then I turned around." Of course, I knew for a fact that Ono had broken the sign. But I wasn't going to implicate a friend.

Ono was pointing and giggling about the sign like a little boy watching cartoons. Then he started walking away. I followed him, but the manager grabbed my shoulder. I shrugged off his arm and kept walking. The manager was quick—his other hand reached around and grasped my tie. I could smell his garlic breath and see spots of scalp oil on his forehead. I tugged his hand off my tie, but then he tried to get me in a choke-hold.

"I didn't do it," I said in English and shoved away both the guy's arms. "So piss off!"

"*Peesu!*" Ono imitated with a laugh. He started running, and I jogged to catch up to him.

The manager chased us. We ran faster, down a back alley. My oxfords were too big, and they were clumsy running shoes. I had to lift my knees high and flex my toes upward so the shoes wouldn't flap off. Ono turned and scampered like a mouse up a narrow stone stairway toward what looked like a graveyard. Then he disappeared into a grove of trees. I didn't have time to follow. I glanced back and saw the manager's bald head. I heard his breathing. Shit—he was chasing me, not Ono!

I didn't know these streets, but a side alley looked like a good bet. It was a bad choice. After a short incline, the alley ended at a concrete wall. I looked back again and saw an arm reach out to grab me. Then I tripped and fell. The asphalt dug into my knee, ripping away flesh like a power sander.

The manager was on me in a second, grunting and cursing. But I didn't resist. He might have a knife, or his henchman could come with meat cleavers and pistols . . . The skinny part of my tie was looped around my arm and made into a knot. This special tie-up seemed to be based on the assumption that if I moved my arm to escape, the tie would tighten around my neck, and I would choke myself—which was absurd—because with my other arm, I could pull the tie over my head and off of my shirt entirely. Besides, the knot was so loose that I could easily slip my hand out. But I pretended to be captured. That was the safest thing. *Yakuza* were known to get violent, especially in a dark alley when no one was looking.

I stood up and allowed myself to be led by the end of my tie, like a dog on a leash. I expected to see more *yakuza* come around the corner any second. But when we got to the main street, and I saw no henchmen, I jerked my hand free and loosened the tie around my neck. The manager twitched and hopped as if he expected me to try something aggressive. But I just kept walking. Then I yanked my tie out of his hand. I made fists and held up my arms to show that I could easily fight if I wanted to. In a funny little prance, skipping and circling his arms, the manager got ready to defend himself. But I didn't hit him. "This is stupid," I said, shaking my head. "I didn't break the sign."

"Police station for you!" said the manager. His chin quivered. Then he grabbed back the tie.

I resisted the temptation to hit the man in the face. "You are stupid," I said. "We will go to the police station together. We will talk about *your* crimes."

A small crowd had formed, and a wide-eyed teenaged Japanese boy seemed to be looking sympathetically at me. I tried to get the boy's moral support. Pointing a finger at the manager, I said confidentially, "*Kare wa baca,*" He is stupid. The *yakuza*'s ears reddened. I felt a little better, but it didn't change the situation much. Where the hell was Ono? He probably just ran off. And I hadn't even seen Ishikawa leave the bar. Some celebration this evening had turned out to be. My leg stung and throbbed, and I could feel blood running down my calf. I wondered how deep the gash was. Was there dirt in it? Would it get infected? My torn pants covered the wound. Out of pride, I wouldn't touch it. I didn't want people to see how bad it was. I didn't want them to laugh. The wool of my trousers clung to my leg, and a large bloodstain had formed at the knee. Good thing it was a thrift-shop suit.

I heard the ululating sound of a siren getting closer, and soon a small black and white Tokyo police car pulled up alongside us, lights flashing and whirling. I decided to cooperate completely with the officers. Fury and belligerence got you nowhere in Japan. "Good evening," I said and greeted the officers with a little bow.

The situation must have already been explained to the police over the phone because I was asked no questions, just put immediately in the back seat of the police car—perhaps this was standard procedure for *gai-jin*. I wasn't shoved, just guided, as if my criminality was so obvious that I wouldn't dare protest. As we drove off, I tried to talk to the officers, but they ignored me like a child being administered *the silent treatment.* I gave up and tied my handkerchief around my knee so I wouldn't bleed all over their police car. In my jacket pocket, I found a comb and slicked back my hair. The teeth of the comb were sharp, like tiny blades. I slipped the comb away before the cops saw. I might need something sharp.

We stopped next to a two-story gray building. In front, a round-tummied man was holding a six-foot wooden staff. He stood alert like a troll guarding a bridge. What the hell kind of police equipment was that stick? Where were we? But then I saw a sign near the entrance: **SHINJUKU POLICE STATION**. It was hardly reassuring.

The man with the staff approached our police car, opened the back door, and escorted me through the main entrance to a smaller room upstairs. Then he held out his hand. *"Passuporto!"* he demanded.

I stared at the man's brownish palm, at the deep folds of skin at the base of his fingers. All foreigners were supposed to carry passports or alien identification with them, but losing the passport was said to be much more of a hassle than getting caught without it. "It is at home," I said, gazing into the beady eyes of the policeman. "I have a business card, though." I took one out of my wallet.

Without blinking, the policeman scrutinized the card, then turned it over. It was printed in English on one side and Japanese on the other, customary for foreigners doing business in two languages. He looked at the company emblem and read it out loud. "Japan Publishing Corporation." His tone softened immediately. "A Japanese company . . ."

"Hai," I affirmed and pointed to the company insignia pin on my lapel. I clasped my hands together in front of me in an attempt to show how cooperative I intended to be, how innocent I was, and how much I ought to be released. I tried not to think about the statistic that in Japan, 99% of *all* accused individuals were eventually found guilty.

The officer took my arm and led me into a tiny side room with a table and two chairs. "You must wait here," he said and closed the door. The stuffy air surrounded me. The room had no ventilation at all. I sat down and glanced at my watch. 1:12 a.m. The crystal had been scraped when I fell, but the watch was still working. Good old Timex! Even took a *Japanese* licking and kept on ticking! I could write a letter to the company and be on TV, like the guy in the commercials whose watch fell into the cement and still worked. I could say that I was chased by *yakuza* and assaulted, but the watch didn't break.

2:31 A.M.

My back ached as if I'd been sleeping with a steel pole lodged right under my shoulders. Needles of pain pierced my spine. I had a searing headache, and my stomach hurt. But I hadn't done anything wrong! I didn't commit any crime! What could I do to make the police believe this? I remembered a half-eaten candy bar on the table near my bed at the boarding house. That would taste good now, if it wasn't swarming with ants—hard-bodied, Japanese fire ants.

The door clicked opened and in walked a uniformed officer, smelling of ramen noodles. *"PASSUPORTO!"* he demanded. It was ridiculous that the other cop hadn't told him I didn't have it. Or maybe this guy was the master of extracting missing passports from prisoners. **'SHOW!"** He stared at me with the same impenetrable glare as the first investigator. This must be their official police glare. They could use it to kill dogs.

I handed the officer another business card instead, and he turned and left without another word. My leg was throbbing again, a beating singe. If the pain had a sound, it would be *"wuhm, wuhm, wuhm, wuhm."* I sucked in my stomach and flexed my abdominal muscles in the same rhythm as the throbs. I felt my pulse. Were the throbs in time with my heartbeat? I put a hand on my left chest and tried to determine this.

The door opened again, and a fat Japanese man with cloudy glasses walked in, holding a photocopy of my business card. *"Passuporto?"* he asked.

I couldn't help laughing, then forced myself to stop. "It is at home," I said.

The man nodded calmly. He sat down at the table in front of me. Then, with the patience of a tired old investigator, he asked many questions. Hours of questions—about the incident and the circumstantial details. I explained the sequence of events truthfully, except that I didn't tell him I saw Ono knock over the sign. I said that I was out in the street and heard the sign fall; I turned around, saw the fire, ran back to stomp it out, then saw Ono *near* it. I said I also saw other people in the street. All of this was true.

The investigator sat back and lit a cigarette. He studied my business card, glancing up at me a few times. I hoped he was considering the possibility that I had not told the full story, since I didn't want to point a finger at a friend—some friend to leave me alone in the street. Still, since prep school, "Never *narc* on a friend" was the golden rule.

This rule presumed friends were equally loyal to each other. And it was not at all clear this was true of Ono. But even if I had told the police he knocked over the sign, I had no guarantee of being believed. In fact, the police might think my incrimination of Ono was an attempt to pass the blame and cover my own guilt . . . There were no solutions.

In another chain of questions, these read from a well-thumbed book, the investigator inquired about my birthplace, vision, height, weight, shoe size, and salary. Then he waddled out to make more photocopies of my business card. This time he left the door ajar.

I could see the balding *yakuza* bar manager sitting at a table in the booking room. He was pounding his fist on the arm of his chair. The back of his head jerked with every blow as if his arm and head were connected with a string like a marionette. He was shouting something, garbled phrases that I couldn't understand at first. Yakuza were supposed to have their own special jargon. But then the words became clearer: I broke the sign. I must pay, or he would *make* me pay. The yakuza overlooked the possibility—the actuality—that I had very little money.

In many ways, reality seemed different for the Japanese. It wasn't a rational organization of facts. It was more how things were *supposed* to be. How they fit into a comfortable framework. It had been impossible for the manager to accept that a meek and polite Japanese restaurant owner, one of his regular customers, would ever cause such damage to the sign. It had to be the American *vandal*—from the land where drivers on freeways shot each other for fun; where politicians were drug addicts and evangelists were pimps; where citizens flaunted the laws and ran amok.

The fat investigator came back into the room with two more copies of my business card. As he sat down, the uniformed officer returned. With an alarmed glance at the papers on the table, the officer announced that he'd better make duplicate copies of the investigator's photocopies of my business card, despite the fact that I had already given both of them actual cards to begin with.

I stifled a smile, took out another business card, and handed it to the officer before he left. At this, I thought I saw the investigator suppress his own smile. He took a long meditative puff on the cigarette, closing his eyes for a moment. Then, blowing smoke out through his nose and mouth at once like a plump drowsy old dragon, he asked, "Why did you come to Japan?"

I also closed my eyes, which burned from second-hand smoke poison in the tiny room. I knew that conversations in Japanese allowed many more pauses than in English, pauses where the parties could feel each other out intuitively, take time to consider their positions, or choose their words carefully. Then I said what I knew the man deep down wanted to hear. "The Japanese culture is very unique. I was very interested in Japan."

The investigator grunted and nodded at the profundity of the statement. He reached for an ashtray and tapped the lit tip of the cigarette into it. The cigarette stopped glowing. Then the investigator left the room, shutting the door. This time, I heard a key set the lock in place.

Twenty years of prison flashed before my eyes . . .

II. JEWEL BEETLE

ONE YEAR EARLIER

The power indicator glowed like a tiny red planet. The plastic keys felt smooth and familiar. I sat with my legs stretched over the futon and played my battery-powered electronic piano. It was a Casio, made in Japan. At first, the New Wave tunes sounded out of place in the Asian room. But then the music blended in—flowing up the walls, encircling the dragon tapestry in the *tokonoma* alcove, and drifting out the wooden hatch window. I was playing chord sequences, composing a new song, but I only had the first part of a melody so far. It was a song about the founder of Japan:

> I think I can appreciate
> Jimmu Tenno's grace
> When I'm under pressure
> And when I'm saving face

I played this part again. The tune needed a bridge. Since I hadn't made one up yet, I just improvised and gazed at the tapestry. The dragon's eyes had some humor in them—sloped brows, puny irises cocked to one side. And the dragon's mouth had full red lips. Between the fangs, a puffy tongue lolled suggestively to the side.

I had left the door to the room half-open, so the music wafted through the halls. The melodies would bless Sanjo Ryokan, a boarding house that had housed travelers for hundreds of years. Perhaps other musicians had been here centuries ago, playing traditional Japanese flutes and drums, strumming on *Biwa*. Only the building itself would hear my music tonight—because no one else was home at Sanjo. It was Sunday night, and all the other travelers were out. They must have had a lot of extra money to go to the expensive discos where beers were fifteen dollars apiece. I had almost no money. I played a series of arpeggios in solemn, minor chords. I had only one hope—a notice for an Advertising Representative was posted in the

Japan Times, the English-language newspaper in Tokyo. On Friday, I'd had a "phone interview" and was told I got the job. Training would start Monday. I wasn't sure what to expect, but I would give it my best shot. I sang a new stanza of my song:

> Is it pure integrity
> Or regimented mold?
> React with sensitivity
> It's written in the code

Then I set my alarm, so I would have plenty of time to get to the Advertising Training, first thing in the morning.

"Japanese business ees very different," said Hamaguchi, president of Japan Publishing Company. He was a portly man in a light green double-breasted sport coat. He spoke in a low voice, as stern as a priest. "Japanese system ees very relaxing, but you must work hard. You must work *seexty* seconds of every minute."

I sat in Hamaguchi's office with the other new sales staff, and we nodded enthusiastically.

"I promise you all unlimited salary," Hamaguchi continued, spreading his hands wide as if he were offering the pearls of heaven. "You will each determine your salary with your sales quota." He paused to let this sink in. "You must learn sales technique. I will explain eet."

Hamaguchi took off his jacket, revealing a white dress shirt with a pointed collar and epaulets, which seemed unusual for a Japanese. But I didn't have time to ponder this because he picked up a copy of Tokyo Time magazine and held it up in front of each one of us so that we could get a good look. We would be selling advertisements in this magazine. "I weel teach you about our business," said Hamaguchi, and cleared his throat. "First, we must find good sales prospect." He ran his thick fingers down a page of the magazine. "Companies which already advertise are the best possibility."

"I brought a Tokyo English Yellow Pages, so I can look for prospects." I took the phonebook out of my briefcase and flipped through the pages. The display ads flashed and disappeared.

Hamaguchi ignored me. He slurped at a cup of tea and wiped his mouth with his fingers. "Now, we are all part of the company. And I am company president. What is best for the company is best for all of us. And we have company pin, and company clip for tie." He bent down to burrow into the bottom drawer of his desk and finally brought out two white boxes. He opened the boxes and doled out tie pins one at a time. They had small brass insignias with the English initials *J.P.C.,* for Japan Publishing Corporation, in blue letters. "We will all wear our company pins. Japanese are very impressed when they see foreigners with Japanese-style pins."

He patted the pin on his own jacket. "I start this company many years ago. In my head, I had idea. I was working for a newspaper, *Japan Economic News,* but I had feeling in my heart. I wanted big company. I wanted success. It was destiny. So now it is your destiny, too."

"And *meishi!* Business cards for each salesman . . ." From another drawer, with less burrowing this time, Hamaguchi took out four boxes and handed one to each of us. "In Japan, you must have *meishi* to be professional."

I opened my box, pulled out a card, and read my name in *katakana,* with the first and family names reversed. Below was my title: "Advertising Director." I felt a quiver of excitement then. The other new employees seemed equally pleased.

The cards were printed in English on one side and Japanese on the other. In the lower left corner of each card was a red and black *J.P.C.* symbol, a stick-figured body with a smiling round face gazing at a magazine—very un-Japanese. But it didn't matter. I had a good job now, a real Tokyo business job.

Hamaguchi spread his arms wide. "In Japan, if you are a foreigner, automatically you will be treated like V.I.P. person. If you speak English, Japanese businessmen will meet you. You have *very* high social rank." He held a hand above his head for emphasis. "I wish all of you good luck." He clenched his fists like a boxing coach. "But you must work hard. You must push beeg for sales. Then you will be a success."

"Here is what you must say. . ." Hamaguchi dictated to us the exact words we were to use when we telephoned a prospect company. He made each of us write out a script, the "sales pitch." Then he showed us to our desks.

I sat down and scanned through my phone book. On page eleven was a full-color advertisement for Sako Department Store with a photo of three happy foreigners buying a kimono from a bowing Japanese salesgirl. I dialed the number and read my lines directly from the sales script: "Good Afternoon. This is Japan Publishing Company—"

"Moshi moshi??" asked the telephone girl.

"Yes, I am calling from Japan Publishing Company and—"

"Moshi moshi??"

I saw that Hamaguchi was watching me, assessing my performance. This was the first sales call by one of his new employees.

"Please may I speak with the advertising manager?" I continued, reading the second line of my script.

"Moshi moshi?"

I didn't answer.

I heard some clicks on the line. Evidently, I was being transferred to an English-speaking manager. Now I was getting somewhere. I gave Hamaguchi a nod to indicate good progress.

A new voice took the call. *"Moshi moshi?"*

"Yes, I—"

"Moshi moshi?"

This was ridiculous. A Monty Python gag. So I switched to Japanese to tell the girl what company I was calling from—I hadn't studied two years for nothing: *"Kochira wa Nihon Shuppansha desu,"*

"Hai!" She acknowledged.

"—You must speak English!" Hamaguchi interrupted. He stepped closer and pressed his fingers like the teeth of a rake onto the top of my desk.

I covered the mouthpiece and whispered, "But they don't understand."

"Then you must hang up."

"Thank you," I said, and hung up the phone like I was told, like an obedient little boy. "I was just going to use Japanese to try to get the advertising manager on the line."

Hamaguchi shook his head. "I know this must be *dee-fi-cult* for you to understand. You must speak only English. Japanese are very impressed to get call from foreigner. You must *expect* that they will speak English."

I'm sure I didn't look convinced because he added, "Very strange system, I know. But you must remember that you have many benefits in sales position."

I was getting tired of Hamaguchi's constant use of the verb *must*.

"Well, what happens if they don't understand and keep repeating *'moshi moshi moshi'?*"

"Then you must say *Thank You* and make other call."

Suddenly, Hamaguchi turned to face all of the office staff. I noted that his suitcoat lapels were cut in an odd manner. I had never seen such a coat. The lapels were slanted back below the waist, creating a V-Shaped opening over his pelvis. Perhaps that was for convenience in the restroom. "I weel be back at three o'clock," he announced, as if declaring a summit meeting. Without another word, he walked out the door.

I sat perfectly still for a moment. I didn't like this "English-only" rule. I didn't like it at all. I had come to Tokyo to speak Japanese. To learn about the culture. Not to speak English to people who didn't understand . . . Did Hamaguchi know from experience that only companies which had English-speaking staff would want to advertise in English-language publications? But that didn't make sense. Sako Department Store had that huge ad in the Tokyo English yellow pages . . .

With a glance to my right and left to make sure no one was listening, I dialed Sako again. I disobeyed Hamaguchi, spoke again in Japanese, and requested to speak with the advertising manager: *"Senden bu no senkininsha onegai shimasu?"*

Instantly, the line was transferred to the advertising department. In Japanese, I explained about <u>Tokyo Time</u> and set an appointment with a "Mr. Arisaka" for that afternoon. Then I couldn't keep a smile from starting. I bit my lip to prevent it. I slipped the advertising samples into my briefcase and stuck the company pin through my lapel. I snapped on the company tie clip and made sure it was perfectly straight. It was my first appointment, my Japanese corporate baptism.

Down by the station in the glare of the afternoon sun, I opened my map book and spread it across a fire hydrant. The subway map showed color-coded train lines, ciliated tracks wiggling through a gray amoeboid oval. This was Tokyo.

I had been on the subway before, but not at a peak hour in the heat of the day. I wedged myself into the crowd of people who surged down the stairs. I was pressed deep into the throng of passengers. At the *kippu* ticket machine, I waited in line, dropped in some change, and the machine spat out a blue ticket which flickered from the slot like a reptile's tongue. I grabbed it. The next train was scheduled for 2:37 p.m. These trains were incredibly prompt. You could set clocks by them. I looked at my watch. Eighty seconds to go.

On the wall hung a huge Toyota advertisement featuring Eddie Murphy, lying with one knee erect, on the hood of a pink car. Along the edge of the platform, the concrete was scuffed at twenty-foot intervals. These marks must be where the doors of the train had opened time and again. I paced over and stood in front of one of the scuff marks. I waited. For exactly fourteen more seconds.

Brakes squealed simultaneously on both sides of the platform as two trains arrived from opposite directions at precisely 2:37 pm. Under vacuum pressure, electric doors slid open, and passengers poured out. There were men in suits, schoolboys with matching hats, and primly dressed office girls. The crowd was expelled from one train and pressed forward into the other. They crossed the platform like Marines fording a stream. Station guards stood behind each boarding line of passengers and literally pushed them through the doors into the car until no more passengers could fit inside. I was shoved from behind and rammed onto the train. My shoulder banged on the door frame, but I grabbed the handrail inside the car and pulled myself out of the way. I squeezed in next to the door where there was a tiny space, just enough for one person flattening himself against the steel support poles. Maybe there would be more air near the door. Maybe enough to breathe. I held my briefcase in front of my chest like a shield.

A whistle sounded, shrill as a steam pipe blast. On the platform, an old Japanese woman with long flaxen hair elbowed between two men, pumped past a group of uniformed schoolboys, and dived into the train. I would have imagined her much meeker. That was the stereotype. But she was an accomplished subway-shover, a practiced old train-dasher, with a dangling tongue.

The old woman's skirt caught in the rubber seal between the doors, and then they wouldn't close. The guards came over and pressed the old lady further into the car. They held her in until the doors could shut all the way. She twisted and wriggled, and soon she was next to me. Her hand, a wrinkled claw, lay against my thigh. Through the tropical wool fabric of my suit pants, I could feel her sharp fingernails clutching my skin. I moved back. My hips pressed into the crotch of a Japanese businessman. With a face as hard as obsidian, the man pretended he hadn't been touched. I moved forward against the old woman's crablike hand again and felt it flex. I shoved the briefcase down my torso until the bottom of it contacted the crustacean hand and scraped it off my body.

To my right sat a pretty girl in a pink dress. Her hair was perfectly cut in an angled bob. Her skin glowed, and her make-up was impeccable. She was a beauty salon dream. She held a Louis Vuitton bag precisely on her knee and rested two hands upon it. I glanced at the other women on the train. Three of them held identical Louis Vuitton bags. This was the ultimate example of "*WA*"— harmony. Absolute brand-name consensus.

The men all wore suits. They relaxed on the crowded train. Some had closed their eyes and reclined against the metal support bars of the train. They seemed to be napping. Others read *manga*, obscene comic books, laying their magazines across the shoulders of the next passenger to turn pages. These were all "salarymen" who worked sixteen-hour days, six days a week. They rode the trains and didn't get nauseous and woozy like me. They knew how to lean as the car rolled around a bend, shoring their chests against each other's shoulders, allowing their legs to intertwine.

After twenty or thirty years, you must get used to the train and lose the need for personal space; you merged with other passengers and let them support you over the bumps. You knew how to conform and wore identical clothing to blend in easily, to fuse. Human beings in perfect co-existence.

The brakes screeched again. Simultaneously, all the passengers staggered as the train jerked to a halt. With sweaty fists and bulging knuckles, I grasped the metal bar to keep steady. The skin of my thigh itched like a rash where the old woman had scratched me. "Welcome to *Ginza*," announced a tinny voice over the intercom. I held my breath until the doors opened. I was the first one onto the platform and, for a very brief moment, luxuriated in the open space. Then the crowd bulldozed me against a metal column. I pivoted to the other side of the column for protection and held my breath again until most of the people had left the platform. Then it was safe.

On the ritzy *Harumi Dori*, land values were the highest in the world. It was said that you could lay a thousand-dollar bill on the sidewalk, and the ground below it would be worth ten times more. I walked past a number of swanky department stores, glittering jewelry stores, high-fashion retailers, and, of all things, a Kentucky Fried Chicken franchise, complete with a picture of the smiling myopic Colonel. KFC customer lines stretched out the door and into the street. Then I saw it—*SAKO DEPAATO!* It wasn't quite as big as the other department stores but looked classier, with polished brass trim around the windows. Two enormous gleaming doors opened automatically to let me in.

A sparkling chrome and gold perfume counter stood close to the entry. It was staffed by two picture-perfect Japanese girls, exactly the same height. They stood at attention, hands clasped, posed still as mannequins.

"Excuse me," I said.

Together, the girls swiveled their heads to look at me. They gave automatic bows. But one of them seemed to be smirking. Was this just my imagination? Was I just nervous?

I spoke Japanese in low, solemn tones. *"Arisaka-san no jimusho wa doko desu ka?"* Where is Arisaka-san's office? He is the advertising manager. We have an appointment.

At the mention of Arisaka's name, there were rapid inhalations. Both girls' expressions changed. Their eyes opened wider. They leaned forward, utterly alert and completely respectful. Now I was royalty. I was anointed. I knew Arisaka-san!

"Hai!" said the girls. They bowed again and asked me to *"sho-sho omatte"*—to have a short, *honorable* wait. One of them ran over to another counter and picked up the phone. She glanced at me nervously. Clearly, she knew that I was not just a stupid tourist looking for imported perfume. I was a revered advertising executive with keys to the city.

Three clerks appeared and bowed together. *"Hai! Hai! Hai!"* they said and escorted me, the esteemed manager-meeter, to a chain of private offices in the back. I was ushered to a green leather couch and given a cup of tea for another honorable wait, while the receptionist made a few frantic phone calls involving frenetic whispers and worried glances as if I might buy the entire store—building, property and all—right out from under her feet. But when she looked up again, I gave her a calm smile, a reassurance that she needn't fret.

Then a younger man escorted me to another office and introduced me to two salarymen. Slowly and deliberately, as if in a Zen ritual, I pulled out my business card and offered it with two hands in the polite Japanese way, so the printing faced the receiver. The men stared at the card. The one on the left tilted his head in a parakeet's twitch and then slid a business card out of his jacket pocket, which he offered with only one hand. It was a gesture soon duplicated by the other man.

I studied their cards. I had read that after careful consideration, the higher-ranking person's card was supposed to be placed above the other cards on the discussion table, available for easy reference during the meeting. But I couldn't tell who was in charge here, so I lay the cards side-by-side. I could only tell *one* thing from these cards: Neither of these men was Arisaka. My abdomen tensed, and I fought back the queasiness in my stomach.

The first man spoke in halting English. "We are very sorry. But Mr. Arisaka-san had emergency meeting. He has asked us to listen to your proposal."

"Thank you," I said, and bent my head forward in a little "seated bow" which I had designed myself but seemed appropriate. I took the advertising samples out of my briefcase and lay them in front of the men. There were copies of the last two issues of <u>Tokyo Time</u>, a letter from one of the big Japanese hotels expressing how much the guests liked the magazine, a notarized statement from U.S. Ambassador Mike Mansfield which said he had read the magazine, and a pamphlet detailing the number of copies distributed per month.

Then I started my sales talk.

The Japanese men nodded. They gave a big nod when I showed them an ad in last month's <u>Tokyo Time</u> from *Seibu Depaato,* one of their competitors. And they nodded again when I pointed to the distribution list and tapped my ballpoint near the list of hotels. I might actually sell an ad, I realized. Yes, I could do it!

I forced myself not to talk too fast. I Japanized my English with throaty syllables, so the men would be sure to understand. I nodded a lot and made earnest expressions and shook my samples. Finally, I brought out the contract and showed all of the different ad spaces and types . . .

But the men nodded enthusiastically at *each* space—and I knew it was all fake. I knew I had no chance. They were nodding mechanically, agreeing automatically like yes-men sidekicks of an inane talk show host. Their nods were not signs of acceptance; they were signs of understanding, validating each point of my presentation. There was no consent. But I thrust my big question, anyway. I was tired of all this nodding and grunting. Now the men had to choose. "So what advertisement size would be appropriate for Sako department store?" I asked bluntly.

"Yes," said the English speaker. "We are very impressed by your publication. Our advertising budget will start in July. We shall consider your <u>Tokyo Time</u>."

My cheeks burned. My knees perspired. It was stupid of me to think that I could convince them to buy. The Great Arisaka wasn't even there. And Japanese businessmen were famed for making decisions very slowly. All facets of a proposal had to be considered by all possible members of the organization. All aspects had to be analyzed and re-analyzed. Then there was a group action. Of course, I shouldn't feel too bad that I hadn't gotten an immediate decision, right?

But there was another possibility. Maybe the men simply weren't interested. Maybe they were just stalling for three months under the guise of "consideration." Pinpoints of heat flashed on the back of my neck. I took a deep breath. "Thank you for considering my proposal," I said.

"Oh, you are most welcome. It ees our pleasure." They smiled at me, then at each other.

"But don't you need more customers before July?"

The men's faces fell, sagged like leaking water bottles. "Yes, of course," said English speaker. "We will consider your proposal very carefully."

I was beaten. "Thank you," I said, and felt the blood rush to my temples.

We all stood up. The non-speaker bowed first. He must be the lower-ranking one. The higher-ranking English speaker bowed afterward. I made sure that I bowed last but started my bow just after the English-speaker so my presumptuousness would be more subtle.

On the top floor of the NDD building, the company cafeteria was surprisingly spacious. Ferns and paintings dotted the walls. A panoramic window offered spectacular views of the city. I sat with Mr. Otosaki, a middle-aged advertising manager, and his assistant—Miss Kawano, highcheek-boned and high-breasted. A pair of heavy reading glasses covered Miss Kawano's eyes.

After our meeting, Otosaki had insisted that I "enjoy" an NDD lunch, even though it was 3:30 in the afternoon. I wasn't hungry. And I had a bit of a stomach ache. But I agreed with an artificial smile and a compliant bow.

The waiter brought our bowls of rice and a plate of *tsunomono* bean appetizer. He gave me a curious glance.

"Do you like Japanese food?" asked Miss Kawano, as if to take my attention away from the waiter. She closed her mouth in a round, lipsticked smile.

Before I could answer, Otosaki clarified the question with a hearty laugh and a slight lean forward. "Do you like Japanese <u>rice</u>?"

"Yes *oishi*— delicious," I said.

Miss Kawano nodded in quick, jerking motions and shot a fast look at Otosaki as if my answer had proven something which they had discussed before.

"Yes, Japanese rice is best," said Otosaki. "Japanese rice is sticky rice. Sticks to chopstick. Better to eat. Better for taste," he explained.

When the waiter served a chicken plate to each of us, I decided to ingratiate myself as much as possible with my possible new clients. I spread both hands over my plate. "I like <u>all</u> Japanese food," I said, "*Sashimi* and bean candy and *natto*," which was a particularly smelly fermented bean paste that I'd never tried—it was known to make most foreigners puke.

Kawano and Otosaki exchanged another glance, almost an "I-told-you-so" look. But I wasn't sure just what they were affirming.

"Miss Kawano has traveled a lot. She has lived in *Bu-ritain* and *Furansu*," said Ototsaki.

"Good." I tried to give a lively nod. Of course, we had to know each other's entire background before we could do business. That was the Japanese custom, right? Business partners had to have total knowledge about each other to engender trust. And in my case, they had to know the exact degree of my love for Japan. They would exhaust all other topics of conversation, and then maybe, just maybe, Otosaki would mention the contract. I would wait. I knew how to wait.

"I had *Furenchu* boifurendo," offered Miss Kawano, wide-eyed and breathless as if I would be eager to hear this.

"Oh, great. Congratulations." What the hell was I supposed to say?

"Are you married?" asked Otosaki, inhaling a piece of chicken.

"No." I shook my head.

"You are single?" he persisted.

"Yes."

Otosaki laughed and ordered some beer from the waiter. "For better or for worse, Miss Kawano is single, too . . ." This time Otosaki didn't look me in the eyes. He pinched a big pile of rice with his chopsticks. Miss Kawano rearranged her napkin and gave me a suggestive, heart-shaped smile and a slight lift of her eyebrows.

I was embarrassed. My thighs were hot. Of course! I was being set up. Like on *The Dating Game*. Miss Kawano had lived abroad and had foreign boyfriends. She was known to desire Western men. Her only option was to find a Western boyfriend, like me, who just happened to be there at the right place at the right time. And Otosaki, like a favorite uncle, was helping her out.

Otosaki gave Miss Kawano another optimistic nod and a soft grunt, and she adjusted her napkin again. "Do you like music?" he asked me.

Now they were closing in. It was time to be aggressive. Time for an affirmative defense. I would ask Miss Kawano a question. "What kind of music do you like?" I inquired.

She quivered and lay a hand on the table to steady herself. Her new suitor had put her to examination. Now she had to perform. "Oh . . ." Her chest rose. "Oh, I don't know . . ." She had a dazed look as if I had asked her about the wonders of the universe, the fabled Spring of Youth or the Mouth of Eden. Shaking, she set down her chopsticks. "It ees, difficult, to eat and to speak, English."

"Unhh . . ." I made an understanding grunt and nodded consolingly. I glanced at Otosaki. He was fully engaged in eating chopsticked mounds of food, and for all intents and purposes, seemed to have left the two prospective lovers, Miss Kawano and I, to our own devices. Otosaki was indeed our chaperone—but a permissive one. His duties were finished. Now he was convinced that his two kindlings were mature enough to go at it alone.

The beer arrived, and Otosaki filled a glass for me, then poured one for himself as well. Miss Kawano wasn't given any beer. "Drink, please," said Otosaki. Simultaneously, we each took a sip of the frothy beer and lowered our glasses. But a millisecond before Otosaki's glass met the table, he spoke. "I'm sorry, we are not interested in your advertising proposal." Then in almost a continuance of the same sentence, he asked, "How was your lunch?"

I was caught by surprise. I managed to mutter, "Oh, very good. Thanks," and reached for my beer again. It was a sudden grab to cover my blush.

<u>Not interested</u>. The words echoed through my head. <u>Not interested in your proposal</u> . . . Otosaki had waited until the beer was served, as if we were all out drinking in the evening. Only in the presence of alcohol was it possible for him to speak frankly. So he had engineered an entire replica of an evening out, complete with female companionship. When businessmen went to drink together, often the biggest deals were made—or *un*made. One of my Japanese guidebooks advised that you literally pour your drinks on the floor (spilling them discreetly, of course), so you wouldn't be too drunk to catch the flicker of business revelations, quick and fleeting as falling stars.

Well, if this was an evening out, and we were all drunk and candid, I could speak openly too, right? I would try. "Your competitor, KTT, Kokusai Telephone, already advertises in our publication," I said.

Otosaki held his chicken bone down with one chopstick and began to scrape off the fat with the other.

"Their market is exactly the same as NDD's," I continued.

With two fingers, in a gentle slide, Otosaki moved his beer glass so it was precisely spaced between the beer bottle and his plate. Then he swiveled it so the grease mark from his mouth faced him directly.

I stopped talking. I sat perfectly still. It was no use. I was being ignored. They had given an answer already, and no amount of evidence would change their minds. If I kept talking, I was only alienating them, convincing them that I was a *rikutsuppoi*, a "reason freak" who speaks in repulsive cold logic.

At that moment, in a surreal epiphany, I saw myself as forever separate from the Japanese, like a lumbering cauliflower-eared boxer in a stadium of slim, agile karate champions wearing matching *gi*. Yes, I could learn Japanese ways, and I could understand the language, but would I ever fit in?

After lunch, I escaped the moist lingering eyes of Miss Kawano with a series of bows, all the way to the elevator. There I was saved by the whirring, humming close of its doors.

Sitting at the edge of a large circular fountain with my suit jacket folded beside me and my back to the bubbling spray of water, I waited. The sun felt good behind my ears. I had left the office as early as possible to get to my appointment with Mazda. I arrived at *Hibiya* station with thirty-five minutes to spare. So I crossed the street to sit and wait in the spacious Hibiya park. To look at a few trees. To watch the children play.

Near the entrance gate, a man was attempting to fly a white-winged kite emblazoned with an emblem of the Rising Sun. But the breeze was faint, and the kite couldn't get off the ground. In the distance, a band sang American Top Forty hits from a pavilion. The park wasn't very crowded by Tokyo standards. Small groups of people roamed and wandered and seemed almost relaxed in the waning afternoon.

Just then, bowing several times and shaking as if the sky were falling, a thirtyish woman wearing one of the blue surgical masks that Japanese put on when they have a cold (to protect others) rushed over to me. "Excuse me!" She trembled and pointed over my shoulder.

I looked at her for a moment, then turned around slowly to follow her gaze. My suit jacket had fallen into the fountain. It was soaking wet and fluttering below the surface near a group of ducklings. Immediately, I leaned over and managed to snatch up the jacket. I held it out at arm's length. A mixture of water, leaves, and possible duck excrement dripped from the collar and sleeves. "Thank you," I said. I gave a nod, a mini-bow, and feigned indifference about the coat as if I had merely dropped a pen or a pencil. No serious problem. *Grace under pressure*, the American virtue.

The woman gave me a curious look, a bewildered twitch of her head. Then she bowed again and rushed off.

I lay the jacket beside me. I had to push it further away, so its wetness didn't reach my pants and stain them like a leaky toilet. I checked my watch. Seventeen minutes until the appointment at Mazda. No problem . . .

But of course, there was a problem. In Japan, a business coat was *required*. All of the Do-Business-In-Japan books said so. Even my manager, Hamaguchi, had carried on about the critical importance of a jacket and tie. What would happen if I walked into the great Mazda headquarters in only shirt sleeves? Would the advertising team still meet with me? Was there time for my underwater-coat to dry in the sun? Maybe it would half-dry to a damp, dark shade that wouldn't look wet—until I sat in a chair and left a puddle. Mazda wouldn't like puddles.

I stared at the glistening silver thirteen-story Mazda building across the street. Maybe I should cancel? But it had taken two weeks to get this appointment. I ran a hand through my hair and felt the heat in my forehead.

Just then, three college-aged Japanese walked toward me, a boy and two girls. They hesitated and stopped a few feet away.

The boy spoke first, with a prefatory grunt. He read questions to me from a clipboard. "Excuse me. What school you go to?"

I spoke very slowly, with an enigmatic raise of my eyebrows. "I do not go to school."

The students exchanged nervous glances. But the boy caught his breath, swallowed, and continued bravely as if he were confronting The Great OZ, blinking from his intensity. "How long, your, summer, vacation is?"

I didn't want to be difficult. I was a good sport, so I answered as if they referred to my job. "Probably two or three weeks."

They all nodded in unison, and the prettier girl spoke—meekly, tentatively, kitten-like. "Two or three?" A little pink tongue came out for a moment on "three."

The boy pressed on, clicking his pen. "What subjects you are studying?"

Then I had enough. I spoke to them in rapid Japanese and explained, "I'm sorry, I'm not a student. I work in Tokyo. In an advertising company."

In their amazement, both girls exhaled and produced odd sounds like electric fans winding to full speed. Their eyes widened. The shorter girl trembled. The boy grunted again. The pink-tongued girl, who also had sensual lips, spoke first. "You, speak, Japanese?"

"Hai," I said, and switched back to English to let them practice. "Can I ask you a question?"

This took a moment to register, but when it did. I was confronted by three looks of undisguised pleasure as if I had just handed out ice cream. The shorter girl spoke for the first time, "Yes. Purease."

"This, is, my, coat," I said, imitating the rhythm of their English and gesturing with an open palm. I enunciated every syllable perfectly like the disembodied voice on a language tape. "My coat just fell in the water. It is very wet. In eleven minutes, I have an appointment over there with Mazda, with their advertising department." I pointed at the gleaming building for effect. "Is it better that I wear a *wet* jacket? Or—" Here, I let my voice swing up to pose the ultimate question: "Is it better that I wear *no* jacket?"

They inhaled at the enormity of the query, the utter quandary. Their brows were knit in thought. Finally, the boy spoke. "In Japan, you must wear jacket." He nodded once, twice, and exhaled through his nose.

"Yes," I said, with a grave look. "Even if the coat is very wet?" This sent the boy into a spasm of lip-tensing thought and produced some additional sounds, including what seemed to be a very soft hiss and a very quiet moan. I waited for a while, but no more answers were forthcoming. In fact, no one moved. Not a step. They were perfectly still, as if in suspended animation.

"Perhaps I should buy another jacket to wear," I prompted.

The boy nodded, and both girls smiled at this solution. They all beamed with expressions of happiness and relief as if imagining the parting of the red sea, or the coming of a divine wind. The sensual one spoke, "Oh yes! That is very-good idea!"

"But there are no shops here. And I have only six minutes . . ."

Their expressions became so sad, so instantly woeful and sympathetic, with watery and beseeching eyes, that I couldn't leave them with only these last words. Besides, there was still an obscure possibility: "Maybe I should tell Mazda that my jacket fell in the water with the ducks," I suggested.

This, however, met with unanimous head-shaking rejection and trembling. Surprisingly, the boy leaned forward and got ready to talk again. I held my breath.

"In Japan," he said, "It ees important, to wear jacket."

I glanced at my watch. I had four minutes. "Thank you all for your help," I said, and tried to give an earnest smile. "I have to go now. Bye-Bye."

"Bye-Bye," chirped the girls.

I stared into the tall one's eyes, "Study your English . . ." Then I stood and picked up my briefcase, gathered the sopping jacket, and took off running in a bee-line for Mazda, hopping over shrubs and dashing into a grove of trees. Safely concealed, I stopped to catch my breath in private gasps.

Now, what the hell was I going to do about the jacket? Of course, I couldn't wear a wet coat. That was absurd. Nor could I carry the muddy dripping thing, oozing duck water. I bunched the jacket into a ball and threw it as hard as I could into the limbs of a tree. It whipped upward through the leaves, then opened a bit on descent, finally coming to rest on a sharp branch where it caught and dangled. The gold buttons on the sleeves flashed and gleamed in the sun. I would come back for the jacket later. Maybe. I straightened my tie. And started running again.

A tall counter stood along the back of the giant Mazda entrance hall, staffed by a flock of exquisite reception girls, corporate decorations. As I stepped through the door, an electric gong sounded, and all the girls looked up. Were they staring at my shirt? They glanced up when anyone came in, right? I rolled back my shoulders and stood straight as a Legionnaire. I walked directly over to the counter. "Advertising department," I said.

"*Hai!*" she squeaked. Then two girls escorted me to the elevator. I didn't dare check to see if they were staring at my shirt. I sucked in my stomach, pushed out my chest, and entered the elevator. There was a noise like air shooting through a pipe. The elevator was extremely rapid yet somehow engineered to avoid the unpleasant stomach-leadening sensation of a quick ascent. In a flash, I was at the ninth floor. The receptionist there was already on the phone announcing my arrival to the advertising manager, Mr. Ishiguru. Two men emerged from a doorway. Their eyes darted around the hall as if checking for vermin—until they saw me and stared at my shirt. This time it was undeniable.

But I stared right back at the men. One fact was irrefutably clear: *These men weren't wearing jackets either* . . . If Mazda wouldn't wear a jacket for me, I didn't have to wear a jacket for them. This realization seemed to hit the Japanese men at exactly the same time. The frowning criticism and tight-lipped disapproval vanished from their faces instantly. We had all disregarded tradition. We had all been very rude, yet we had all "lost face" to precisely the same extent, so everything was still in balance. Everything was okay.

After quick bows, one of the advertising men stepped forward. "I am Ishiguru," he said.

We exchanged business cards and sat down at a table near the window overlooking the perilous fountain itself. "Your building has a beautiful view of the park," I said.

"Yes," said Ishiguro, "It is . . . refreshing."

This seemed to be a curious choice of words, and I wondered if the men had actually witnessed the jacket episode. But Ishiguro's expression was blank. "Where are you from?" he asked.

"I grew up in California."

"California, with the movie stars and surfing." Ishiguro laughed. "My daughter wants to visit California to attend Stanford. However, I prefer British English."

Ishiguro's pronunciation of English vowels did seem to have a British cadence which combined with his Japanese accent in an odd way. "Our Tokyo Time magazine has Burberry ads in it," I said, and opened it to show a half-page advertisement for the English company, featuring a scarf, an umbrella, and a British flag. But Ishiguro seemed unimpressed.

I started my advertising presentation. The men nodded at every point and nodded every time I touched the sample magazines. Ishiguro's associate said *Wakarimashita*—"I understand," at least twelve times. But at the end of the sales pitch, he lowered his glance and waited.

"We are sorry," said Ishiguru. "This magazine is not suitable for Mazda."

Surprisingly, I chuckled. Then I controlled my mouth, so I didn't grin. I had gotten a straight answer right away! Ishiguru told the truth, with no hedging his response to save face. Maybe he didn't want to waste my time. Maybe my Japanese social skills were getting better, and Ishiguro trusted me enough to be honest. This was almost as good as a contract itself. "Well, that's all right," I said, and smiled. "I'll just take a Mazda Miata sports car in compensation."

But neither of the men laughed. They glanced at each other in alarm.

"*Jodan da yo*—Joke," I clarified.

"*Ohhh.*"

But it wasn't funny. "Thanks." I stood up and bowed. The men bowed back and then were still, as if uncertain what to do next. So I found my own way to the elevator, held my breath on the ride down, and clumped across the mezzanine. Its floors were so polished that I could see my reflection. I could see the soles of my heavy, thudding feet.

At my first Nissan appointment, Tokyo Time magazine had only gotten a lukewarm reception. I was given a *tamamushi* decision. The term related to a beautiful species of Japanese beetle, famous for the iridescent spectrum of the colors on its back: *tamamushi iro no*—"jewel beetle." Depending upon which way you looked at the creature, which angle of observation, the beetle's back reflected different colors. The phenomenon referred to the relativism of *all* matters—in life, in business, perhaps even in the after-life. Miss Ishi, the early-thirtyish advertising representative with an odd face but a very curvy figure, had told me that she had to discuss my offer with the "Advertising Team," which gave me hope, but promised nothing. I had pressed her to meet with me again in two weeks. And now it was time. It was the final moment.

I stepped off the elevator on the sixth floor of the Nissan building in Ginza. In front of me lay several partitioned corridors, maze-like and circuitous. I turned left but soon found myself wandering through unfamiliar offices. These were huge wide rooms crammed with tiny desks and mounds of paperwork. I turned around and paced toward the elevators—or where I thought the elevators should be. There was only a dead-end corridor. So I headed back around the other way. Finally, a bowing young Nissanite tapped me on the shoulders and, polite and contrite as a choir boy, pointed me down the right passageway. He followed me until I was safely seated in just the right place, behind a potted tree, and brought a cup of dark green tea.

The tea was bitter, absinthian, which I took as a compliment. Nissan assumed that I was Japanized enough to like strong *ocha*, green tea, and that I wouldn't demand only coffee like a pushy foreigner.

Miss Ishi hurried over, rushing as much as she could in a pencil skirt, which forced her into a knock-kneed trot. Her lower lip pouted a bit as she said, "Ummm . . . We are very sorry that after, considering—"

"—Oh!" I interrupted. "I brought something very interesting to show you." I wasn't going to give her the time to reject the contract.

"You did?" she asked, cocking her head.

"Yes." I opened my magazine to a glossy Mercedes advertisement, rolling back the pages and spreading them like a sacred scroll.

"No." Miss Ishi shook her nose. "We have already seen this."

"You saw this two-page ad?"

"I theenk you showed us smaller one."

"Oh, because I wanted to show you the large ad," I stalled—then I had an idea, a grand idea. "This is the advertisement size that

Toyota was very interested in."

"**TOYOTA!**" Miss Ishi twitched into instant alertness. She stood very still and even seemed to stop breathing.

"Yes," I said again, trying not to laugh, "Because with Toyota, we had discussed the full-size, two-page ad." —Which wasn't entirely true. I did have an appointment with Toyota's advertising company, and they had given me the usual answer: They were *considering* it. But if the Japanese used tamamushi decisions with me, I would use tamamushi statements back at them. Fair is fair.

"Toyota will advertise in Tokyo Time?" Miss Ishi asked.

"Well, we're just finalizing negotiations, but Toyota is interested for the next period."

"Just a minute purease," she said, and walked away again.

I waited. I could feel the tingle on the fishing line now, the jiggle at the end of the pole. It was a "we-too" fish! Whatever the competition does, we must do it too . . .

Soon Miss Ishi came back. She was walking more relaxedly now, clicking along like an off-duty shop girl. "Okay, so please you will let us know if Toyota will advertise." She closed her notebook.

But I wasn't finished. "Yes, I will do that. Do you think that Nissan would like to advertise next to Toyota advertisement?"

"Eet it is very possible." She gave me an encouraging smile.

"Oh good. Only—" Here I frowned, creased my forehead as if the notion pained me terribly, as if I were reporting a death in the family. "I cannot promise you that we will still have advertising space. Our magazine is very popular now you know, what with Toyota and so on. All the spaces may be filling up."

"*Ah!*" Miss Ishi's look got intense again. She let out a small gasp. "Just a minute, purease." And I got to watch the walk once more.

When Ms. Ishi marched back again, I tried to appear as nonchalant as possible. I leaned back in my chair and rubbed my chin. That was what you did when you made ten-thousand-dollar deals with Toyota and Nissan every day.

"Wheech space was Toyota interested in?" she asked again. Now she was talking.

"Well, we had promised them the center two-page spread, but still, we have available C-space, single-page. That was the space I discussed with Rolls Royce, Japan. But I told them I could not reserve it without payment."

Miss Ishi was studying the page like a designer dress—flipping it back and forth, holding it up to the window, rubbing its surface with her index finger and sighing. Finally, she spoke. "All right. Nissan will take C-Space."

I nodded and clenched my teeth so my smile wouldn't be too wide, so my cheeks wouldn't glow like airport landing lights. "Yes, very good. Excellent decision. Nissan and Toyota. Let me just get the paperwork."

I reached into my briefcase and pulled out the yellow contract sheet. Then Ms. Ishi squinted as if to shield her eyes from a blazing desert sun. Japanese didn't like contracts, hated them, in fact. They much preferred oral agreements, thinking that anything which purported to force two parties to rigid conditions smacked of deceit. Just one last push was necessary . . .

"So a copy of this paper we give to our printer, then he knows exactly what size to reserve, and we will have space for Nissan ad." I clicked out the ballpoint of my pen and wrote "Nissan July," and checked "C-space." Then I offered Ms. Ishi the pen.

"Just a minute purease," she said again, and stood up.

Dammit! Just when I was so close. Just when I could see my co-workers' jealous smirks. Just when I could feel Hamaguchi's pat on the back, recommending me for a promotion . . . Shit.

When Ms. Ishi came back, I didn't look up from the table.

Then she spoke. "Here," she said. "I have *hanko* now." A *hanko* was a Japanese stamp used in place of a signature on important documents. It was a traditional seal of approval.

I guided her hand to just the right spot. There . . . Finally. Finally, I was a success.

And bending the truth to sell the ad really didn't matter, right?

III. SPRATS

Lizzie and her cousin were giggling like schoolgirls inside their room at Sanjo boarding house. I had helped Lizzie move in the day before, carrying her numerous flowered Laura Ashley suitcases up the stairs. I knocked on her door, softly at first, then louder—three virile raps. Lizzie opened the door. She was wearing pink pajama pants and a lacy T-shirt. "It's the American . . ." she smiled. "Come join the cultural fire. We'll let you." Her cousin, Kate, wearing business clothes, sat on the futon bed.

"What fire is that?" I asked.

"The British cultural fire. Don't all Americans secretly wish they were British?"

"Liz . . ." Kate scolded.

"Well, don't they?" Lizzie lifted her chin. "And all the Japanese want to speak British English. That's why they pay us so much to teach at Stanton."

Kate busied herself rearranging suitcases. She snuck a worried glance at Lizzie. Then Kate picked up a paperback textbook. "Off to teach . . . Today, we're studying *Business Protocol*." She imitated a lecture: "Mr. Hirasawa, would you, like to buy, a green, umbrella?" Then she cocked her head the other direction to imitate the student's response: "Yes. Sank you."

"May, I, buy, a, pink, umbrella?" Lizzie continued.

"No. You have far too many pink items already. We're drowning in pink," said Kate. "See you later." She waved and walked out the door.

"Do you teach them *American* English?" asked Lizzie.

"No. I work in Advertising,"

"Oh . . ." She blinked a few times. "So you can afford to take me out to dinner."

"Only if there's a good dessert."

She didn't answer.

"All right, we can go for sushi."

"Sushi??? Raw fish?" She groaned. "Disgusting."

"You have to know what to order. Come on . . ." I pulled her arm. "I'm a sushi expert."

"I have to get dressed first." She opened one of the suitcases and took out a skirt. "Turn around and don't look."

We walked to a sushi stand near the station and sat out front, where there were metal tables and rickety wooden chairs. "I like to eat outside," I said. Then a taxi blew its horn and screeched past, leaving a waft of exhaust in its wake.

"Glorious," said Lizzie.

"We'll get the shrimp, the tuna roll—*tekka maki*, and the cucumber roll." I bought the sushi at the counter and brought it back to our table. "Let's try the *tekka-maki* first. It will give you a good overall sushi sensation. The fish is wrapped in rice."

I used my key to puncture the plastic wrap on the sushi container. Lizzie's nose quivered. She took one section of *tekka maki* in her fingers and carefully took a bite. She started to chew, then dropped her jaw and left it hanging open. Her face blanched—she held the unswallowed sushi at the bottom of her mouth in front of her rolled tongue. Then she grabbed a napkin, spit out the sushi, and dropped the whole mess onto the ground. "I think I'm going to vomit."

"What's wrong? It can't be that bad." I took a hefty bite of the sushi to prove my point, crammed half a roll into my mouth—then shuddered as I bit into a hard fish muscle, rigid in the middle like jerky. It must have been sitting in the case all day. But I made myself swallow it anyway and held back a gag. I tried to force a calm expression. "A bit old, possibly."

Lizzie folded her hands in her lap and frowned.

"I guess it's not too good here, huh?" I said.

"Well, from a *sushi expert*, that's a correct analysis." There was a hint of a smile.

"We'll go somewhere else. I know a good noodle house." I tried to sound excited.

"No thanks."

"Okay, we'll go to McDonald's—or, I saw this spaghetti place near the bus stop."

"I think I'll just go home and have my *favorite* dinner." She brushed back a few strands of her strawberry-blonde hair. Her hand rested on her neck for a moment.

"What's your favorite dinner?"

"Chocolate. Lots of it. Then go to bed."

I must have smiled a little.

"Alone . . ." she continued.

I shrugged. "Can't argue too much with that logic. One of these days, we'll have a rain check."

She stood up and walked back to Sanjo, leaving me to ponder my strategies. Evidently, I needed new techniques.

I sat there a few minutes, trying to decide if I was still hungry or nauseous. Then, slowly, I made my way back up the block. There was a vending machine just outside the boarding house, and I bought a can of dark Oolong tea. Perhaps that would soothe my stomach. I opened it and took a sip. Because it seemed like a good idea, I also bought a small bottle of whisky from the machine and slipped that into my pocket.

Then I heard Lizzie's voice behind me. "How can you stand to drink that awful tea with your Western palate?"

I turned around. "So you're following me. I thought you were supposed to be in bed."

"I couldn't sleep. I'm bored . . . How can you stand that stuff?" She shook her head.

"It's an acquired taste. I'm bored too. Let's—" My mind raced . . . "Play cards or something."

"Play cards! You have a dirty mind, don't you?"

"I'm very respectable. And half-English, by the way." I used a slight English accent on the "a" in *half* as a form of proof.

"Well, if you're part British, I suppose it's all right."

We went back to my room and sat down across from each other on the futon. I had a deck of cards from the airplane and opened it. "What shall we play? Rummy?"

"Oh, I don't care. Anything stupid," said Lizzie.

"What do you mean?"

"I like *stupid* games. Where you don't have to think." She glanced around the room and stared at the jumble of clothes and magazines on my table, half of which had fallen into a messy pile, and at the mounds of Japanese coins I had left right where they fell on the tatami mat. "We didn't have time to tidy up today, did we?" She clucked her tongue.

"I'll show you a stupid game. It's called *Slap*. Each of us gets half the deck. Then we slap cards down—up or down—by number. First player out of cards wins. It's a matter of speed."

I handed her half the deck. "Take out the face cards and jokers, then shuffle twice. Now we play like this . . ." I demonstrated with a few cards and put them back in my stack. "Ready. Let's start." I turned over the first card—a **9**.

Lizzie scanned through her cards, squealed, and flipped down an **8** and a **9**, then another **8**, **7**, and **6**. "Oh, this is a good game!" she giggled, and put down more cards.

I tried to play faster, flicking through my cards to find the right numbers. Several times Lizzie beat me to it, and my hand landed on top of her fingers, warm and smooth under my palm. I left my hand there, just a little too long.

She got better and better at the game until she only had three more cards, and then—"I've won!" she proclaimed, face glowing, hands clapping.

"Very good. Let's have another game."

"All right, but first, I have to go to the bog."

"The *bog*? I thought you called it the *loo* in 'English.'"

"Well, that too."

"What's the difference?"

"If you're nasty, you call it the 'bog.'"

"Are you nasty?"

"Yes." She stood up with a little hop.

"Good."

In a few minutes, she came back in, smiling, peeking around the door.

"Like the game?" I asked.

"Yes. It's perfectly stupid."

"You seem intelligent, though. I would have thought you were a Bridge or Canasta champion. Where did you go to school?"

"*Cam*-bridge," she said, drawing out the first syllable.

"What did you study?"

"Engineering."

"Did you like it?"

"Hated it."

"Then why'd you study it?"

"Don't know 'till you try, do you?"

"No, I guess not."

"—Let's play again."

Outside, it had started to rain. Gray droplets spattered and oozed on the window panes. We played another game, but Lizzie wasn't as happy this time. She played fiercely, thrusting her cards like knives, bending and creasing them as she placed them down. A few times, I got my card down first, and her hand pounded on top of it—pummeled it—hurting my fingers. "Oww. You know, it's cheating if you injure your opponent during the game."

She ignored me. "Damn it. It's raining."

"Just a light rain. It rains quite a bit in England, doesn't it?"

"What's that supposed to mean?" Her eyes flashed.

You couldn't say *anything* right with this girl. "I mean—" and I changed tactics, "Maybe that's why the Redcoats lost the revolutionary war with the Colonies. Too much rain. Not enough green brellies."

She had to laugh. "It's *brolly*," she corrected. And we kept playing cards. But soon, the game was over.

"Let's watch TV," I said, and moved my suit jacket, which was draped over a large red plastic television set on the table.

"It only gets Japanese stations."

"Might be something interesting on though." I pushed the power button, and the screen flashed to a commercial featuring Paul Newman walking through hills covered with wildflowers in the Japanese countryside. There was no talking in the commercial and no sound except for the rush of the wind and the chirping of birds. A company logo flashed—Japan Electric Company. Then the commercial was over. No insipid dramatized situation, no annoying announcer's explanation, no hideous jingle—just a captivating view of nature and the company emblem. The viewer would associate Japan Electric with the beauty of nature and develop loyalty to the company for that reason alone.

"Why do the Japs want all these foreigners in their commercials?" asked Lizzie.

"Want a lecture on it?"

She fluttered her eyelids facetiously. "Just the highlights, please."

"Well, at first, companies which had foreigners in their commercials were set apart. They could *tame* the old enemies and turn them into pets. Now there are so many foreigners, it just adds a little flair."

"Oh," said Lizzie, sarcasm gone and an amorous glint in her eyes—I'd have to remember that.

A mock documentary began on TV, featuring a clownish Japanese "professor" in huge thick eyeglasses. He lined up five Japanese girls, naked from the waist up, then re-positioned them until they were standing in order of their breast size, from smallest to largest. With a pointer, he poked each breast and gave a lecture on its shape in correlation to different types of fruit, whether the breast was more like a balloon or a headlight, or if the nipple pointed East or West.

"They're very sexist, aren't they?" said Lizzie.

I chuckled.

"Don't laugh!" said Lizzie. "It's grotesque."

"Well—our movies have the same thing, just not on television. Except maybe your *Benny Hill*."

Lizzie changed the TV channel, then, with a groan, turned down the volume. "You know what one of the students asked me today?" Her eyes widened. "The audacity . . . He asked me how come my father <u>let</u> me come to Tokyo? Can you believe it? I told him it was my decision, not my father's. And that Daddy respected it. But he still gave me this skeptical look, as if I were up to something *suspicious*."

I patted her knee. "Well, they just have different ideas about things. That's all."

"I'll say. Medi-eval ideas . . ." She laughed, despite herself, and turned back up the volume on the television, where a horse-faced blonde American woman was bleating out a sorry, honking rendition of "Hey, Mr. Tambourine Man." Lizzie held her hands over her ears. "God, she's awful."

"The Japanese don't know that, though. They can't judge Western performers. All that matters is her hair. Then she's on TV."

"—Oh, I know! They can't get over red hair. They'll start following me in the street, or their eyes will pop out of their heads." She changed the channels again, rapidly now, and finding nothing to her satisfaction, shut off the TV entirely.

"We'll play *Slap* again. But no hand injuries this time," I said.

She didn't protest.

"Care for a drink?" I took out the bottle of whiskey.

She nodded.

I found some paper cups, poured a splash in each cup, and raised my cup in a toast. "Cheers."

Her eyes met mine for a second, then she lowered them, and looked at me again. I thought I saw a gleam of romance, and we kissed. Soon, she kissed with abandon, her mouth and jaws reaching for me, pushing. Her hands caressed my neck and hair. We didn't even start the game. I had her clothes off in five minutes. Yes, everything in Japan was going swimmingly well now.

I woke up to a loud crash from downstairs. It sounded like someone had kicked over the shoe cabinet in the entryway. Probably a new resident. Maybe drunk . . . Loud footsteps ascended the stairs, and then a male began to sing loudly. Surprisingly he had a Cockney accent, replete with dropped consonants.

> Not long ago, in Westminster
> There lived a rat-catcher's dau—er.
> But-she-didn't-quite live in Westminster,
> 'Cause-she-lived t'other side of the wa-er.

Now he was in the hall just outside my room. The singing continued. He trilled certain words together, in what seemed an authentic British folksong.

> Her father-caught-rats and she sold sprats,
> All-around and about that qua-ter,
> And-the-gentlefolks, all took-off their hats
> To-the-pretty-little rat-catcher's Dau-er.

His singing stopped. The door across the hall was opened, shut, and locked. The concert was over.

Lizzie had awakened as well. She pulled a pillow to her body and sat up. Her red hair flowed over her bare shoulders. "What's all the bloody noise?"

"One of your countrymen just moved in."

"God, I'll never get back to sleep. Have you any more of that whiskey?"

We drank out of the bottle.

"What are *sprats*?" I asked. "He was singing about sprats."

"Oh. Little fishes."

"Maybe good for sushi."

She hit my leg, then kissed me. We lay down, had sex again, and fell asleep once more.

A few hours later, I woke up when I heard Lizzie's sniffle and a tiny whimper. I pushed myself up on my elbows. She was crying.

"What's wrong?" I asked gently.

"I don't know. I hate it here."

I blinked.

"No—It's not your fault."

"Well, that's good."

She wiped her eyes with the sheet. "I miss my parents . . . Dad's a minister, you know?" She twisted over on her stomach and turned her head to face me. "I hate Japan."

"Why?"

"I was on the train today . . ." She spoke softly. "All alone in the car except one businessman. And he was watching me." She touched her hair. "I looked away. Then I looked back, and he had a band-aid on his crotch—only it wasn't a band-aid. His fly was down, and he was *exposing* himself." Her eyes narrowed. "Next time, I'll <u>cut</u> it off." She hit the word *cut* hard. "I'll slice it, with a knife."

Every muscle in my body tensed. I sat perfectly still, conscious only of my heartbeat and breathing. What could I do? Ride with her on all the trains? Beat the guy up? "I'm sorry," I said at last.

I held her. Her warm tears trickled down my cheek and neck. Gently, I rubbed her back in little S-shapes, until her breaths smoothed. We lay down, and finally, she fell asleep again. A deep, snoring sleep.

I lay there, staring at blurred dark of the ceiling, wondering how to deal with a crisis when there are no options at all . . .

Somewhere outside, a cricket chirped its evening finale.

IV. SALARYMAN

Early Friday morning when I arrived at the publishing office, the blinds were drawn shut. Most of the other employees hadn't come in yet. Tanaka-san, a middle-aged Japanese advertising salesman, was already working—face down to his books, pen wiggling like a Geiger counter needle. He didn't even glance up when I came in. I took out my new Nissan contract and lay it on top of the desk. Tanaka was too busy to see. I heard the company president, Hamaguchi, inside his office, then waited until his snorting laughter stopped. I walked over and knocked softly on his door. "*Shachou*," I said, "I have some good news. I got an advertisement with Nissan."

Hamaguchi's eyes bulged. "Let me see!"

I handed him the contract and watched his round face fill with glee. His cheeks puffed up, and his lips curled into a smile. "Urrh! Ve-ry Good! Ve-ry Good. NISSAN! Ve-ry Beeg Space!"

"I had to push them, *Shachou*."

"Um, Yes . . . a long, long time ago, ten years ago maybe, we had very leetle, teensy Nissan ad." He squinted up his eyes and pressed a fat thumb and index finger together to demonstrate. "But at that time, we had to give free advertisement. They were not advertising much back then in the magazines for foreigners. Now we are getting bigger. Now they like Tokyo Time. Very good!" He rubbed his belly. "I theenk maybe you will be the next manager. But still, we have time to find out. You must keep working hard. *Gokorosan*," Good luck. It was the first time he ever had spoken to me in Japanese.

I went back to my desk, took out my notebook, and straightened a row of pencils and pens in my top drawer until they lay together perfectly, side-by-side, like bullets in a cartridge belt.

"NISSAN!" said Tanaka. He must have been eavesdropping. He smiled widely, revealing a line of crooked teeth. "*Emedetoo gozaimasu*, Congratulations." His face was red. "Nissan!" he repeated, pumped the word with false excitement. "You—Nissan . . ." He aimed a finger at me. Then he pointed back at his nose, pressing his finger against it, so the nostrils spread. "Me—Toyota! Tomorrow, Me,

Toyota. *Appointo . . .*" His lips trembled and jerked as he tried to verbalize in English. Ultimately, his need to speak overcame his squelching of Japanese, and words poured out like beans from a bursting sack. "*Ato de Nissan to Toyota no koukoku ga issho ni deru,*" Then Nissan and Toyota advertisements will be together.

"*Ii to omou yo,*" That will be good, I said, trying to inject enthusiasm into my voice to match Tanaka's. I had already met Toyota, though. Tanaka might be screwing up what little chance I had of getting a Toyota ad. Oh well, they didn't seem very interested anyway. Besides, maybe he had called another division. Maybe he had special contacts, or special Japanese intuition, to get an ad. Perhaps just <u>being</u> Japanese would do the trick.

Hamaguchi came out of his office. He walked over to my desk and tapped on it with a pen. "Even if you do not sell more right away, you must not give up. In Japan, we have lifetime employment system. You must keep working hard. Then you will be rewarded." He grunted, a single marked grunt to emphasize gut-level truth. "Now I must go. I will play *golfu*. One day, if you are successful, maybe you will play *golfu*, like me—if you do your best." He walked out the door.

I checked my phone book lists and appointment notes. I decided to call "Nodo Tokyo View Tourister Bus Tours." I dialed the number and spoke exactly the way Hamaguchi had instructed us. "Hello, I am calling from Japan Publishing Company. Please may I speak with the Advertising Manager?"

"This is Nodo," answered a gruff voice. "Why are you calling me?"

"Our magazine, <u>Tokyo Time</u>, has many transportation advertisements," I explained. "Perhaps your bus company would like to discuss an advertisement."

"You work for a Japanese company?" asked Nodo.

"Yes."

"You are American?" Nodo's voice had a hint of accusation now.

"Yes, we have salesmen of many different nationalities here." I tried to sound friendly.

"I see . . ." Nodo didn't finish his sentence. I didn't understand what there was to "see"—except that Nodo must have had some spare time because he made sighing noises for at least a minute. Finally, he spoke again. "You are very polite," he began.

"Thank you."

"Yes, you are polite, but most Americans are so rude and self-centered—except for you."

"Oh?"

"It is a pleasure to speak with you," Nodo continued. His English was perfect. "Because most Americans are so egotistical. They like to think only of themselves—but not you."

I almost laughed. Nodo was so bold-faced in his criticisms and his attempts to hide them in the guise of compliments, like a toll booth agent insulting drivers, protected by the roar of an expressway.

"Perhaps an advertisement in <u>Tokyo Time</u> will bring you more business, of all nationalities," I suggested.

Nodo wasn't finished. "Yes, most Americans are selfish, but *you* understand that the Japanese have, a selflessness."

"Great." I allowed a mild sarcasm, then softened my tone, "Shall we set an appointment so I can show you our publication? I glanced around the office. Tanaka had left, and I was alone, so I threw in an old Japanese proverb. "*Chansu wa jibun de tsukuru mono,*" You create your own opportunities.

The proverb must have taken Nodo by surprise. He was silent for a moment. No sighs this time. Then he agreed to an appointment later that afternoon.

Nodo was a plump Japanese man with carefully brushed hair. He wore a checkered three-button suit with outdated lapels and slightly bell-bottomed trousers. I gave him my advertising presentation, and at first, Nodo feigned interest—he sat forward and nodded. Then his eyes dulled, and his semi-inquisitive look deteriorated into a bored gape.

I tried to think of something to say that would get his attention. "We're starting a special feature in the magazine . . ." I opened it to the back, where there was a removable paper insert. "There is a guide-map now, with the advertisers' marked on it. The foreign visitors take this out of the magazine and keep it with them." Carefully, I tore out the map, folded it, and slipped it into my jacket pocket. "They carry the map to look at again and again."

"They carry it like the *bible*," said Nodo. His eyes sparkled.

I laughed. "Exactly. And it will show them just the right path to your Tokyo View Tourist Buses."

Now Nodo looked much more alert. "—Just a minute," he said suddenly and pressed an intercom switch on his telephone. He spoke in long syllables, drawing out his authority. "Brenda, please bring in my eyeglasses," He sat back in his chair to wait. And to watch me sit and wait. Only then was it clear why . . .

A busty, Caucasian platinum-blonde girl in a too-tight skirt bounced into the room. She held the eyeglasses in one hand and a magazine in the other. I smiled at her, but she wouldn't look at me, just handed Nodo the glasses and swiveled back to sashay the other way, revealing the acne scab on her left temple.

"Thanks, Love," said Nodo, apparently trying the British expression. His eyes followed Brenda as she sashayed out of the office. Then he turned back to me, clearly awaiting my appraisal of his gaudy secretary.

I smiled approvingly. I didn't want to ruin the sale—Jesus, the nauseating things you had to do to sell . . ." She's quite attractive," I lied.

Nodo beamed. "Yes, I found her in a little coffee shop in Roppongi."

He *found* her—as if he were a Hollywood talent scout. "Well done," I said. "So let me show you some more sample ads."

After thirty minutes of extended discussion about other <u>Tokyo Time</u> advertisements (the mere length of which Nodo seemed to enjoy); and many details about advertisement sizes, finally, with a royal nod, Nodo decided to buy a "Z" space. It was the smallest possible size—one square inch. Still, it was a sale. One more contract to add to the chart in the office.

That evening when I got back to the office, again, only Tanaka was in. He was working diligently in his notebook. I took out my prospect list and double-checked the names and addresses for Kenwood and Sony listings. Then I opened my Tokyo English yellow pages and made a list of new sales prospects—Ginza Beishu Japanese Dolls, Mitsubishi Automobiles, Fuji Bank, and Longo-Longo Diving school, with its motto, "We train people who cannot swim until they can obtain the international certification cards!" Obviously, Longo-Longo needed some advertising help.

Antennae waving, brown wings fluttering, a roach skittered across my desk and hid under the phone. I decided to ignore it, instead of causing a commotion by chasing it. Then I felt Tanaka's eyes on my back—a tingling heat. I turned around. He was nodding at me with a thin-lipped smile. "*Yoko hattari ku, ne,*" You work hard, he said. "*Nihon no sutairu da ne,*" in the Japanese style.

I smiled and bowed my head. It was a compliment. "*Gokurosan,* Good luck," said Tanaka.

"*Domo,*" Thanks, I said, and flipped more phone book pages, trying to look as industrious as an insect. Then I put my notebook in my briefcase and stood up to leave.

Tanaka was writing on a small pad. He quickly tore out the page, folded it, and put it in his jacket pocket. Then he also stood up. His chair screeched against the side of his desk. "*Gokurosan,*" he said again, and stared at me for a long time. He was nodding, brow wrinkled as if in deep thought. Finally, he spoke, in rounded melodic vowels as if reciting a poem. "*Boku-tachi no kaisha wa onagi,*" Our company is the same. "*Boku-tachi wa kazoku da,*" We are family. Here he interlocked his fingers to show the connection. "*Issho ni nomubeki,*" We should drink together.

This was an invitation, and I couldn't say no. "*Domo arigatou,*" Thanks very much. I bowed, then waited while Tanaka locked up the office. I followed him out into the shadowed street, allowing him to walk a half pace in front as he seemed to prefer. We walked in silence through some tiny back alleys and around a small playground. Tanaka stared straight ahead. On one corner stood a plain two-story building with glowing Japanese lanterns in the windows. We climbed up a narrow stairwell to a dimly lit bar.

"*Irrashai,*" Welcome, the cook called out from behind the counter. The bar was half-full of Japanese men sitting in groups, sipping drinks or eating "yakitori," roasted chicken appetizers on sharp sticks. Their faces were flushed, their ties loosened. It was the end of a long day.

I followed Tanaka to a table. We were served drinks automatically, tart *shochu*, which was said to have a higher alcohol content than *saki*. Instantly, Tanaka's somber face metamorphosed into a huge grin. He lifted his drink, "*Kampai!*" he said, and drained the glass.

I didn't know if I was supposed to be impressed, but this wasn't a drinking contest. It was a bonding of employees. Or maybe an initiation.

"*Anata wa ii kaishain desu,*" You are a good company worker, said Tanaka.

"*Domo,*" Thanks, I answered—in essentially the only word I had uttered in the past forty minutes—but that was okay. That's the way it was supposed to be.

Tanaka made a fist and grabbed it with the palm of his other hand. "In Japan, company spirit is important." He took another long gulp of his shochu, which had been immediately re-filled by the waiter. The liquor pulsed down his throat. Out of the corner of my eye, I could see the other Japanese men in the bar staring at us, examining the gai-jin with his Japanese business associate. But Tanaka didn't seem to notice. He sat in silence and finished two more drinks. Now his face flushed carmine. "*Kaisha no seishin*!" Company spirit! His head bobbed, and he sloped forward in his chair.

My vision was blurring slightly—maybe the drinks were stronger than I had realized. I took another sip, raising the glass in exact synchronization with Tanaka. I blinked and the room seemed to grow hazier. A trinkling Japanese melody flowed from behind the counter. All the tables had filled up now, and the gentle buzz of quiet talk permeated the room.

Suddenly, Tanaka sat up straight. "I will *help*," he said, using the English word, thrusting two hands forward as if he were offering a gift.

"*Arigatou.*" I bowed my head again—but I didn't know what this meant. Would he accompany me to an appointment? Would he intercede to get me a promotion? A raise? Did he think the mere communal spirit of drinking together would help on its own? Whatever it was, I knew I shouldn't take the offer lightly. In Japan, a favor wasn't an isolated event. It meant an ongoing connection. It created *On,* a burden of gratitude. A single favor established on an endless chain of return favors and reciprocations. Tanaka was ready to allow me into this cycle of obligations, *forever.*

For a moment, I wondered if it wouldn't be better to avoid any debts—of gratitude or otherwise. But that was the Japanese way. Here, a man was not autonomous; he was part of the group, fused into it through cooperation and support.

Tanaka began patting the left outside breast of his suit jacket, over his heart. He made a low humming sound—a single tone. Then he reached inside his jacket pocket and face impassive, handed me a folded note. I opened it and read its lopsided letters:

BRaSSERIE SYMPHO-NIKU
FRENCH RESTaURANT

MISTER MaTSUMOTO
832-2447
D-SPACE AD

It was a tip for an advertisement sale! "Domo Arigatou," Thank you very much, I said and smiled. I read the note again: *BRASSERIE SYMPHONIKU*. The word should have been "Symphonique," but in katakana a vowel "U" was added to almost any syllable. "*Ni-ku*" itself meant "meat" or "flesh"—so according to the message, I would be selling an ad for *symphony meat*. "Domo," I said again and bowed my head. I slipped the note into my shirt pocket.

Suddenly, Ono's gesture to help me itself seemed a symphonic moment.

When I glanced up, Tanaka's pupils were swiveled far to the side, and—immediately—they jerked forward again. From the bar, three Japanese businessmen were staring at us. Their stares had broken our *Wa*, our harmony. Then the men laughed, and Tanaka reached quickly for another guzzle of shochu. I reached for my drink too, so Tanaka wouldn't be drinking alone. Again, I felt honored that he allowed me into this inner sphere. Was he taking a chance by helping me? Why had he picked me, and not one of the others? Was it just the overtime work?

If, as I suspected, by Japanese standards our company president Hamaguchi was something of a buffoon—driving teams of gai-jin to sell ads with high-pressure, Western-style telephone sales—and Tanaka was more of the typical "salaryman" type, then Tanaka himself might feel isolated at the office. He was the only Japanese salesman, constantly surrounded by loud, gabbing foreigners. Maybe he craved a peer, a company pal, and since no other Japanese men were at the office, I was the best choice—a makeshift Japanese chum!

Now the drinks weighed heavy on Tanaka's lids, and his head drooped. He took out a 10,000 yen note and placed it on the table. Slowly, he stood up, and I followed him downstairs. Each of us swayed a bit—tottering in our own ways—holding the banister for balance.

Outside, the street was crowded, teeming with Japanese businessmen—many more than I had expected. There were hundreds of them sauntering down the sidewalk. The drunkest ones clung to their friends' shoulders for support, staggering and stumbling.

We stepped into the crowd and shuffled behind another group, all of us walking at exactly the same pace. We were part of the human herd, trudging toward the train station. We were salarymen in our nightly routine of drinking with co-workers after a long day. The company, as Tanaka said, was a second family. Many of the men likely went on company retreats together, where they took communal steam baths and meditated and memorized company philosophy. Their actual families, their wives and children, the salarymen usually only saw on Sundays. Now I was a full member of a company family too . . .

Next to a convenience store, beside a trash pile, a red-faced Japanese man was urinating—squirting against the wall. Tanaka didn't seem to notice. His head was tilted back, and he gazed at the night sky. There were bright pointed stars and a sliver of a moon, a "fingernail moon," the shape of keratin crescents which fell out of a nail clipper. Tanaka was gaping at the moon, and as he walked, a long low moan came from deep in his throat. But directly in front of us lay a reeking pool of yellow vomit, splattered with gummy chunks of regurgitated food . . . Tanaka was oblivious to the vomit—so, without thinking much, I put my hand on his shoulder—"*Abunai!*" Watch Out!, I said, and pushed him hard to the side so he didn't step in the barf.

Tanaka grunted, and his eyes narrowed. He clenched his jaw and glared at me. Then he saw the slimy pool and realized the necessity. But he didn't say anything. His gaze swept over the vomit, lingered on a building, and focused back on the night sky.

We kept walking in silence. At the subway entrance, we bowed to each other. Tanaka held the bow longer than usual. Then we turned and went our separate ways.

Inside my shirt pocket, over my heart, I could feel the warm outline of the folded note he had given me. I patted my breast pocket and made a low, humming sound, just like Tanaka did . . .

V. PERSISTENCE

Early Monday morning, Sanjo boarding house was as quiet as a tomb. Everyone else was still asleep. At least there would be warm water left for the shower. Sanjo's tiny shower was located in the basement, at the bottom of a rickety old stairway. The shower was coin-operated. Five minutes of water cost two hundred yen. You had to shower fast and rinse furiously. I managed to finish before my time ran out and opened the shower door to grab my towel—suddenly, a middle-aged Japanese woman stepped out from behind the bathroom closet. She gazed up at me as if I were a mirage.

Quickly, I covered myself with the towel. "Excuse me," I said. "I didn't realize anybody was in here."

The woman stared at my naked chest. She was attractive. Fine-featured and slim. She held a dirty scrub brush. With the back of her hand, she wiped the moisture off her brow. Then she spoke. "I am finished. I am Fujiwara. Sanjo manager."

"I live in room number seven."

Her eyes swept over me now, lingering for a moment on the towel wrapped around my waist. "Nice young boy," she said.

"Well, thank you. Not so young, really."

"Nice boy. Young. Like my daughter." She squinted at me. Perspiration glistened on her upper lip. "You are early! You must teach *Engurish?*"

"No, I work for an advertising company."

Her brow wrinkled.

"Advertising company—*Koukoku no kaisha desu.*"

She made a low humming sound. "A Japanese company?"

"Yes. Our company is called Japan Publishing Corporation."

'Salaryman!" Fujiwara stared at my face now. "Nice boy. Young," she said again, and let out a long sigh.

I pulled the towel closer. "Bye-Bye," I said, and brushed past her into the hall. Then I caught a whiff, closed off my nose. Fujiwara must have worked hard scrubbing . . .

Holding onto the loose banister, I climbed back upstairs. At the

top stair, I readjusted my towel and—

"ARA!" A woman screamed from downstairs, *"EHHHHH!"*

I rushed back downstairs and peered into the steamy shower room. Fujiwara was bent over, holding two wires with bare stripped ends which led to an electrical outlet. She was motionless and peered straight ahead. Her skin had a grayish hue. A burning odor, oddly sweet, hung in the air.

"Are you okay?" I asked.

She shuddered and spoke in a higher-pitched voice than before. "Yes—only small electric problem. *Denki* . . . Electricity . . ." Her hands shook.

"*Amenai.* Dangerous," I said. "We need an electrical expert."

Fujiwara nodded slowly. Her eyes widened. *"You* fix electricity?"

"No."

"Here. You hold," she said, and offered out a bare strand of wire.

"No thanks. Sorry I have to go to work now," I said. "Work. *Isogashi.* Busy. I have an appointment." Then I left her standing there in the humid shower room, and I hoped she had the sense to let the wires go.

That evening when I got back to my room, I decided to reorganize. I was a respectable salaryman now. No reason to live in sloth. First, I took my suits out of the garment bag and lay them on the futon bed. I collected socks and tossed them into the green trash bag that was my bureau. I folded my boxer shorts and stuffed them into the bag as well. Where could I put the suits? They were getting wrinkled in the garment bag. I needed more space, but that was impossible. I considered the options. Put the suits out on the balcony? Ridiculous. I might get arrested for breaking some city laundry ordinance, not to mention the frequent rain . . . Were there any ceiling beams to hang the suits from? Any window edges that would work?

The solution—I would take down the *Tokonoma* dragon tapestry, pull away the prayer table, move a tiny etched mirror, and hang all the suits from the span of wood which ran across the back wall. Then I wavered. The Tokonoma was the spiritual center of a Japanese room. If I took it down, I was ripping out the sacred heart of the room.

Remove the heart and save the patient.

Using my Swiss army knife, I worked to dig out the antique nail from which hung the long silk tapestry. It gave up with a vicious squeak. Fluttering and ruffling, the tapestry fell into a colorful pile on the floor. Filaments of red and gold lay quivering, exposing black ink marks on the dragon's back, the signature of its maker. The tapestry lay still and lifeless. What would Manager Fujiwara say? Would she be shocked? Would she yell? Would she understand that I had done only what was necessary? Would she realize that anything which occurs is in fact *destiny*?

I hung up my suits, wedging the hangers behind the wooden plank. Then I felt a sudden ache in the pit of my stomach. My vision blurred. The hatch-window bobbed like a porthole. The tapestry swayed, and my head swam. I walked and whirled through the spinning room toward my futon bed. I lay down. Instantly it was too hot in the room. Stifling hot! I managed to stand again and slide open the window to let in some cool night air. There was a moment of relief. But only a moment. Soon I heard the insidious whine of a mosquito and saw its tiny form. I slapped at it—but missed. Damned mosquito. I couldn't see it, but knew the insect was still there . . . I stood perfectly still and utterly alert until I heard its high-pitched singe, as fine and sharp as a dentist's drill, right over my head. Then there were more mosquitoes. Many more. Hundreds. They had been waiting outside the window. And now they had been summoned to swarm.

Closing the window didn't help. The mosquitoes were already inside, on the attack. I had no weapons to fight back. They bit, simultaneously inserting their piercing proboscises into the skin on my neck, my forearms, and my legs—even through the fabric of my pants. The itching was immediate and intense, but I couldn't scratch all the bites at once. And now the mosquitoes were on my face, too . . . I dashed out of the room and into the street.

A few blocks away, on a corner under a green awning, stood one of the tiny jam-packed Japanese appliance stores. It was chock full of alarm clocks, bikes, locks, portable fishing rods, fans, flashlights, screwdrivers, radios, nylon rope, needle-nose tweezers—the place had everything. A hunched and wrinkled man crept around the counter when I entered the store. He looked up at me over the frames of his thick glasses. "*Irrashai.* Wel-come," he croaked.

"Do you have anything to kill mosquitoes?" I inquired, breathing heavily. "For the inside of a room."

The man closed his eyes halfway and gave a prescient nod as if he could visualize the rooms in Sanjo swarming with insects, the foreigners slapping and cursing. He motioned with an open palm to a tall glass display. I was glad to see that he had quite a good selection of mosquito-killing devices, including a silver electric zapper with a spiked top and two strange horseshoe-shaped machines, a big one and a little one. Each horseshoe machine came with a stack of tan wafers.

"Which one is the best?" I asked. "The bugs bite again and again." I made quick pinching gestures on my hand, pulling at the hairs for emphasis.

The man closed his eyes completely and gave a wide smile, a grin which understood the world and all things within it. All people, animals, plant life, and insects. And especially, all insect-plagued foreigners. He nodded for a long time. Finally, he spoke. "Japanese mosquitoes are unique," he said. "Very persistent."

I grit my teeth. "What's best to kill them?"

"The big one, you know." The man's eyes slid toward the shelf. Then, reverently, he lifted out the larger of the white horseshoes, its cord trailing like a stingray barb.

I pointed at the wafers. "What do you do with those?"

What happened next transcended the bounds of language. It obviated the need for words. In an amazing series of noises, grunts, and gestures, the tiny old man showed me exactly what occurred when you slid in a wafer: "SUHHHHH" and a hand jerk >>> shut the catch: "CCCKK" and a clenched fist >>> plugged the machine in so the wafer heated and sent up a poison mist: "PWFFF, PWFFF" circling hands, fingers wiggling >>> reached a mosquito: "EEEEET" and a wide-eyed clap >>> asphyxiated the bug: UGUH—UHHHRRR," hands around neck >>> and sent the bug tumbling to the floor dead: "SHIIIIII-NN KAH," head shaking in mortis tremens. Exhausted, the old man stared down at the floor.

"Good," I said, and bought the thing. Happily, I carried it back to Sanjo, back to my soon-to-be-mosquito-less chamber.

When I opened the door to my room, my chest tightened. The breath left my lungs. I blinked and stood motionless. Kneeling in front of me with her hands on her knees, staring at the wall as if in a trance, her small frail body hunched forward—was Fujiwara, the Sanjo Manager. She wore a white silk kimono. Her hair was more neatly brushed than before. Her face was scrubbed and clean. She had reattached the dragon tapestry to the wall and moved the prayer table back into position. All of my suits were neatly folded in little piles on the futon bed. Fujiwara was gazing at the Tokonoma dragon. Its serpentine body had uncoiled. Its piercing eyes were vibrant and triumphant.

She didn't look at me for a moment, didn't make a sound. We were motionless, co-existing in the silence. Then she turned. The twist of her neck was slow and staggered. Her eyes seemed clouded and far away, but her expression was calm and patient as if she had awaited me for a hundred years, pondered the moment, and knew that I would arrive. Now she was savoring the experience. She spoke softly, "I fix . . . your room."

"Thank you," I said.

Fujiwara nodded for a long while, then leaned further forward and placed both hands on the floor in front of her, as if in Arabic prayer. With a tremble and a lift of her small buttocks, she stood up. She wavered for a moment, pushing down on the balls of her feet as if they were numb. Then she took a step toward me and stumbled— I rushed forward to catch her, but she was all right. She found her balance and walked toward the door. Then she turned to me, exposing her long white neck like a floating swan. Her eyes opened and closed in sloe-eyed blinks. "I want . . . to show you . . . something," she said, beckoning with two slender fingers.

I dropped the mosquito-killer on the tatami mat and followed her out into the hall. Together, we descended the stairway. Each stair had a different sound, a musical wail in the night. Downstairs in the entryway, Fujiwara's eyes had a quiet expectation. Somehow she looked more attractive in the evening. "This way," she whispered and turned to unlatch a door under the stairs.

I ducked under the stairwell and was surprised to find myself in a dusty, hidden suite. Ancient tatami mats lay underfoot. There was a large Western-style double bed and a tall brass lamp, black with age marks. In the back of the room were wooden shelves clogged with yellowing books and papers. An armoire stood in the corner, and a pant leg was caught between its doors. I inhaled and felt the stuffy air wrap around me like a musty blanket. It was hard to breathe.

"Look!" said Fujiwara, holding out a stained photo of a very pretty but buck-toothed girl who sat smiling under an oak tree. "This ees my daughter. She is in New York." Her voice lilted like a guitar string being tuned. "She told me she has American *boifurendo* who looks, like you." Fujiwara stared at me and moved closer. I could feel the heat of her body. I could smell her jasmine perfume.

Fujiwara pointed toward the bed. "This ees where my husband slept. This was our bed." She opened her palm, gesturing toward the shelves. "These were his books and his papers." She reached for a framed photograph, dusted off the glass, and held it out to me. It was a picture of a foreign man with a beard. He was big-framed, handsome but very thin, with a jutting Adam's apple and a protruding collar bone as if he had lost a lot of weight very quickly.

"You see . . ." Fujiwara's eyes were moist now. Her words seemed to choke in the back of her throat. "He was like, cherry blossom. He was, most beautiful, before he . . . died." She said the last word slowly, reverently. More heat emanated from her body. In the darkened room, she seemed to glow. Again, her eyes had a trance-like, faraway look. "I told him, go to Nara." Her voice was hoarse, nasal. "I told him go, go to Pokkuri temple to pray for . . . for . . ." She struggled as if unable to get out the words, then shivered and continued, "to pray for peace . . ."

I took a step back and something crumbled under my foot like an old cracker, powder now. At Pokkuri temple, the dying Japanese went to pray for a quick and easy death. They brought their underclothes as an offering to put on the stone shrine.

"He would not go to Pokkuri." Fujiwara closed her eyes as if this refusal implied an unspeakably horrible period of suffering for the man. "But I said I would go to pray for him." She nodded as if it was a profound solution. "But then, too much time . . ." She shook her head. "I was too late."

My dry tongue pressed against the roof of my mouth. The tongue felt hard, extraneous, swollen. Dust from the room clung to the back of my throat and made each breath painful, an arid spear of air. Instinctively I moved—two steps only—toward a tiny window, half-obscured by piles of cups and saucers and a thick leather belt which snaked across the glass.

Fujiwara shuffled forward. Her expression had softened. She was more relaxed, as if somehow she had swept her memories aside. Her hand grasped my arm, and her hot fingers burned my skin. "I had other boyfriend," she said. "From Egypt, like movie-star Omar. But after five years, he also got sick."

"I'm sorry . . ." I coughed and wanted to shove out of the room, to clear a path toward the door and out into the cool air. But I only stood and looked at Fujiwara. She was trembling again now.

"My Omar told me if I ever sleep with another man, he would come back in next life to kill me." She gazed down at the floor.

I didn't know what to say. I glanced at the bed, which seemed to have a dark stain near the pillow.

Fujiwara tucked a stray wisp of long black hair behind her ear. "He said he would come back—but I do not believe him."

"That's good." I nodded slowly.

"This was our room together." Fujiwara looked around. "Omar slept here. You can sleep here too. You can use closet."

I felt my eyebrows rise, my chest tighten. I coughed to clear my throat until I could speak. "Thanks, but my room is okay."

"You don't like this room?" Fujiwara had a sad expression. She leaned against the wall for support.

"Yes, it's nice, but . . ."

"Something is right when the heart is quiet." She touched her chest. Then she laughed—a sharp and insane note in the darkness. She moved toward the bed and stroked it. "Feel . . . Feel my bed. Feel how soft it is."

"Well thanks, but I better go." I took a step backward toward the stairway, back toward my own room. "I have to—go. Thanks again."

Fujiwara let out a soft moan. "I want to make tea ceremony for you now. I want to show you tea leaves at the bottom." She inhaled rapidly, as if she were about to cry, and closed her eyes. "I can make tea for you, every night . . ." She tip-toed closer to me, closer to the bed.

I side-stepped, avoiding her, avoiding her arms which were extended and spotted like tentacles in the strange light of the room. "Unfortunately, I'm allergic to tea." I rushed an answer, any answer.

Fujiwara stood perfectly still, a statue in the evening, a stone-sculpted maiden of the night. Her white kimono shone and hinted, glimmered like a diaphanous specter. Then it stopped shining. The whiteness paled and the old room came back into focus. The sadness was written on her face, written in her sagging cheeks and lips, and in her dulled eyes. But suddenly, the sadness went away. The sorrow was gone. The pain had left and been replaced, amazingly, by a tight-lipped smile. A resignation. Then the smile opened wider, opened up into her cheeks; and her eyes gleamed in a poignant bliss, an utter acceptance, almost an enjoyment of suffering as one enjoys life . . . She didn't move from her spot in the center of the room.

Neither of us spoke. I walked around Fujiwara, barely brushing her shoulder. I found my way to the door and to the street outside, where the cold night air stung my face.

But I had nowhere to go, so I turned back. The Sanjo entryway was dark. Pitch black. The naked single light bulb on the landing had burnt out. I found the stairway and took a step up. The wood creaked and sang out. Step by step, holding on to the banister which wobbled on old nails, I groped my way upstairs.

Safe inside my room, I immediately unwrapped the mosquito-killing machine. I inserted a wafer in the appropriate slot and plugged the cord into an outlet. I touched the device, felt it vibrate. An acrid smell filled the room. Soon, overhead, a mosquito was flying in a skewed circle. Then it fell from the air and landed directly in front of me on the tatami mat. I could see its swollen, blood-engorged body and twisted wings. I could see its twitching legs. Then it stopped moving.

The killing machine throbbed with an electric pulse.

VI. SYMPHONY OF MEAT

Tuesday morning was hot and humid, bright as an arc welder. I walked up the stairs from Shibuya Station and found myself next to another foreigner from the office. He was dark-haired and dark-skinned. He wore a gray pin-striped, double-breasted suit, made of a shimmering sharkskin fabric not popular in the States.

"Hi," I said. "I think we work at the same office."

"Yes. I am Maximillian. You can call me 'Max'." He had a friendly chortle. "How is the job going?"

"Good. I have an appointment with SONY today."

"SONY!" said Max, "Oh, boy!" He chuckled and let out a high-pitched, wavering whistle. "I knew you could do it. When I saw you, I said to myself, 'That guy—he can sell!'"

"Well, thanks. How did you know?"

"—Not like the other new salesman."

I wasn't sure what to say. Was I being tested? Tricked? "I don't know them very well."

Max patted me on the back. "I weel help you be the next <u>Tokyo Time</u> manager. I sell for a different publication called <u>Tokyo Today</u>. So there is no competition between us. Sounds good, huh?" He grinned, revealing tobacco-stained teeth.

"Yeah," I said, trying to seem excited. But a salesman from another established publication might be even more of a competition . . . I didn't press the issue. "How long have you been here?" I asked.

"Ten years. I am from Iraq, but I grew up in Turkey. I lived in U.S., too—like you! Now my home is here, and I have Japanese wife. You must work to prove that you are Number One! You must sell the most."

"I'll do my best," I said, listening to the echo of Hamaguchi's *must* in Max's sentences.

"*Shachou* did not tell you," Max continued, "But he needs a manager very soon for <u>Tokyo Time</u>. He will not pick a woman. It will be you, or one of the others."

I leaned forward to hear better.

"I do not like the others," Max said bluntly, shaking his head. "I will help you. We will be buddies." He smiled again and patted my shoulder now, grasping it for a moment, an odd moment. There was something so arbitrary, so pre-determined in Max's proclamation that we were buddies—almost naive, like the announcement of a young boy to his classmate that they're best friends since they both play marbles. I could feel the spot on my shoulder where Max had held it. But the grasp wasn't a homosexual gesture, more brotherly. I snuck a quick glance at Max's profile: a rounded forehead and slightly beaked nose—a middle-eastern Eastern nose. Max grew up in Turkey, did he say? Did male friendships have a different tone where he came from? More immediate? More cliquish?

Side-by-side, we turned the corner onto the stumpy street toward the office. "Is it helpful to have a Japanese wife to get advertising sales?" I asked.

"No. She is female. She doesn't understand." His brow wrinkled. "I tell you honestly, I married a Japanese, and I am glad. But some-times . . ." He squinted and looked up, as if to see something far away. "Sometimes, I am afraid, I am losing . . ." He struggled for words. "Sometimes I am thinking too much like a Japanese. Ten years . . . All the time I am with them, you know?"

I nodded and swallowed hard. But I didn't really know. I didn't understand. It was fascinating, this notion of losing your identity in another culture—of succumbing to it, unless you struggled to hold on to your own values. Especially interesting here in Japan, where the foreigner was an outsider. Was that it? Had Max worked so hard to fit in all these years, put so much energy into it, that he was for-getting how he used to be?

"You can make a lot of money here, like me." Max's eyes wid-ened. "You are young. How old are you?"

"Twenty-four."

"Yes, you are young. In a few years—two, maybe three—you will have beeg salary. I will help."

"Thanks. Tanaka-san said he'd help me, too."

Instantly, Max's eyes narrowed, and he took one step back. "Lis-ten to me," he said in a deep voice, almost rough. "Do not trust the others. Only me. We are foreigners. We must stick together." He nodded and patted my shoulder again. His face was stern.

Shoulder-to-shoulder, we walked up the stairs into the company office. Then I turned and pushed into the restroom. "See you later,"

I said, and closed the bathroom door.

On the single hand towel in the bathroom, a lone yellowed thing, I searched to find a cleanish spot, rinsed the towel, and wiped my forehead. Ninety-five percent humidity today in Tokyo, that's what the news said. I straightened my tie—dammit! Drops of water had spotted the silk. They would leave odd polka-dotted stains . . . So I wet the hand towel again, got it sopping wet. Then I used an emergency technique: When your tie got stained, you wet the entire tie to cover the blemish—not just the individual spots—turning the whole tie a few shades darker, disguising the individual sully with one enormous smear. It worked. The only challenge was the knot. I rubbed it harder. There. You couldn't even see the water marks. The entire tie was now crimson instead of red; blood-colored, not gaudy . . . Proud of my newly scarlet tie, I sat down at my desk.

At 9:00 a.m. exactly, Tanaka-san arrived at the office. It was the first time I had seen him since he gave me the tip for the advertisement sale. "Domo Arigatou," Thank you, I said again.

Tanaka's eyes had a kindly gleam.

I had waited until Tanaka was in the office to call about his advertising sales tip, just in case he needed to back me up. I picked up the phone and dialed the number. "Hai! Matsumoto desu," a gruff male voice answered.

I gave my sales pitch, just like I was supposed to.

"*Wakarimasen*," I don't understand, Matusmoto answered. So again, I switched to Japanese, and speaking in a quiet voice, set an appointment for that afternoon.

Brasserie "Symphoniku" was in Nogizaka—not too far from the office. I decided to walk in the afternoon, despite the heat. I headed down Gaien Nishi Dori, past the park and the salaryman bar from the night before. I paused at the corner. Someone had cleaned up the vomit.

I looked at the building numbers but couldn't find the restaurant, even after walking up and down the street where it should have been. Finally, I spotted a small blue sign: "Brasserie Symphoniku French Cuisine." It had an image of a finger pointing towards a very steep metal stairway under a bank. No wonder the Brasserie needed to advertise . . .

The restaurant was small, more of a cafe-bar, and Matsumoto—in a chef's smock and a maroon beret—sat at one of the tables underneath a French flag.

"Your restaurant is pretty. Truly French," I said. At least the flag looked authentic.

"*Oui*," said Matsumoto, and laughed.

I opened my sample magazine and began to explain, but Matsumoto interrupted. "I like D-space," he said. "I will take D-Space."

And that was that.

I felt a rush of adrenaline—a flutter in my chest. But I tried not to seem too excited. I slowed down my words and folded my hands under the table—all the while imagining the expressions on the other salesmens' faces when I walked back into the office with yet another contract!

Matsumoto signed with a clumsy squiggle. I realized that I couldn't have gotten the contract without speaking Japanese. I had to disobey Hamaguchi—again. I had to follow my own intuition and analyses. Of course, I only got the sale with Tanaka's help. But that was also a function of intuition, and my sense of the Japanese frame of mind . . .

"*Merci beaucoup*," I said to Matsumoto (Hamaguchi hadn't said anything about not speaking *French*. . .) Then I stood up, bowed, and climbed the stairs to the street. As I walked toward the office, I swung my legs in long happy strides, giant floating steps. Somehow, my feet seemed lighter than before. Yes, things were working out in Tokyo now. I was learning to function here, learning to fit in. It took a while to get the hang of the system, though. It took someone culturally sensitive like me to master the Japanese ways.

My tongue was dry, parched. I was thirsty after all the talking and the hard work. Big Bunyan work. I only drank a can of orange juice at breakfast. Half a glass of water at lunch. No coffee all day! And I didn't even crave it! Must have been a couple of years since my last coffee-less day. Yes, one adapts . . .

To peek at the contract again, I opened my briefcase. The yellow paper nested next to my dictionary. Just wait until Hamaguchi saw that contract! And Max. And the other salesmen . . . I visualized myself marking the ad on the office chart, creating a long path of marks all the way to the manager position at the end!

¥

Back at the office, I immediately brought out the yellow contract paper and lay it on my desk. It glowed and shimmered in the light from the window. I wouldn't wave it around, though. Hamaguchi had said to put all new contracts on his desk, right? So I got up—carrying a paper out in front of you was normal, right? I glanced at Paul, another American salesman from somewhere in Mississippi. He was leaning on his elbow, leafing through a magazine. Max was on the phone. Hamaguchi came out of his office and spotted the contract paper right away. "You have other contract?"

"*Hai, so desu, ne,*" Yes, that's right, I said. I had earned the right to speak Japanese.

"*Emedeto gozaimasu!*" Congratulations! said Hamaguchi.

Paul jerked to his feet. "You got a contract!" His voice was shrill. "Lemme see." Then he pursed his lips and clicked his ballpoint pen in and out. He continued in his high-pitched Southern drawl, "Ah'm gonna meet with McDonald's tomorrow. We were talkin' 'bout A-space, a full-page ad!"

"Great," I said, and glanced over at Tanaka, who was smiling and nodding.

I smiled back at him. We had a tacit understanding. We wouldn't tell about the tip-off. It was our secret. A Japanese secret.

"Good job!" said Vanessa, another American just hired as part of the new sales staff, while taking her junior year off from college and studying Japanese literature. She wiggled in her seat and smoothed back her hair.

Max had come into the office and was listening. "Oh-Hoh!" he said. "CONTRACT!" he bellowed and walked over to put his arm around my shoulder and stood too close to me.

Abruptly—as if someone just cursed at him—Tanaka stopped smiling. He looked back down at his notebooks.

"Congratulations!" said Max, patting my shoulder, massaging it. He gazed at Paul who now sat glumly at his desk as if at a doctor's office recovering from bad news. Max kept talking, "Paul, you better hurry up and sell, or there will be no more contracts!" Max sniggered and wiped his big nose. He took hold of the contract paper—with two hands—shaking it a little, reading it again and again. He turned back to me. "You have Nissan ad, too. What size is Nissan ad?" The size was clearly circled on the wall chart with a thick marker, but Max asked anyway. "What size space is Nissan?" he asked again.

"C-Space," I answered.

"Ohhh! Big space!" said Max. He pointed at the chart. "Paul, do you know what size C-space ad is?"

I felt a little guilty. Max really knew how to rub it in, and I wished he would just shut up.

Tanaka was staring at Max. Tanaka's cheeks were set, rigid as ice. The two men definitely didn't get along. I could feel their hostility. But I couldn't worry about stupid office politics like this. I was just here to do my job. To work hard. To learn about Japan . . . I glanced out the window. In a breeze, a stream of reddish leaves blew past the building. One leaf caught on the porch rail and trembled in the wind. Mistaking it for an insect perhaps, a black bird darted over and took the leaf in its mouth, then spit it back out—head quivering, beak twitching. Did birds have saliva or just a natural beak lubricant?

"Are you busy?" asked Tanaka. He seemed to be smirking at me, a Japanese smirk with narrowed, glinting eyes.

"*Hai, so desu,* " Yes, that's right. I stared down at the scratched, cloudy glass top of my desk, nodding as if in deep thought about the complexity and responsibility of my job, and the range of obligations, which extended even into the zoological kingdom.

"*Gambatte, gambatte kudasai.* Do your best," said Tanaka, closing his eyes, lowering his head as if his real vision—the optic lens—were in his crown. I could no longer determine if he was sincere or mocking.

I took out the phone book and searched for new ad prospects. Then I shuddered when another large brown roach squirmed up the side of the drawer and darted up my forearm. It hesitated on my elbow, tentacles waving, digging its tiny feet into my skin. In one continuous motion, I slapped the thing off my arm and stepped on it, grinding the bug down hard into the rug—reducing it to a chitinous crushed abdomen, a lumpy pool of white internal organs, and a stain of brown liquid. One of the insect's hind legs stuck out from the carpet fibers and trembled—was that just a nerve reaction, or the pliancy of the rug? Could the bottom half of the bug still be alive?

I gagged.

"*Cocku-roachi?*" asked Tanaka, who was eating his lunch with loud chews. It was a "*bento*" combination take-out plate. He took a bite of shredded pickled cabbage into his mouth. A strand of lettuce wiggled above his bottom lip.

"*Shindeiru cocku-roachi,*" Dead cockroach, I corrected.

Tanaka paled.

In my mind, from long ago, I heard the Buddhist coda: *Better luck in the next life . . .*

The following day, side by side, Max and I walked from the office through the humid afternoon toward a restaurant he called "the secret lunch spot." As usual, my T-shirt clung to my back in the heat. But at least I wasn't ruining the two-hundred-thread-count, pinpoint cotton oxford. Traditionally, a man wore a T-shirt under a dress shirt—it actually kept you cooler. Max, I noted, had large perspiration stains under the arms of his striped polyester shirt. "Do you eat at this secret restaurant a lot?" I asked.

"Yes, almost every day. It ees good food. Japanese food, but beeg portion." He licked his bottom lip. "There it ees!" On the second floor of a shabby two-story building, with all the windows open for ventilation, was the restaurant. I could just make out a table or two— I blinked. Yes, I had been here before. Max must have taken different back streets to get to the restaurant, but this was the same place that Tanaka had taken me to go drinking. It looked different in the day, less inviting and somewhat dilapidated even, with nail-split boards under the windows.

Max led me up the same rickety stairs and into the hot little table area with only a few customers. Two fans blew cross-currents of warm, moist air through the restaurant. One of the fans sat on the counter blowing a garlic wind right at us. "*Irrashaimassen!*" Welcome! The cook called out from behind the stove.

I smiled, enjoying the uncomplicated acceptance. Even though Max was a foreigner, he seemed well-liked—and as his friend, so was I . . . We sat down at a table in the corner. The menu was all in *kanji* for traditional Japanese dishes. There were several kanji I didn't recognize. "What's this one?" I asked, pointing.

Max squinted down at it, puffing his cheeks, making an odd, gusting noise. Finally, he spoke. "I don't know. I don't read kanji."

"How do you know what to order?"

"I always order the same thing, *yakumi no buta niku*. Spicy pork meat. It ees good." Max patted his belly.

I wasn't in the mood for a heavy meat dish, but I didn't seem to have much choice when Max ordered for both of us. Soon the food was brought to our table.

"Do you know how to use chopsticks?" Max asked.

"I'm a chopsticks expert." With a quick pinch, I picked up some of the grayish meat. It didn't taste bad, despite the garlic. From behind the menu rack, Max pulled out a small wooden bowl that I hadn't noticed before. It contained inch-long speckled eggs. He grabbed a metal tool with two handles, like a nutcracker, and split open one of the eggs over his rice. The orange yolk spurted out, as if under pressure.

"You like quail egg?" he asked.

"No. I don't think so. Thanks, anyway."

"Tanaka-san doesn't like quail egg either," said Max, in an odd change of subject. "I make a lot more money than Tanaka." He leaned forward and spoke in a confidential whisper. "He has been weeth the company eight years longer, but I sell much more. And Hamaguchi lets me use his office sometimes."

I took a sip of beer which had also been brought to our table, unrequested. Why was Max revealing this information? No wonder Tanaka didn't like Max. If Max had worked a shorter time for the company, his larger salary went against the Japanese tradition of rewarding seniority and loyalty, not individual merit. In paying Max more, Hamaguchi was violating the whole tradition of bonding among Japanese employees, undermining their cohesive spirit. And Max was a foreigner . . . Of course, Tanaka would be jealous. I had read that in many Japanese companies, even a pedestrian clerk of twenty-five years' service—a janitor of twenty-five years for that matter—made more money than a white-collar manager of fifteen years' employment. Hamaguchi was trying to combine established Japanese business customs with Western sales practices, fusing them together in some odd mutation. And Tanaka didn't like it one bit.

Why was Hamaguchi so different from the other Japanese? So different from the traditional Tanaka? I looked up and realized that Max had been studying me while he ate. "Hamaguchi doesn't seem to me so much like a typical Japanese," I said. "Where is he from?"

Max mixed some meat into his rice. He made me wait for an answer while he chewed a big mouthful, used the napkin, all greased up now, and gulped some more beer. Eventually, he answered. "Once he told me his family is from Fussa, near Yokota U.S. Military Base. He lived in Hawaii and started selling guidebook advertisements there. But he knew more money is in Tokyo. So he moved back here."

"Hard to imagine how he fits in with the conservative Japanese." I said, thinking of Hamaguchi's beady eyes, epaulets, and suit jackets with oddly cut lapels. Hamaguchi was almost another species.

Max cracked a third egg, a big splotched egg. It lumped and oozed around the glutinous rice like mucous. He was quiet now, mixing and poking at his food. Had I said too much? Taken liberties in talking about the boss? Max said we were buddies, right? Buddies talked about things. "It's odd," I continued, "Hamaguchi told me not to speak Japanese."

This time Max laughed. "Yes, he likes to tell people what to do."

I finished the meat—as much off it as I wanted, anyway. Then I started on the rice, pouring soy sauce over it first.

"Why don't you eat rice with your meat?" asked Max, with a funny half-smile.

"I don't know. I guess I like to save the rice for last. It's my dessert."

Max pointed with two stubby fingers. "Well, if you go out to lunch with Japanese businessmen, you cannot eat like that." He shook his head.

"Why not?"

"Because they will theenk you are weird. And they won't want to do business with you. It is not normal to eat the rice separately."

"Not normal??" The tie gripped my neck, squeezed like a garrote. "I don't care if they think it's *normal.* You mean just because of the order I eat my food, they won't sign a contract?" I set my chopsticks down on the table.

Max seemed amused. "You're in their country."

I stared out the window at the blistering street below—no trees. Then I glanced around, away from Max, to look at the other patrons. The restaurant had filled up. At the next table, a man was reading a magazine—an efficient combination for the automobile/soft-porn enthusiast. On the open page, next to a transmission diagram, a buxom Japanese girl sat on top of a pink Nissan. She was in the act of removing her brassiere, exposing a wide nipple. Of course, she wore her underwear. In Japan, it was illegal to show pubic hair, even in the full, pornographic "meat-market" magazines.

Apparently, every country had different rules for meat . . .

"We must go back to the office now," said Max. "Or we will be late."

VII. THE CHERRY TREE

From far away, Ace looked like a blond, Nordic giant. He was another American from the boarding house. At six-foot-four, he towered above the sea of Japanese who passed him on the sidewalk. Next to Ace stood a tall girl. She had long wavy hair, flashing black eyes, and dark skin. "Have you met my girlfriend, Noriko?" he asked.

I walked with the two of them to the train station. Noriko carried herself with graceful, long-legged strides. But her head drooped, and she gazed only at the few feet of concrete directly in front of her. On Noriko's wrist hung a leather bracelet interwoven with red stones and small pieces of metal, almost too clumsy for her slender arm. "That's a nice bracelet," I said.

She didn't look at me but glanced up at Ace as if for approval. He had an ironic smile. We were all quiet for a few steps. Then I couldn't resist asking, "Is that a special bracelet? A charm bracelet?"

"No, it's . . . it's . . ." Noriko didn't finish her sentence.

Ace was grinning. "I guess we can tell, can't we?"

"Sure, you can tell me anything. I'm sworn to secrecy." I nodded and tried to look knowledgeable and trustworthy like a wise old mountain man, an omniscient mushroom-eater who wouldn't be shocked even by the wildest revelations. Then I glanced down, so I didn't seem too curious.

"It's kind of an amulet," said Ace. "You know for good luck. But this one's for something else." He hesitated for a moment. "It keeps her from getting pregnant."

I thought I heard a squeak from Noriko, but then she was quiet. Ace's ears reddened.

It wasn't such a big deal, right? Sophisticated people could discuss the weather, sports, restaurants, wrist-thong-hanging-rock birth control methods—all small matters. "Does it work?" I asked.

Ace shrugged.

"Well, it's a good method. More comfortable than . . ."

Ace caught my eye, winked, and changed the subject. "When's the rent due? Do you know the Sanjo manager, Fujiwara? Noriko calls her a *haba*."

"*Haba!*" Noriko tossed her hair. "*Shiwa no haba*—<u>wrinkled</u> haba." She stopped walking suddenly. "*Haba* ees Okinawa lizard," she announced.

"She thinks Fujiwara is an old bitch," Ace explained like a true American. No hedging of words.

"Why is she a *haba?*"

"I guess they just don't get along."

"*HABA,*" Noriko said again, enjoying the attention.

Soon we were out of the curved back streets and on the busy main street, *Tokiwa Dori*. Noriko moved over to walk closer to Ace. Her face was turned toward him, so she didn't make eye contact with the other Japanese on the sidewalk. She avoided their passing stares. But then an extremely short woman, her head and spiny neck bent forward in an obscene ninety-degree malformation, staggered out of a shop and stood dead still in the middle of the sidewalk. The woman glared at Noriko. Ace put his arm around Noriko as if in protection—but she only let him hold her for a moment. In Japan, a long display of public affection was inconceivable.

I tried to make conversation. "What subway line are you taking?"

Noriko answered almost curtly in Japanese, "*Marunouchi sen kara Tozai.*" She gave a nervous laugh. "Sor-ree, I meanu—"

"It's okay, I understood."

"*Honto?*" Really? Then she spoke in a quick stream of Japanese, speaking faster and faster until her words gushed out at a frantic pace. She described in detail all the subway stops on her train line, all the transfers and two bus lifts to her final destination, her Aunt's house, the fence, the shrubs . . .

Ace was glancing around uneasily, linguistically isolated like a child forced to attend a foreign school. So at the end of Noriko's string of flower descriptions, just as she appeared to be launching into a narration of the arrangement of her Aunt's kitchen, I interrupted and said the first thing that came to me. "I got a new mosquito-killer yesterday."

"Great," said Ace, with a ponderous look. And Noriko stopped talking. Perhaps she needed a chance to catch her breath. We walked a few blocks down the street, and soon we were standing near the top of the stairwell leading into the subway station. Noriko started to walk away. She turned her head back for a moment to give us a weak smile. We waved to her until she began to descend the stairs and was engulfed by the crowd, which took exactly three steps down.

Ace slapped me on the shoulder. "Where are we drinkin'?" he asked in a low voice. He clenched his jaw.

I didn't feel like drinking in the middle of the day, but for some reason, I didn't have the heart to tell him this. "I know a place," I said.

We walked quickly down the smaller, strangely-angling streets near the station, cutting through smelly lanes with glittering porno bars, pachinko parlors, and sushi take-out stands. At one of these stands, the electricity was off, and inside glass display cabinets, the sashimi lay in pools of half-melted ice. Striated muscles of halibut and tuna glistened and slid toward the watery depths of the display— a final submergence.

We turned and headed northwest, past the boarding house to a quaint little street with flying banners, kite-shaped lanterns, closet-sized fruit stands, and microscopic laundromats. We moved to the side of the five-foot-wide street to make room for an old woman on a bicycle. Her groceries were stuffed into a basket. She was riding so slowly she seemed ready to topple over, especially when she stared too long at Ace's blond hair.

I surveyed the view ahead like a film buff enjoying the cinematography of his favorite movie. But Ace enjoyed none of this scene. He scanned the horizon as if looking for a hole in a distant line of artillery. "Where's the damn bar?" he asked sharply. Each word stung.

"Well, I thought we'd find one up this way. Away from downtown. It's nicer here." I squinted and peered down the lane. After a few more steps, I caught a glimpse through a window of two elderly Japanese men sitting at a corner table, one pouring beer into his friend's raised glass. Then in reciprocation, the man lifted his own glass, which was filled by the friend. It was an *akachochin* watering spot. "Look," I pointed. "This looks like a good place, huh?" I opened the slight door with rice-paper windows. It was a feather-door, an angel's wing.

Inside, the room was dim and smelled of liquor, garlic, and celery. But there was just enough light for us to see. Just enough light for us to observe the drinking men stop talking and turn around. A gaunt-cheeked bartender behind the counter held a towel in one hand and a heavy wooden bowl in the other. As soon as he saw us, he banged the bowl down hard on the counter—a loud clatter cut through the room. Then he yelled, *"GAI-JIN WA KOKO HAI CHYA IKE-NAI!"* NO GAI-JIN INSIDE HERE !

A flash of heat ran through my body—and suddenly, I felt light-headed, as if freed from the pull of gravity. I spoke loudly. "We are *Gai-KOKU-jin! Foreign COUNTRY people!"* I said, emphasiz-ing the most formal and polite designation. I took a step forward. The righteousness surged through my chest, *"GAI-KOKU-JIN!"* I repeated. **"SAY IT RIGHT!"**

One of the seated old men made a nasty grunt. It was a course sound as if emanating from nose and throat at the same time. Then the bar owner was shouting a stream of curses. It was a spray of insolent sounds from a shaking face with a jutting chin. The other men stood up to join the yammer like chimpanzees gathering to oust intruders. I stepped back until Ace and I stood side-by-side. Then I backed up further—with a quick glance to make sure the door was still there . . .

Ace looked around the room and stepped back as well.

We made a quick exit and took fast strides down the street. But after about twenty paces, we slowed down. "It's the hundred-year war," said Ace. "It started in 1939. And we're losing . . ."

"Is that it?"

"Sure. They can't fight anymore, so now they'll buy the world."

"Well, I don't think they want to buy—"

"You know what they do? You know what?" He didn't give me time to answer. He spoke faster now, getting more upset with each word. "They sell at twenty percent below market value and buy at twenty percent above market for everything. And smile and bow. That's their plan. To buy us up slowly. It's only here in Tokyo that we see what it's really like. How they really feel. They think they're safe here. Especially when they're drinking . . ." Suddenly he wheeled around. "I'm gonna go kick that fucker's ass!" He made a fist. The anger ripped across his face in a wave, distorting his mouth and red-dening his neck.

He turned and pushed through two Japanese men, each a head shorter and half as wide as Ace and probably less than half his weight. He shouldered through them like a Mack truck plowing through milkweed. He was a blond-haired giant, a Viking out for vengeance.

I jogged after him. "Wait!" I touched his shoulder, then ducked to avoid his powerful arm shoving me away. My voice was urgent, "Ace, forget about them. We'll just get in trouble with the cops and—what about Noriko?"

That stopped him. He stood perfectly still in the street. His arms were spread wide. He didn't blink. And his chest swelled with each heavy breath.

"Come on, I know another bar. A good one this time, where they like us." I forced myself to smile. "Just forget about it."

We turned onto another street and walked away, out of trouble's range. I hoped I could remember which direction to go. We strode past a tiny park with children playing. Thank God the kids didn't shout anything. On instinct, I cut between two dilapidated buildings and through a walkway I thought I recognized. There it was! A low building with the door propped open. A greenish glow from inside washed into the street. Nailed to the door was a wooden sign with English words routed out and painted red: **THE CHERRY TREE**.

"Here," I said. "You can meet Moe-san."

Inside the bar was lit by glass lamps with green shades. Small tables were arranged in rows, and to the right was a bar crammed with liquor bottles and glasses. On the wall hung blurred photographs, postcards with grayed edges, and faded newspaper articles from time immemorial. A Bob Dylan song played over the stereo, that unmistakable gravel-voice wafting out of a pair of old walnut-cabineted AR speakers.

There were no other customers.

Then Moe-san stepped from behind the bar. He was an Asian man with long hair tied in a ponytail, gold-rimmed glasses, and a tie-dyed T-shirt emblazoned with a wobbly black peace sign. His eyes seemed only half-open, giving him the sage, contemplative demeanor of a monk. Gently, he lay down the knife he was using to chop vegetables. "Hello," said Moe-san. He had a pure and honest expression. It was a Zen master's tranquil gaze. Instantly, Ace relaxed.

"This is my friend, Ace," I said.

Moe-san nodded humbly and gestured toward the tables. We sat down, and I ordered beers. Ace wiped his forehead with the back of his hand. Soon, eyes still half-closed, Moe-san brought out—glided over—two gigantic bottles of Sapporo beer and a tray of shelled peanuts. I filled Ace's glass first, then my own. "Cheers," I said.

But Ace's expression didn't change, so I continued, "A toast . . ." I spoke loudly and waited until Ace looked up. "To HONOR! Get on her and stay honor!"

This time Ace laughed, just as Moe-san slid in a new cassette.

There was soft jazz now, piano and bass.

Ace leaned towards me. "Secretly, you know the Japs are pretty racist," he whispered.

I glanced over my shoulder to make sure Moe-san was out of hearing range. "Some of them," I said.

"_Most_ of them."

I tried to change the subject. "How much rent do you pay?"

"Rent? To Fujiwara? She's an old witch. That's what Noriko calls her. _Kimu_—Old Witch."

"I thought she calls her a _haba_-lizard."

"Well, that too."

"Why doesn't Noriko like Fujiwara?"

Ace leaned back his head. "It's a long story." But his tone was encouraging.

"We've got lots of beer left, and I've got ten thousand yen in my pocket. More fun to spend it on beer than rent anyway . . ."

Ace took a handful of peanuts and, one-by-one, ate them out of his hand as he spoke.

"Noriko was explaining it all to me. How just being Japanese isn't enough. There are special kinds of Japanese that are like, low class. The _Burakumin_ who handle butchered meat, and then some others—Anus or _Ainu_ or something—who have a lot of body hair, but rounder eyes. They're from the north. But the other Japanese don't like them either for some reason. I forgot."

I glanced past Ace and gazed up at the postcards and tapestries on the walls. On the shelf above Ace sat a cassette deck and an enviably large collection of music—jazz, rock, classical, folk. "You can put on whatever you want here," I pointed.

Ace didn't look. His expression didn't change. He just kept talking. "And the mainland Japs don't like Okinawans, either. They think Okinawans are country bumpkins." Like a baby grabbing for its bottle, Ace grasped his beer with two hands and finished it off. Then, eyes tearing, he looked at me and spoke quietly. "Noriko is Okinawan. And Fujiwara doesn't like her."

I felt a flush of sympathy. "But Noriko is a great girl. She's pretty and nice and funny and—"

"Of course she is!" Ace's eyes were ablaze. His hair was in disarray, and one side stood straight up as if he were a cartoon victim of electric shock. "The Okinawans are good people, and they're friendlier than Tokyo Japanese. Tokyo Japs have a saying—_With women as_ *with rice, the whiter the better.* And Okinawans have darker skin, so Fujiwara is kind of prejudiced against Noriko."

"Well, Fujiwara's crazy," I said quickly. "Noriko must have other people she likes here. Her Aunt or some things she likes about Tokyo . . ."

"She hates it here!" Ace laughed, a hysterical peal of laughter which dissolved into a twisted smile. He took another slurp of beer, from his glass this time. Then he grabbed another handful of peanuts, too. Before he put the peanuts in his mouth, he squinted and examined them in his palm. He frowned. A nauseated expression gripped his face, and he stared down as if the peanuts had released writhing larvae. He dumped them into the ashtray. The whole handful didn't fit, and a few nuts rolled across the table. Ace didn't notice. He spoke bitterly, "There's also kind of a bad feeling between Okinawans and mainland Japanese, because in World War II, the mainland army, the Yamato army, told Okinawa to fight for Japan then left them totally unprotected. Sacrificed them. For nothing."

"I'll be right back," I said.

In the corner of the bar was a little bathroom, a tiny room only about four-foot square. But it had a Western-style toilet, not just a hole in the floor like in most Japanese restrooms. When I came out, Ace was staring at me and baring his soul like he would to a confessional priest—or to his mother. His eyes were red from alcohol. He had drunk most of our two enormous beer bottles and then almost another full one, which had been quickly and silently brought over by the telepathic Moe-san.

Ace coughed and spoke hoarsely. "You know, Noriko's parents aren't too happy she's going out with an American, either . . . When Americans invaded Okinawa, the Okinawan women and children were told that American soldiers were going to rape and butcher them, so they hid up in caves. A lot of the women committed suicide. Even killing their kids, throwing them off the cliffs. And then the G.I.'s came to look for the kids, but . . ." Ace was crying now. Tears ran down each of his ruddy cheeks. His voice wavered and cracked. "You know what the G.I.s had for them?"

I didn't know. I looked down at my empty glass.

"They had fuckin' Hershey bars to give the kids. And food . . ."

I crushed a peanut on the table. Half of it spun off onto the floor. Ace reached for my beer bottle, but I filled his glass for him. Then I poured a little more beer into my own glass to make it appear that

Ace wasn't getting drunk alone. I took a deep breath, but said nothing. That was best. I would let Ace sit quietly for a moment. Let him relax after getting out all his emotion. But he wasn't finished.

"Noriko's father tried to scare her." Ace wiped his eyes with the back of his hand. "He told her that Westerners have a different body temperature and a different kind of brain, so that if children are born, they'll be *deformed*." He spoke this last word angrily, like a curse. Automatically, he reached for his beer bottle, which of course was empty. Again I filled his glass from my bottle.

Moe-san didn't bring any more beer. Perhaps old Moe-san knew that we had drunk enough. Ace slid his glass across the wooden table. A few inches from the edge, he stopped pushing and held the glass in place. He stared at the rim of the glass for a long while as if it reflected something I couldn't see. Then he looked at me. "I didn't tell you the truth before," he said slowly.

"What do you mean?"

"About why Noriko doesn't like Tokyo."

"Oh?"

He spoke as if each word required immense effort and concentration. "She was crying, because her father . . . beats her. He hits her, because she sees me . . . But still, she comes back to me." He stared at his perspiring hands.

In a rare instance, I didn't know what to say. I didn't know what to do. We both sat there looking down at the scratched, yellowed resin on top of the wooden table. The scratches formed an intricate pattern of interlaced lines, like a road map. But at the edge of the table, all of the lines ended in oblivion.

Moe-san quietly approached our table again. He carried a white platter. Without a word, he placed it in front of us. There were slices of apples and pears, halved cherries, sections of mandarin oranges— all arranged in beautiful symmetry.

Silently, we ate the fruit. When the platter was empty, we stood up and walked over to the counter where Moe-san was arranging glasses in a cabinet. *"Domo Arigatou,"* I said quietly. *"Gochiso sama.* It was a feast." I held out a ten-thousand yen note.

Moe-san handed back our change. He leaned down. Then, from under the counter, he pulled out a huge vintage Polaroid camera and peered through the viewfinder. "Okayee," he said. The bulb flashed and sizzled and captured a sudden picture—Ace had a stunned expression, I'm sure.

"Why did he do that?" Ace asked and rubbed his eyes.

"He takes a picture of every foreigner, every time they come in, and puts them in those books back there." I pointed to a shelf along the wall stocked with photo albums marked by year, dating back to 1968.

"Everybody since '68?"

"Yeah. And that's probably not all of them. He's got more in the back. Years later, you can come back to this place. You can find your picture and see how you were."

Moe-san closed his eyes and bowed low. He held the bow for a long moment, his head perfectly still above the tall countertop. When he looked back up, his eyes were wide open and brilliantly clear.

Then the lids closed again.

VIII. THE ART OF YEN

With a slam of the door, at 2:00 pm, Hamaguchi entered the office. "*TODAIMA!*" I'VE ARRIVED, he said. Then he began his daily sales pressuring questions, strutting from person to person and thumping on the desktops. "Do you have any good news?" Of course, he would have known already, because all new contracts were marked on the wall chart.

Nobody had any sales to report.

Hamaguchi grunted. "You must keep working harder." As usual, he stopped very close by Vanessa's desk and looked down at her blouse. "Mees Vanessa, I theenku you are gaining weight."

An apricot-colored blush crept up her neck, but she tried to act nonchalant and, with trembling fingers and delicately manicured nails, kept writing in her notebook. "Oh, I don't know," she said lightly. "My weight goes up and down."

"Now, I theenk it ees up," Hamaguchi continued. He stepped closer and leaned forward to look at her body. "Yes, you are, fatter than before. Huhr," he laughed. Vanessa stared at her desk. She sat absolutely still. Her blush darkened.

I caught Max's conspiratorial smile across the room but didn't smile back. I tried to think of something consoling to say to Vanessa but decided it might be best just to pretend that I hadn't heard Hamaguchi's comments.

Two hands on his stomach now, Hamaguchi gazed at the <u>Tokyo Time</u> contract chart on the wall. Then he wheeled around to face the staff. "All right," he said, "I have made a decision. The salesman weeth the most contracts by the end of September weel be the new manager!"

"Ohhhh!" Max burbled and stood up. "*Shachou*, you mean by September 30th, the salesman who brings in the most money will be next <u>Tokyo Time</u> manager?"

"Yes, that ees what I said," responded Hamaguchi. "So everyone must work their hardest!"

Part of this hard work involved typing *Thank You* letters to prospective clients, as Hamaguchi had explained. So I wrote out a list of addresses in order to type them up, one by one, on the electronic typewriter. This was a tedious process since the machine's *auto-correct* ribbon frequently malfunctioned. And the typewriter was perched on a coffee table, so the user had to sit on a couch and lean far forward to reach it.

After two hours of total focus and painstaking typing, my lower back hurt. My neck ached. The job was almost finished. I had typed seventeen letters. Now I only had to type the addresses and return addresses on the envelopes. But I could tell that I was just at the point of over-work where I would probably start making errors, which would result in another ninety minutes of typing and back pain . . . I didn't understand why the office had no word processor. Was there something honorific about using the actual typewriter? Or was it just punishment? It didn't seem to be a matter of lacking technologies. The Japanese loved Fax machines—There were three in the office, and their electronic chirping was incessant.

With the Japanese quest for nuanced perfection, mistakes on the very front of an envelope would be unforgivable. Companies might not even open such a poor letter, just put it in the trash—while wearing rubber gloves . . . A letter that I personally had received from a prospective client had been addressed in lovely calligraphy, with a gold-embossed seal.

Then I had an idea. I took all the typed letters over to the photocopy machine—a new refrigerator-sized, color-copy Canon brand which was advertised as so good it could copy American currency (the ad showed a befuddled American businessman trying to differentiate between a real dollar bill and a copy)—and made two duplicates of each letter. Sitting at my desk, I put one copy aside for my files; then, with precise cuts of my scissors, I snipped out all the addresses, trimming them, so they were perfectly square. Carefully, cautiously, I glued each address onto the front of my envelopes, in both the TO and FROM positions. I made sure the paper cuttings were perfectly aligned, and pressed each down with another clean paper so the photocopy toner didn't smear.

I felt Tanaka staring at me. I glanced quickly at him but said nothing. No one else was in the main office, since Max and Vanessa had both left, and Paul hadn't even come in that day. I ran my hands over the top of my desk, brushing together a pile of cut-up letters so they would be easy to toss into the trash can.

Then Hamaguchi came out of the back room and saw the pile of paper fragments on my desk. "Unhhh?" He stared at the pile. "WHAT IS THEES MESS?" He stood dead still, gaping as if the entire desk was covered with refuse. "What ees all thees mess?"

I gave him a nervous smile. "Oh, I just figured out a new way to save time on the letters and get more contracts." I pointed at the stack of finished envelopes. "See, I just make copies of the letters— the *Thank-You* letters . . . Then it's easy to cut out the addresses and paste them on the envelopes. It saves time, so I have more time to get new contracts."

Hamaguchi was shaking his head, lips pursed, and eyebrows knit in utter disapproval. "No. Thees ees no good. You must type all the letters."

I explained gently, "I did type the letters, seventeen letters. All I did was copy the—"

"NO! You must not do it like these," he said, in a final pronouncement.

"Okay. Next time I'll type all the . . ."

But Hamaguchi had turned and walked back into his office.

A few minutes later, Max returned. I didn't look up. "MAXIMIL-IAN!" Hamaguchi yelled from his desk, and Max went for a closed-door conference. Soon Max emerged and walked an arrow-straight line over to me. "*Shachou* said for me to tell you that you shouldn't type the letters like these."

I crumpled the paper I was holding, squeezed it tight. The tendons and veins on the inside of my wrists—where people slit them— bulged. "I know," I said slowly. "He told me. I don't understand why he even needed to mention it again. Besides, it's not the typing he doesn't like, it's the addresses on the envelopes." I held up an envelope and showed Max how I glued on the address. "Does this look bad?"

"It looks fine to me," Max admitted. "But eet is not the Japanese way."

"You mean the—"

With a wag of his hand, a secretive wave, Max beckoned me into the hall.

I clenched my teeth and held my breath until we stood safely in the entryway by the coat racks—as private as things got at the office. Then my words came out. "You mean the Japanese way is for me to waste my time? You mean only Hamaguchi can be different with his epaulets and stupid suit jackets? And everyone else has to be exactly alike? For Chrissake, I already told him I wouldn't do it anymore."

Max just stood there with a bemused smile until I was finished. Then he spoke. "Thees is Japanese way. You have to do things *exactly*. That ees how they think." He tapped his forehead.

"It doesn't matter anyway," I said. "I guess it just doesn't matter. A waste of a day, that's all . . ." I exhaled slowly. Then I walked back to my desk and threw all of my envelopes with address labels, cut-up letters, and snippets of paper into the trash can. At least I had copies of the letters themselves. Maybe I would sneak them into newly typed envelopes.

Max had tried to explain the Japanese mindset, although he didn't need to. I had read hundreds of books and articles on Japanese business, philosophy, and culture. The bottom line: stick to tradition and procedure no matter how inefficient. There was a saying: *Deru kugi wa utareru* - The nail that sticks up will be hammered down. Back when I was a little kid who needed help putting new tires on a bicycle, my grandfather, who fought in World War II, used to say, "There's the *right* way, the *wrong* way, and the *Japanese* way . . . Although, to be fair, I had heard him make the same generalizations about the *right* way, the *wrong* way, and the *Army* way. Perhaps the two were related.

Part of the problem was Hamaguchi himself, flaunting his command. I vaguely recalled another saying—was it American? *Give someone authority, and they will use it.* This seemed to be true, no matter what hemisphere. What did it mean when one has to resort to tired proverbs to try and understand the world?

Vanessa came back into the office and sat down at her desk. She took out a compact mirror, then began to apply lipstick. I couldn't help watching her expertly apply the tip of the ruby-colored lipstick to her mouth. She caught my gaze. "Well, you look interested . . . And maybe a little depressed. Bad night last night?" She gave me a flirtatious smile and raised her eyebrows.

"No, it was a good night—or just a regular night. Not so sure about today though."

"It's all about attitude," she said, as if reciting from a *Cosmopolitan* article. She took out a brush from her purse, pouted at the mirror in her compact, and briskly fluffed her blonde hair. "Everything is attitude!"

"Right," I said, and opened my top drawer, where I had been tossing all of my Japanese change. An inch-thick layer of Japanese coins took up a good part of the drawer. Mostly cheap copper one-yen pieces, worth even less than American pennies. The coins were a real bother. They lay heavy in your pockets if you carried them, and you couldn't spend them on anything much. A big waste of time. A waste of your life. With two hands, I felt the weight of the drawer. I'd better take some of the coins out, or else the aluminum sliders in the desk might break. Hamaguchi would love that . . . "Vanessa, what do you do with all these stupid one-yens? Kind of a hassle, huh?" I grabbed a handful of the coins and let them fall back into the drawer in a metallic shower.

"I have this one friend that lugs them down to the station to buy a train pass. The station has to take them—because they're government property.

"Who counts them?

"She counts them out first, then wraps them in foil."

"Foil? I wouldn't waste the time. I'd use them to make a sculpture or something. I'd solder them together—New Age art. Like Picasso." I opened the drawer again and gazed at copper coins, running my fingers through them, raking them. The ridges of the coins tickled the skin between my fingers. The coins made a loud, scratching sound as they slid and rolled in the bottom of the drawer.

I stole a glance to the side to see if Tanaka had heard. No—thankfully, he was on the telephone, and speaking in an artificially cheerful voice like an insincere T.V. host. Now he was laughing and joking with a client, much louder than he usually spoke—his mouth frozen in a fake smile. His hands trembled as he gripped the phone.

In the back of my drawer, I found my artist's eraser, soft, gray, malleable, the consistency of play dough. I had bought the eraser in the stationary section of the convenience store near the office. You could squeeze and pinch it to diffuse any ink stains and make them disappear. I rolled the clay-like eraser in my hand until it was a perfect sphere, then I pressed it between my palms and rolled it into an oblong shape, a gray mound about four inches long. Coin-by-coin, I stuck one-yens into the soft rubber, so they protruded like squamous ridges of an armadillo, or maybe porcupine quills.

I counted the coins as I pushed them in: Sixteen. Then underneath, carefully, I inserted four more coins: wheel-feet. There. All it needed was ears—two ballpoint pen caps. Great! It looked surprisingly good. A desk animal. "Vanessa," I said. "Look . . ."

"Oh my God! How cute!" she squealed. "What is it?"

"A yen animal. An armadillo-porcupine thing, I guess."

Vanessa turned to try to get Max's attention. "Look, Max. He made a creature. It's a yen animal."

But Max was on the phone. I thumbed through my dictionary until I found the translation and read it out loud: "*Mogura* - porcupine."

Vanessa stood up. Then she knelt down beside me so that she could see the creature at eye level. She blinked at it like a little friend. "*Kawaii so!*" It's so cute! She giggled.

Tanaka saw Vanessa kneeling beside me and glanced over. The false glee was still frozen on his face like a mask. "Unh? *Nani?*" What?

"*En no mogura desu,*" It's a yen porcupine, Vanessa explained.

"AH!" Tanaka shrieked. He jumped up from his desk. "***NANI?***" **WHAT?**

An electric shock ran down my spine—I needed to take control of this situation fast. "*Jodan da yo?*" A joke, you know?" I said. "*En no geijutsu,*" Yen art. I smiled up at Tanaka's red face.

Tanaka's lips drooped and became paralyzed in a frown of horror, as if I were actually eating a raw porcupine—quills, entrails, intestines and all—right there at the desk.

"*Okashi geijutsu . . .*" Funny art, I said, in a mollifying tone, playfully pushing the creature with an index finger. But one of its coin-feet came off and rolled across the desktop, then fell into the trash can, where it landed with a metallic clang.

"*DAME!*" **BAD!** shouted Tanaka. His face had turned beet-colored now. "***En no gijutsu wa—kinshi sarette iru!***" **Yen art is— forbidden!** Tanaka took a clumsy step toward me, and for a moment I thought I might get hit. Vanessa's eyes were wide in alarm.

Tanaka moved closer. "***Seifu no mochi mono da!***" **Government property!** He yelled, as if I were some juvenile delinquent. "***KENO GEIJUTSU WA DAME DA! FUHOO DA!***" **THIS ART IS BAD! IT'S ILLEGAL!** He took a final step forward and lowered his face down toward the yen porcupine. "***KONNA GEIJUTSU SONZAI SURU DEKI J' YA NAI.***" **THIS ART SHOULD NOT EXIST**, he said, like a Japanese Reich Minister of Culture. I felt his hot saliva spray on my arm and smelled his horseradish breath.

My cheeks burned. But I wouldn't cower and grovel. I wouldn't hang my head and whimper. I would keep my graceful resolve. "*Ah, so desu, ne?"* Is that right? I asked casually.

"HAI!" YES! Tanaka shouted back.

Taking my time, I carefully lifted up the sculpture and set it down in my drawer. Then I closed the drawer slowly, counted one-and-two-and-three until it was shut—the perfect speed for dramatic effect. I stood up. *"Sumimasen,"* excuse me, I said, and walked past the glowering Tanaka and the quivering Vanessa. I walked into the bathroom, locked myself in, ran my hands under the cold water, and rubbed my face. My cheeks were hot. The cool water felt refreshing. I took a long breath and washed my face again. Then I washed my hands, taking time to scrub the skin just behind the fingernails, rubbing them hard to get out all the dirt—until my knuckles grew raw. I sat on the toilet for a while with the seat cover down. I just sat there. Then I flushed the toilet, in case someone was listening. Was there a hidden toilet monitor?

Tanaka had flown off the handle—went berserk. Tsk-Tsk, very un-Japanese. Did he get upset because he felt I had flaunted government authority? Or was it simply that he didn't know how to act, since there were no established guidelines about how a Japanese should behave when a gai-jin made yen-porcupines. There were no rules for controlling feelings in such a situation, so he went *ape-shit.*

Finally, I was ready to face the office again. I heard Max and Paul joking in the entryway. Curiously, I was glad to hear their voices, to take cover in the mere presence of others. When I entered the office, I saw that even Hamaguchi was back, talking quietly with Tanaka over in the corner. I sat down, flopped into my chair, and looked up to find Hamaguchi staring at me. His eyes swept over me from head to toe, and back to my face, lingering on my hair. "You have very fine hair," he said. "Like a *woman's* hair . . ."

At that moment, time seemed to stop. I saw the office from above, as if I were hovering, floating up near the fluorescent lights. I heard Paul scoff behind my back and saw Vanessa watching me with moist, sensitive eyes. Tanaka sat face down, hunched over his books.

"Yes," said Hamaguchi again in his deep voice, "Very thin hair, like a fee-male."

When I answered, I controlled my tone, made it smooth, even unresponsive. "Well, thank you for pointing that out about my hair," I said, and let my voice swing up a bit. "Kind of you to notice—and compliment." I felt the blood in my ears, a seething rush—but forced an ironic smile, clenching my teeth. I reached into my desk drawer and found the yen porcupine, then I squeezed it as hard as I could until the eraser-embedded coins dug into my fingers and palms.

The pain felt good.

IX. GRACE UNDER PRESSURE

At rush hour, a *shikan*—a train pervert—rode the same subway line I did. According to an article in the *JAPAN TIMES*, two German girls wearing sundresses on the *Yamanote Line* had reported that they were molested by a Japanese man. The girls said that even though he was wearing pants, they could feel the poke of his genital organ against their buttocks during the subway ride. The man had been detained, but he claimed the contact was accidental since the train was too crowded and passengers were jammed against each other. Surveillance footage on the platform prior to boarding showed him cutting in line to stand behind the girls. But the article went on to explain that technically, since the man had remained clothed, and he had merely been "pressing"—not "fondling," "stroking," "thrusting," "patting," or "caressing"—no criminal behavior had occurred.

During rush hour, at 300% capacity, the trains were rather indecent. Sub-human. Subway guards literally pushed passengers through the doors onto the train until no more could fit, and passengers were breathing down each other's necks . . . If you know you will be forced to press against someone, is it a "molestation" to select the person you prefer?

As I read the article, my face flushed—because twice I had made such a selection, just before the subway guards began their shoving. Of course, I had not cut in line. But I had chosen the boarding line with the most attractive woman standing in front of me, instead of a salaryman. Was I a *shikan?* Was I a train pervert?

I played the two incidents in my mind. The first one still made me smile. Astoundingly, after we were in the train and pressed together by the force of the crowd, the twentyish office girl in front of me had <u>not</u> tried to move away. In fact—and this was the amazing part—she had leaned her head back against my shoulder. And then, slowly, she moved her hips up and down, and side to side . . . We were so close that I could feel her breathe.

The second time was different. When the guards shoved me into the train, and I was pushed into the woman ahead of me, I felt her back and shoulders tense. She tried to move forward, but it was not possible. And I tried to step back, but I was up against the door. There was nowhere to go. So I just stood there, wedged against the woman. On the tracks, the train vibrated around the bends and shifted to and fro.

Instead of choosing the line with a pretty woman, should I have just walked to the nearest line and allowed myself to be pressed into a sweaty salaryman? The thought made me nauseous. And if he had disliked the contact, would the situation have been any better? What if someone selected a boarding line in order to be pressed into *me*? All of this was a moral quagmire. Was there a solution? What could I do? I had to commute to work every day. I certainly couldn't afford taxis five days a week. And the office was definitely too far to walk.

But then, like a mathematician in a pointed hat with astrological symbols finds the hidden code, the elegant solution—I had the answer: I would buy a bicycle! I would ride it to work every day.

I studied my map book and determined how to ride around Hotel Metropolitan and down *Edonimae Dori* to the office. It wasn't that far, maybe eight or nine miles. I was so excited about the idea that I had trouble falling asleep. It took a bold and inventive mind to turn the hell of a Tokyo subway squash into a healthy morning bike ride. At 1:47 a.m., I took my emergency money out from under the insole of my right shoe. I had hidden thirty thousand yen there, almost two hundred and forty dollars. I stuck the money in my wallet and lay down again. Eventually, my eyelids closed. Just before I fell asleep, visions of spinning circumferences and prismatic ratios of distance-rate-time danced before my eyes.

In the early morning haze, I was the first customer to the little general store near the station. The wrinkled old owner was bracing his awning. I walked directly to the back of the shop, where propped against a shelf were two shiny bicycles. A red one and a blue one. I wanted the blue one. Then I spotted a bike helmet and grabbed that, too. The store had everything, from ointments to octopus tentacles encased in plastic, all in a sixteen-by-sixteen room crammed to the ceiling like the hull of a nineteenth-century trading ship.

I pulled out my wad of money and walked over to the shopkeeper, who was twisting the dial of a combination lock attached to his awning. "I would like to buy a bicycle," I said.

The shopkeeper took off his thick glasses and looked at me. He raised his eyebrows quizzically. In Japan, evidently, a bicycle wasn't a 7:00-A.M.-Thursday-morning purchase. It was a Sunday-afternoon purchase or an evening purchase.

"One bicycle and one helmet," I said with some finality, like Alexander the Great purchasing his fine horse "Bucephalus" and requisitioning battle equipment. I lay my money on the front counter, which was still covered with a film of dew.

Now the shopkeeper gave me a bizarre look with one eye half shut, as if I took baths with my clothes on or sucked up rice through a straw. With an examining gaze that started at my oxfords, swept over my suit (thrift-shop Armani), and lingered on the Japanese company pin in my lapel, the man decided I was serious. He determined that this wasn't a foreigner's trick. It was a *gai-jin's* aberration, an obsession, a bike fixation. "Just a minute," he said.

"The blue bicycle, please."

Then the bike was out front—gleaming and new, promising and grand. The helmet was there too, all black with a little sliding air vent. *"Ii no jidensha*—Good bicycle," I said and realized this sounded oddly anthropomorphic, as if I were comforting a pet. So I patted the money pile instead and paid 19,000 yen, about $160 for the bike, 4,000 yen for the helmet, and 3,000 yen for a snap-on headlight and taillight set, which the shopkeeper had brought out as well. "One lock," I added, and forked over an additional thousand yen.

With a shiver of excitement, I swung a leg over the bike, latched the helmet, and began to pedal down the wet street—

"MATTE! WAIT!" The old man yelled. **"STOP!"**

I set the pedal brake.

"You must register bike. You must buy insurance," he said.

Was it true? Was this the law? "Where do I register?" I asked, annoyed now. I would definitely be late for work.

The shopkeeper opened an old filing cabinet with ornate brass knobs. Carefully, he removed several notebooks and a sheaf of forms. After filling out three forms, showing my business card and Sanjo key for proof of residence, paying thirty dollars more in fees (which left me twenty dollars for food for the rest of the week), I was free to go.

¥

The bike was smooth. And quick, too. Not like my racing bike back home, but fast for a one-speed, 1940's-style, big-seated, square-basketed old lady's bike. There was no cross-bar, no horizontal between the seat and stem, like on Western men's bikes. The frame angled down in front. All Japanese rode women's bikes . . .

I stopped back at Sanjo for a quick change into a T-shirt, so I didn't sweat up my suit on the ride to the office. I stuck my jacket, tie, dress shirt, fresh undershirt, comb, map, and deodorant (American deodorant) into a gym bag, then headed out to the main street. At first, I rode slowly on the sidewalk, passing other bicyclists and dodging pedestrians, until the crowd got too thick. Soon, in the joy of maximizing Tokyo transportation, the delight of whirring tires, I hopped my bike off the curb and onto the street, making sure I pulled up the front wheel for a solid landing.

I rode even faster now, standing up and tugging on the handlebars, pressing the bike frame from side to side as I pedaled. Every few blocks, I overtook another cyclist. But no one passed me. Why hadn't I thought of this sooner? This bicycle was ideal. Sublime . . . Wearing my helmet and sunglasses, I knew I looked like a dedicated cyclist. The Japanese probably couldn't even tell I was a foreigner.

I headed under a bridge, which I didn't recognize, so I stopped to take out the map and look for street signs. I asked directions from a polite bowing man. Everyone was friendly today. Friendly about my bike. And I had only five more miles to go. Up a steep incline I rode, straining at the pedals, feeling the pull of the handlebars in my triceps and the pressure of exertion in my thighs. But I wouldn't grunt and pant. I would maintain a certain grace. I would control my body for maximum efficiency, breathing in through my nose and out through my mouth like a true athlete. *Grace under pressure.*

At the top of the hill, I rested, coasting for a moment, and began to pick up speed again as the road sloped down. Then I couldn't resist. The adrenaline surge of bicycle ecstasy came again, shooting through my arms and surging in my chest. I let out a shout of joy and pumped as fast as I could, whizzing through a traffic-locked intersection and rocketing ahead of all the cars. I was a professional cyclist, a triathlete in his best event. No slow sidewalk riding. This was expert cycling. The street merged, and I was side-by-side with moving cars now, straining to pass them. Slowly, surely, I could.

A huge bus loomed up ahead. In the midst of heavy traffic, it was traveling rapidly for such a large vehicle. I pedaled with all my might and gained some headway. Soon I was behind the gigantic bus, veering to the side to avoid its gray puffs of acrid exhaust. With each stroke of the pedals, I moved closer until I was alongside. Inside the bus, the Japanese passengers had spotted me, and they were applauding. They smiled and cheered. I waived back and pumped even faster, harder. The Japanese clapped more. They tapped on the bus windows, made pedaling motions with their fists, and waved two-fingered peace signs.

Near an old cemetery, I had to stop to get my bearings again. But soon I saw the *Aoyama* twin towers and knew my location. Just a few more minutes to the office. I glanced at my watch. A half-hour late for work. That was the price of transportation maximization.

The morning sun was bright. A piercing white. I squinted and unfastened the strap of my helmet. I was a block from the office, beside a park with a children's jungle gym, where I had decided to stow the bike. I locked the rear wheel to a chain-link fence. A blanket of warm perspiration covered my shoulders, and my T-shirt clung to my back. Sweat ran down my ears and forehead. The perspiration seemed almost to gather its own energy from the hot, humid air.

I walked over to the playground outhouse—the kind construction workers use, with a plastic door and a chemical toilet. Then I stopped, frozen in my tracks. Inside a laundromat, a row of women had lined up in front of a window to watch me. A foreigner in the morning must have been a very surprising sight for them, a Ripley's believe-it-or-not. One of the women had a snaggle-toothed smile. Two more stared vacantly. The last woman frowned, with a crease in her lips that accentuated her jowls.

I felt good after the bike ride, strong and proud. The exercise had given me more energy than usual in the morning, enough energy to deal with these women, to combat their gapes. I swung my gym bag over my shoulders and turned to face them head-on. I gave them my biggest grin, a wide pearly beam. Maybe the buck-toothed woman would notice the effect of five years of orthodontia and take it to heart.

My smile completely altered the women's expressions—turning innocent stares into alarm, and hostile glances into surprise. Now they knew I was not just an ordinary foreigner. I was not just a sweaty *gai-jin*; I was an insane barbarian with delusions of happiness. Fantasies of flowery bliss. And it got them to muttering. And shaking their heads. But then I went into the outhouse and disappeared.

When I came back out, like Clark Kent in the flash of a minutes' metamorphosis, I was a new man. My hair was slicked back. I was clothed in a gray suit and yellow tie like an ad from Gentleman's Quarterly magazine. I looped around to pass by the Laundromat window. I walked right next to it, just to check the women's reactions. I even paused to watch them laboring, arms scrubbing and folding, rounded backs hunched over. One woman spotted me, stared, and stood perfectly still, as if I were a feral animal which might frighten and run. She gave a low-pitched call to alert the others, and they all gawked together, eyes wide with amazement. Soon, they were grinning and nodding in admiration of my miraculous transformation. And I realized the profound truth about the importance of a suit jacket in Tokyo. It was pure magic—Japanese magic.

That evening after work, I ate dinner at a tiny restaurant near the office where the grandmotherly *obaa-san* talked softly to herself as she made me *yasai itame,* sauteed vegetables served in a wooden bowl. The food was fresh and tasty. I felt well-nourished and revitalized as I unlocked my bicycle, snapped on the battery-powered headlight and taillight, and started the long ride home through the dark.

It was a warm, sticky night. At first, I rode slowly on the sidewalks only. But I had to swerve into the street to dodge a urinating man—his stream had pooled in the middle of the sidewalk. In the dark, as if aboard a whirring alien vessel, I rode alongside cars and secretly gazed at the occupants through the windows. I stared down at blue-suited bodies and tired faces. There were only a few other bicyclists on the road, delivery boys with boxes of food and bowls of soup strapped to their baskets. Easily, I out-pedaled them all. I streamed past with an effortless rush.

Near *Yoyogi Park*, I spotted two other cyclists riding faster than most. They wore cycling shorts and rode 10-speed bikes. They were standing up while they pedaled. I set eyes on them and fixated as if peering through a rifle scope. I grasped the handgrips tightly, stood up, and pedaled as hard as I could. Steady pumps of my legs. Triathlon kicks, timed and tuned years ago cycling along San Diego beaches. Again, I felt my adrenaline building and glanced up at the flickering lights and enormous buildings of Tokyo. I needed to concentrate.

There were no gears to shift, so I pedaled faster and faster. Soon I was shoulder-to-shoulder with the two Japanese cyclists, then overtaking them. I heard their grunts of surprise and couldn't resist winking as I passed.

But the Japanese riders sped up, too! This was undeniable. They almost caught up to me. It was a race, no doubt. A *Tour de France* in Tokyo. A contest of wills. A contest of countries . . .

I glanced down at the spinning front tire and rushing asphalt. I increased the pressure of my pedaling, torquing down harder and harder. I leaned forward so that my body was almost parallel with the ground, but I kept my forearms and abdomen tight, holding the bike perfectly straight. Going this fast, swaying the frame cut your speed and control. Soon I was leaving the two gasping Japanese riders far behind again. Then I sat back down in my seat, let go of the handlebars, and lifted both my arms in the air. The surging wind of victory streamed through my hair. It was a good night.

In Shibuya, neon signs burned their hideously bright colors into the darkness of the sky, forming yellow, red, and blue streaks among the stars. The signs were everywhere. Enormous blazing billboards. A glowing orange reflection from a Fuji Film sign shone on my knuckles in eerie illumination. I tried to pedal harder to escape the lights, but it was no use. My entire body was aflame in psychedelic stripes.

Soon the streets became very crowded. And the sidewalks were worse. So I slowed and cut in beside a row of cars near the center of the street. I was heading out of the business district now, past a row of noodle shops, Pachinko halls, and leafless trees. Then I had to jerk my front tire hard to the left to avoid running over the body of a crow, dead on its back with one wing extended. Its bloody beak pointed to the sky. "Better luck in the next life," I said out loud.

Down an incline, I sped. Now the air was cold against my damp hair. It chilled my ears and temples like an antiseptic spray. But soon, I was in a warehouse district with only a few cars on the road. The dimmed lights from factory windows cast strange and distorted shadows, patches of white and gray on the street. I heard the buzzing, chopping engine of a motorcycle behind me. Then it was next to me. And suddenly—no warning—turning in front of me, cutting me off, broadsiding—

I crashed.

The front tire of my bicycle hit the fiberglass tank of the motor-cycle. Then strangely calm and removed, I felt myself flying over the bicycle's handlebars through the air until I hit the ground, shoulder first—a hard, sudden impact. I rolled and rolled to decrease the force, as I had learned from years of skateboarding. I fought to keep my neck straight as I spun—dozens of turns, dizzy jerking spirals, spinal twists . . . Finally, I lay still in the road. The buildings reeled. My hands were numb. I couldn't feel my body. The rough surface of the asphalt dug into the side of my face. I lay there motionless, gazing at the curb and wondering if I was paralyzed. All I could hear was the rasping sound of my own breaths.

In a blurred glance, I made out the knobby front tire of the mo-torcycle. I could see a yellow insignia on the forks: KAWASAKI. A foot stepped off the bike. A foot clad in Nike athletic shoes. I tried to sit up, but long needles of pain shot through my hip and back. My neck throbbed. The motorcyclist took off his helmet, and I stared up into the frightened eyes of a teenaged Japanese boy. *"Daijobu?* Are you okay?" the boy asked. His voice wavered.

Before I could answer, a car had pulled up alongside us, and the driver leaned out the window to scream at the motorcyclist— *"WATCH OUT! YOU'LL KILL SOMEBODY ON THAT MOTORCYCLE!"* The car sped away, leaving only exhaust trails in its wake. Carbon fumes coated my throat. I coughed and managed to prop myself up on one arm. I pried open the plastic buckle and took off my helmet. It fell clattering onto the pavement.

The boy saw my Western features and let out a gasp. Trembling, he took two steps back. With my good arm, I tried to push myself up and get my legs underneath me. It was a feeble effort. The pain in my hip seized like huge pliers. I lay back down again to catch my breath. The boy opened his mouth, horror rippling across his face. Once more, I tried to stand. The boy glanced at his motorcycle, turned to walk toward it, then retraced his steps back to me. *"Dai-jobu?"* he asked again, bending forward and blinking too frequently.

"I don't know," I said and stifled a groan. Pressing both arms down and wedging my good knee underneath me, I was slowly able to stand up. The weight was brutal on my hip. A jackhammer pounded inside my skull. I staggered over to the side of the road and leaned against a streetlamp. The boy dragged my twisted, ruined bike out of the street. He tugged it up the curb, swung out the kickstand, and tried to stand the bicycle on the sidewalk. It fell over with a hateful clank and lay there, a few feet from a trash can.

I reached into my jacket pocket and pulled out one of my business cards, smudging the printing with a bleeding thumb. The boy was shaking. He took my card, bowed, and tried to read my name through the blood. But he didn't offer his own card. "Do you have a business card?" I asked.

This set the boy trembling even more.

"Just write your name," I said.

But neither of us had a pen. The boy offered to look for one and, before I could protest, he was pacing back toward his motorcycle. He didn't try to escape, though. He lifted the seat, searched in a tool kit, but found no pen.

I tried to adjust my weight to lessen the pain in my leg. I rested my left foot on its heel and wrapped an arm around the streetlamp for support. Then the boy walked away, and I watched him go from shop to shop until he disappeared into a store. Soon he reemerged with a pencil in one hand and paper in the other. I touched my elbow and felt the hot, wet, pulpy skin of the wound. Despite the sting, I pressed down with my palm to try and clot it. Where was I? I squinted to try and make out a street or a landmark. Nothing.

The boy held out the paper. His name was printed in uneven English letters: SHIRO HAMADA. There was a phone number, too. I nodded and tried to walk away but stumbled. I kept going and passed the boy's motorcycle—I had to fight myself not to knock it over. "I will call you," I said.

"Yes *purease*," Shiro answered obediently, and took this as a dismissal. Right away, he hopped on the motorcycle and started it. Then he was speeding off into the night without another look back.

I stared again at my bike. The front wheel was bent, the handlebars were crooked, the frame was scraped, and one of the pedals had broken off. The bicycle had been smooth and fast. Now it was garbage.

Tottering, with one hand over my bleeding arm, I made my way toward a subway sign down the street. It was a slow process. I took a big step forward with my good leg, stopped, then dragged my bad leg ahead, again and again—for two ugly blocks. Finally, I was at the subway entrance and propped myself against the door.

I had tried to optimize Tokyo transportation, but I had failed. Maybe I just tried too hard. Or was this my karmic punishment for being a *shikan*, a train pervert, if that's what I was? I couldn't think clearly anymore. All I knew was that my head was throbbing. It hurt like hell. And I just wanted to sleep.

Inside the station, the fluorescent ceiling bulbs made a bitter electric hiss. I paused in front of the subway route diagram, a blur of tangled lines, to try and make out the intersection of the light blue *Tozai* line and the *Yamanote* line back to the boarding house. Suddenly, behind me, there was laughter and nasal guffaws. I turned to see two Japanese men pointing at me. More people stared, and the laughter got even louder when I walked away, exposing my bloody arm and dragging my lame leg. Then more snickers across the hall. Four young girls giggled and covered their mouths. They were extremely amused to see a funny, limping *gai-jin*.

I glowered at them, but then up ahead were more chuckles. A group of chortling boys. Suddenly, everywhere I looked, someone was pointing and joking about my ripped pants or my odd shuffling walk, my mussed hair, or bloody hand. All around, by the scores, they were laughing—a sea of open mouths, stretched lips, and crooked teeth. My eyes burned. I clenched my teeth and glared back at the crowd. But it roared even louder. I almost cursed—but that would have gotten the Japanese rolling in the aisles, I knew. So I hobbled to what seemed like the least populated hall in the station, where I encountered a new bunch of sneers from a line of women. Their eyes glinted with mirth. Yes, I was a comical injured foreigner. Incredibly humorous. A laugh and a half . . .

With searing hot cheeks and a few stinging tears (tears of rage, right?), I staggered along the darkest passageway until I spotted the bathroom. Then I was safe behind its doors. Of course, there was no toilet to sit on, just a gaping, brownish hole in the concrete floor. But there was a wall to lean against—clean or not. And I could catch my breath and press paper towels over my wounds. I unlaced my shoes and tied the shoelaces around the paper towels to hold them in place. These were my *gai-jin* bandages.

The subway passengers had all laughed as if I were a clown. Were pain and injury so amusing? Japanese thought foreigners were innately odd to begin with. I knew that. But why was an injured foreigner so comical? Japanese were supposed to have a different sense of humor than Americans, and incongruity or incompatibility was funnier to them. But how could you laugh when a person gets hurt? Was I slapstick humor? Was I a *stooge*?

I wrapped my elbow in a wad of toilet tissue, rolled up my shirt sleeve to hold it in place, and shuffled back toward the trains. Soon I was immersed in a new crowd and more laugher, but not as much as in the first groups. Now that the towels and toilet paper covered my cuts, there was less hilarious blood to see.

At least I was alive. And not paralyzed. Always plenty to be thankful for . . . I should write down my blessings when I got home—give thanks that I wasn't being scraped off the road by a huge, whisk-brushing Japanese street cleaning machine. I took a deep breath and let the air out slowly. I wasn't limping so much now, only dragging my left leg a little. It hurt worst on the stairs.

But I had a good story to tell—a tale of a championship bicycle ride and motorcycle peril. I saw myself in a continuing melodrama, narrating the action in a somber tone: "He trudged through the train station and the sneering masses. Back to his meager little room in the decaying old *ryokan,* to the dubious comfort of his futon bed."

After two numbing train rides back to Ikebukuro, I was safe at Sanjo. I stood at the hall sink outside my room. I had taken off my ruined suit and thrown it outside the hatch window where I had been putting all my trash lately. I had gulped down four extra-strength Tylenol to ease the pain in my neck and hip. Now I rinsed my elbow in the cold spray of the faucet. The water swirled crimson and pink with blood.

I took a deep breath and decided that I was not a slapstick stooge. I was not a punished train pervert. I was a wounded warrior. And a tired one at that. I lay down in my futon, closed my eyes, and almost instantly fell asleep. It was a deep hibernation of a sleep. My one escape, doubtless and pure.

Outside, the night sounds played like a junkyard orchestra.

X. ENTRANCE TO PARADISE

After a long week, on Friday night, when I got back to the boarding house, Lizzie was in my bed. She wasn't asleep, just lying on her back and staring at the ceiling. She was voluptuous, Rubenesque in the full sense of the word, and even beneath the covers, her body had an array of inviting curves. "This is a nice surprise," I said.

"Yes, and a bit of an escape . . . My cousin had gas, and I had to get out of the room."

"I see." Just for that, I'd make her wait for her own surprise. "I have a secret," I said. Then I picked up a newspaper and pretended to read.

Lizzie sat up. She was wearing a pink nightgown. "Well, what kind of silly little secret could that be?"

"A Japanese surprise. But it's secret." I turned and made an elaborate effort at folding and arranging my suit coat so it was perfectly centered on top of my briefcase. Lizzie loved secrets.

"It's in *there*, isn't it?" She pointed at the briefcase and jumped out of bed to make a grab for the case, but I picked it up just in time. I unzipped the side pocket, pulled out a magazine, and held it open to a display photo of a tea ceremony: kimono-clad Japanese women sitting perfectly still and placid, holding cups of greenish-brown tea and staring at a teapot. Their eyes were half-closed, as if in meditation.

"I got us tea ceremony lessons. Two months' worth," I said.

Lizzie frowned. "You would . . ." Wrinkles formed at the corners of her pretty mouth, destroying her expectant look centimeter by centimeter. She sank down into the pillows and pulled the bed covers up to her chin.

But then, with a dramatic flourish, I brought out the real surprise—a folded brochure with photographs: a huge crowd at last year's Mt Fuji Jazz Festival, the wild clapping and cheering of the audience, Miles Davis playing trumpet, a bandstand decorated with thousands of purple flowers, dreadlocked Rastafarians in sunglasses, and rows of shiny brass instruments. "I was just kidding. Look, I got us tickets to the Mt. Fuji Jazz Festival!"

Lizzie gazed up at me then, slightly disoriented. She was happy, but uncertain whether I was joking again. She held out a hand, grasped the brochure, and pulled it closer.

"I bought the tickets today. We'll go tomorrow morning. We'll get out of Tokyo for the whole day."

Instantly, she was jubilant. Her face glowed. Her eyes lit up, and her cheeks flushed. She was elated, shown the entrance to paradise. "You!" She got up from bed and kissed me. "How over the top! Who's there? Jahzzz!" She put her arms around me. "Oh, I can't believe it! We're getting out! To see a concert! Oh, let's celebrate . . . Get your piano! Play something!"

I started to open the case, but Lizzie slid down the shoulder straps of her nightgown and let it fall to the floor. "I know another way to celebrate . . ." she said. Then she slipped back into bed and lifted the covers invitingly. That night, in a variety of ways, she showed me just how happy she was.

I had set the alarm for 4:00 a.m., and Lizzie got up without a fuss, which alone was a miracle. Humming and singing, she went to take her shower. We caught a taxi to the station and boarded the three-hour express train to Mt. Fuji—or as near an express train as I could gather from the schedule.

"Are you sure we took the right train?" she asked.

"Utterly certain." I was only fairly sure, but I wasn't going to let anything ruin our morning.

A half-hour into the ride, I saw a Japanese couple holding the same Mt. Fuji Jazz Festival brochure as I had gotten from the ticket agency. "See . . ." I pointed at their brochure. Immediately, Lizzie kissed me twice, flagrantly, right in front of the other passengers. She didn't seem to care anymore what was proper and what was not. She rubbed the back of my head, which apparently was enough to excite one Japanese man, even this early in the morning. He spread two fingers over his lips and stuck out his tongue, wiggling it back and forth in a lascivious slither. Fortunately, Lizzie was facing the other way. Just to be sure, I pointed out the window. "Look! I think we're getting closer to O-Fuji," I said, using the prefix "O"—for *honorable* Mt. Fuji. "I can see mountains in the distance."

With a gentle glance, she followed my gaze. "Those aren't

mountains, silly. Those are *hills.*" She patted my leg.

"Quite," I said.

"That sounded very British."

"If you're lucky, I'll teach you to speak *American.*"

We leaned back in our seats. Lizzie hummed some more and played with the hem of her skirt. If I saw a Japanese man staring at her body, I would try to point out something else through the window. But when I thought Lizzie might be catching on, I had to stop and just hope for the best.

We were about an hour and a half outside Tokyo now, in a far more rural area with meadows and flowers and small wooden gates. Several of the men boarding the train wore their pants too short as if the bottoms might get wet in the fields. I lay my head back against the seat cushion. Yes, we were far away from the city already . . .

But the country people gawked even more than the other Japanese on the train. One of them chuckled and gave a lewd laugh, jabbing an elbow to alert his friend about the way Lizzie sat, leaning her head on my shoulder with her long white throat exposed and her reddish-blonde hair dangling around me like gold lace.

Many of the Japanese only had information about foreign girls from television shows or movies—the vixens from TV's *Dallas* or the prostitutes of *Pretty Woman.* They seemed to think that foreign girls simply had sexual intercourse on their minds all the time. Lizzie had told me that when she first got to the airport in Tokyo, a Japanese man had walked up to her and asked, bold-faced and earnest, "*Haro.* You wantu fuckee?"

I gestured out the window toward a jagged boulder at the top of a hill. "That's an interesting stone formation," I said.

"I didn't know you were such a nature buff."

"I'm just buff." I flexed a bicep.

Lizzie groaned. She turned to look out the window and then lay back against me. Outside, the sky was gray and overcast. "It might storm," she said absently.

"No. It should clear up."

"Look," she whispered. "All the Japanese keep staring at us. They can't stop."

"They hope we'll do something interesting," I lied. "So they can go home and tell their friends. Watch . . ." I tensed my lips, tightened my throat, and made beeping noises. Then I produced a loud cat meow, a perfect feline imitation that got all the Japanese around us to smile. Even Lizzie, horrified at first, had to laugh herself when soon the whole train was filled with beeping and mewing Japanese, all giggling and telling each other how the *gai-jin* communicated. One man leaned back his head and let out a rooster crow, which earned him a swat from his wife.

"See, we made their day," I said. "They'll have stories for generations."

Lizzie giggled and kissed my neck. She closed her eyes. Soon her breaths lengthened, and her head swayed with the gentle side-to-side motion of the train. Then she was asleep. Her body was warm and soft beside me. Delicately, I pulled away one of her hairs, which was encircling my face and tickling my cheek. I glanced at her long eyelashes. Behind closed lids, her eyes were moving. Maybe she was dreaming. I took a deep breath and decided that this was a perfect moment. In life, such moments only come from time to time, and they must be savored.

A few minutes later, I found myself dozing off as well. Before I fell asleep, the last thing I thought of was how Lizzie and I were breathing together at just the same rate, which was odd. Usually, she breathed faster.

A horrid screech!—the shudder of the train jerked me awake. I blinked. There was rain now, torrential rain, Noah's flood pouring down outside the windows. Thick clouds obscured the sky. A jolt of alarm shot through the train like a power surge. A baby screamed in one of the front seats. Then Lizzie was awake and grabbing me, digging her fingernails into my arm, terror in her eyes. "WHAT? What's wrong?" she asked, trembling and frightened as a child herself.

The intercom crackled, and I strained to understand the tinny, distorted Japanese voice. I only caught a few words: "Arrival . . . Typhoon . . . Four hours duration."

"What did it say?" Lizzie asked, suddenly calm and resigned now as if the whole thing were predestined; as if she had already prepared herself for the worst, primed for a train crash, bloody bodies, Ninja torturers . . .

"A storm," I answered in a controlled voice. "A small typhoon. They said it would be four hours."

She let out a long razor of a sigh that hinted of tears. I put my arm around her, but she was perfectly still, neither stiff nor pliant, simply inert and immobile as a sack of flour.

"Shall we play a word game?" I asked cheerily. I would stay upbeat like a soldier who remains composed and clean-shaven even at the bottom of a muddy trench. "You think of a letter," I offered. "Then I'll add another, and the first person to—"

Her look gave its own answer. It was a stare which had endured years of tedious bingo matches and scrabble games in stuffy parlors; survived monotonous cribbage tourneys and infuriating Tiddly Winks bouts . . .

We were both quiet for a few moments. Soon I had another idea. "Shall we play mental chess?"

It was a joke. A bad joke. Lizzie didn't laugh. She sighed and spoke in bland, lethargic words which hovered in the air and clung to the wall like fat moths. "I, just, want, to, sit." She turned to gape out the window at the huge drops of water which splattered on the glass. Perhaps she looked at the scarred earth, where an unused old track lay under the gray darkness of the sky.

After three hours, the smell of human bodies in close contact—a warm, damp, pungent, vaguely sickening smell—had settled in on the train like an evil spirit. Lizzie looked pale and slightly blue-colored. Her breaths were loud wheezes, even though she barely moved a muscle. Her eyes were wide open, staring straight ahead and bulging so you could see the whites above the eyeballs.

I was tired. Exhausted. I offered Lizzie the brochure for the Mt. Fuji Festival to look at. It was my only offer left. "Want to read this?"

Of course, she didn't. So I read the brochure myself. The spectators in the photo didn't look as happy now for some reason. They seemed dazed and somnambulant. And the Rastafarians looked dirty and sweaty. I turned the photo over. On the back was a blank section, so I found a pen in my shirt pocket and drew a flower—a tulip with four petals, shaded, so it looked three-dimensional. Carefully, I tore out the flower picture and placed it in Lizzie's lap.

No response. Nothing. I may as well have offered diamonds to a fish, dropped them in a pond to fall through fetid water, and sink into the murky bottom. I found another blank section in the brochure and drew a new picture—an intricate, hour-long illustration of a castle with turrets, archers, rippling flags, and three drawbridges. As an afterthought, I sketched in five palm trees and a row of surfboards leaning up against one of the castle walls and dancing musicians on the roof.

Just as I was trying to remember the difference between a sham-isen, a sitar, and a zither, the intercom crackled again with another announcement, seven hours after the first: "Our train is in the center of a typhoon. This train cannot travel in heavy rain. Five hours additional delay estimated."

Lizzie didn't ask for a translation this time. She just stood up and muttered "bathroom," then pushed past me into the aisle. When she came back, her hair was wet. She seemed even paler than before. Yellowish now. She sat down, and I put a hand on her arm—she flung up her elbow, and it almost struck my face. Then she let out a gasp. Her head was down. I couldn't see her eyes, but she was crying. Tears ran down her cheeks in long streams.

I lifted my hand to touch her shoulder, then held back. My palm hovered an inch from her body, feeling the sparking tension pulsing off her through billions of electrocuted synapses. I wouldn't touch her. I leaned back in my seat—and caught the fascinated expression of a middle-aged Japanese man, round-faced in a fishing hat, eating rice cakes from a basket and watching us as if we were a bizarrely interesting foreign film.

The man reached into his basket to take out another rice cake. Then he realized that I was looking back at him. He didn't move for a second but sat there clutching his rice cake above the open basket, as if unsure whether to offer it to us or eat it himself. He glanced at Lizzie and saw her tears, then dropped the rice cake back into his basket.

A few minutes later, the man was peering at me again. But I was too tired to stare. Too tired to glare. Too tired to turn my head the other way. Then—and it was most unfortunate that Lizzie had to look just then—the man made a small curving gesture around his abdomen. He cupped his hand and rolled his wrist as if stroking a swollen uterus. "*Ninshin shite iru?* Pregnant?" he asked.

The noise that Lizzie made was not really a human sound—more simian—an orangutan's snarl. I was frightened to touch her, as if she might bite or shriek—or just sob, with her head in her hands. She stood up suddenly as if an exit sign had been illuminated, as if her name had been called from above. She forced past me into the aisle, looked to her left then to her right, took a few paces toward the bathroom, and collapsed into a cross-legged pile on the floor, head in her hands, weeping. Then automatically, I was up too—no decision now. I walked over to her and touched her shoulder softly.

Her punch caught me in the groin, a vicious jab. Stunned—I took a step back. My eyes watered with the pain. But I wouldn't grimace. In blurred steps, I managed to sit down again. The Japanese man was still watching. A piece of rice cake had caught in the corner of his mouth like a wart. After a few minutes, I wiped my own mouth to give the guy a hint. But it didn't work. "She is pregnant?" the man asked again.

I shook my head. "No." I felt dizzy. "She's just tired."

The man stood up and gathered a rumpled canvas sack that he had tucked under his seat. He took a step toward the disheveled, glowering Lizzie, approaching slowly, as one approaches a cornered stray dog or a swaying snake. He reached into his bag, and I had absolutely no idea what the guy was doing—let him do what he wants . . . He groped around in the sack until his hand found what it was searching for and pulled it out: a box of chocolate malt balls. With one arm extended, keeping his distance, he dangled the candy towards Lizzie's mouth. Then he shook the box and jiggled the malt balls near her ear. But she didn't move, didn't even twitch. So he set the box on the floor and crept back to his seat, shaking his head. The battle was lost.

After another hour, which brought the total train prison time to eleven and a half hours so far, Lizzie still sat in the aisle. Japanese passengers stepped around her as they made their way to the bathroom, avoiding her like a mound of dead fish on the beach.

A small boy about six years old walked up the aisle, groping chair by chair and touching each armrest, singing softly to himself. Eyes wide, he saw the hulking ominous form of Lizzie and stopped. He also spotted the box of chocolates, untouched and alluring, which seemed to give him just enough courage for one more step and one more wide-eyed blink. He grasped a seat and leaned forward—that was all. That was all he could muster. He stood there motionless, staring at the candy on the floor.

Then I was on my feet again. I walked toward Lizzie and cautiously reached down for the malt balls, covering my face with the brochure as a shield. Quickly I picked up the box. Then I held it out to the boy. Speechless, he gazed down at the candy, took it slowly from my hand, and gave a tiny quivering bow. He turned and ran back to his seat.

An hour later, the intercom crackled again as another train pulled up alongside us on the second set of tracks. We were instructed to switch trains since the new one was better equipped for storms. All of the Japanese passengers stood up. There was a fresh stir of energy, a grab for parcels and coats and hats.

Lizzie didn't move. I went over to her again, keeping my distance—at least three feet. "Liz, we have to change trains, honey . . ." I tried to soften my voice at the end of the sentence. Isn't that what a good psychiatrist would do? She didn't move. I lifted my hand to touch her, then thought better of it. Hell, she was a big girl. She could figure it out. I couldn't take anymore. But then she was standing, staring blankly at the surge of passengers ahead and following them, leaving me behind to take her sweater home for her.

I turned around to see a tall Japanese man looking down at me and nodding. But he wasn't glaring. He had a kindly glow in his eyes, a gleam which must have witnessed Lizzie's breakdown and seen my resignation. "Eet has been, long day," said the man. And I could only nod.

Finally, back in Ikebukuro, the sky was an odd beige color just before sunset. When the replacement train arrived at the station, I spotted Lizzie exiting through another door, two cars down. I called to her, but she ignored me. She just kept walking. I followed her up the pitted sidewalk toward Sanjo.

Some wonderful vacation. Some great escape from Tokyo . . . I stared at Lizzie's back, watched her heavy strides. Then I couldn't look anymore and stopped to lean against a building. I gazed up at the evening clouds. Suddenly I turned around and walked the other direction toward the station again—although I wasn't sure why. So I turned back and made my way back to Sanjo.

In my room, my suit jacket was on the floor, and the electric piano was half out of its case in joyous disarray. I switched on the keyboard and played a few somber tones. The music soothed and depressed at the same time, so I put the thing away.

I wasn't hungry. I wasn't tired. I didn't feel like reading. I wasn't thirsty. I didn't have to use the bathroom. I wrapped my face in a towel, lay down on the futon, and counted slowly to myself, "3, 6, 9, 12 . . ." all the multiples of three up to 999, the way I had learned in grammar school. Then I counted multiples of four. And fives were easy. Somewhere in the midst of the sevens, I drifted off.

That night I dreamed of lost, buried treasure.

The next morning, I woke up much later than usual. I went to check on Lizzie. Her door was open—but the room was entirely empty. No suitcases, no shoes, no books. The two futons were folded up against the wall, and the room looked freshly cleaned.

Fujiwara, the Sanjo manager, crept up the stairwell, carrying a stack of pillowcases. She saw me staring into the empty room. "They go home," she said. "They go bye-bye." Then she walked away.

Suddenly, the world seemed a little smaller.

XI. THE STARTING OF A THING

On the morning of October 1st, it seemed that the heat of Tokyo summer had begun to dissipate, but I wasn't certain if that was only my imagination. I was pretty sure I had more contracts than the other foreigners on the sales staff, although new contracts could be signed any day, or reported late, and Hamaguchi had been close-lipped about his choice for manager.

As soon as I walked into the office, Paul called to me. "How many contracts ya got?"

"Oh, about ten."

"Exactly how many contracts, though?"

"Ten or eleven, I think."

"What size are your contracts?"

"I don't remember—look at the chart if you want." I caught Max's *Paul's-a-dummy* smirk.

Hamaguchi must have heard us too, because he swaggered out of his office. "So, who has the most sales?"

"Ah have nine, and he's got eleven, but ah'll catch up to him soon," Paul brayed. "I'm supposed to hear from Kentucky Fried Chicken today. They liked me a lot."

"But today is decision date," said Hamaguchi. He looked at the chart, then at me. "Congratulations. You will weel be the next manager for Tokyo Time!"

I felt a curious rush of pride—and anti-climax. The success had an unexpected hollowness to it. "*Domo Arigatou.*" I gave a little bow.

Paul stood up from his desk. "But I've also got a big contrac' brewin' with Ginza Hotels for an A-Space. I think we should wait a couple days to decide on manager."

"No. Decision is made."

"Oh-hoh!" Max gave me two thumbs up.

Tanaka stared down at his desk.

Paul sat there blinking.

I bowed again. "*Domo Arigatou. Ima wa appointo,*" Thanks, I have an appointment. And I left the office. I was surprised by my lack of excitement, after all of the anticipation about becoming manager and all the appointments. All of the phone calls, train rides, business cards . . . All of the searching for addresses, elevator rides, typing, bowing, strategizing, pen-clicking, and waiting . . . But I didn't have much time for introspection because I was on the verge of being late.

In one of the gleaming mirrored towers of the Shinjuku business district, next to the very modern Keio Plaza Hotel, overlooking a maze of contemporary shops, walkways, and sculpted landscapes, was the main office of Canon camera. I got in the elevator and wiped the sweat from my brow with the only thing I had to wipe it off—the back of my tie. Just before the door slid opened on the seventh floor, I stuffed the tie back under my jacket. Perfect timing. I walked through the huge reception area and told the girls at the front desk that I had an appointment with Mr. Matsuda. Soon a tiny cup of steaming coffee was brought to me, with two containers of cream and two packets of sugar. I waited at a little table to the side, puckered my lips to fit around the cup, and drank all the coffee in one scalding gulp.

A man with hair longer than the usual Japanese walked to the desk and, in perfect unison, both receptionists bowed to him reverently, their heads almost touching the top of the counter. The length of their bows indicated his high status. He approached me and gave a dignified bow, which I reciprocated. I looked into his steady eyes. They sparkled and calmed at the same time. I glanced at the business card—**Matsuda Hiroshi, Director of Worldwide Advertising**.

Matsuda was <u>not</u> a mere associate manager; he wasn't a lower-level employee whom I could manipulate; he was not even just manager of the International Division—Matsuda was, in fact, the Advertising Supreme Being.

"*Hajimemashite*," Nice to meet you. I bowed again, then followed Matsuda to a plush conference room. Three more office girls brought us green tea and then backed out of the room with a chain of mini-bows, leaving us seated across from each other at a glowing mahogany table.

Matsuda nodded his head slowly and took a contemplative sip of his tea, without making any slurping noise. It was a smooth, sophisticated sip. "Thank you for coming," he said, in excellent English. "I was very interested in how a young man would decide to come from America, and to *Jah-pahn* . . ." There was a veneration for the word "Japan," and Matsuda bowed his head as he uttered it, almost as if it were a prayer.

"Thank you. I am honored to meet you."

"I come from Kyoto," said Matsuda. "It is the oldest capital of Japan. I have worked with Canon Camera for thirty-eight years." His eyes met mine. "I desire to have good relations with America." Matsuda paused and looked down as if to meditate on this.

"Yes, this is important for our countries." I nodded and attempted a sage squint—which blurred my vision like a stray eyelash—so I looked down at the table instead. At last, after ninety-plus appointments, I was meeting with the type of people whom I had envisioned in Japanese business—subtle, polite, honorable, intelligent. Not egotistical, smug, and xenophobic. Evidently, there simply weren't many businessmen like Matsuda around anymore. Was Matsuda part of a dying breed? Was it just Tokyo? Maybe I should leave and go to Kyoto—but I wouldn't have a job . . .

"It is important for our countries to understand each other," said Matsuda, closing his eyes again.

I studied his face. I could almost feel his contemplation. Had I found the heartbeat of true Japan? The ancient and admirable Japan? The Japan that had been lost to modern Tokyo in the churning and shoving of economic life; in the race for export markets; in the hubris of the increasingly valued yen . . .

I looked at the Matsuda's smooth features, his large forehead, chiseled cheeks, and—could it be? An aquiline nose? He had an aristocratic air about him, an educated and studied elegance. This wasn't due to his age. It was his entire persona. Matsuda was a rare and treasured relic. I knew it from the depths of my stomach. I felt it—and we had barely even spoken yet.

"How long have you been in Tokyo?" he asked.

"About eleven months—*juuikkagetsu.*"

He smiled slightly at my lapse into Japanese, and again bowed his head as if I had given a minor compliment, which also somehow also had a hint of humor to it. "Yes, Japanese business is different," said Matsuda. "Do you know the game, *GO?*"

I nodded enthusiastically. I knew the game well and played it on the beach in California. I loved *GO*, with its symmetric stones and amorphous strategies—

"Japanese business is like *GO*. American business is like Chess, and also like poker, *ne*?" right? "In chess, you must analyze what will be the exact probability; and what will maximize your chance to win. In poker, a man can bluff—and he wins an immediate result. In *GO*, we have a saying, *isseki o tozuru* . . . Do you know what that means?"

I tried to think fast, but I didn't know.

"It means *the starting of a thing* which cannot be foreseen. The development of a pattern, a deeply hidden consequence." Matsuda spread his hands out over the table and extended his slender fingers. His palms hovered over the table, trembling slightly as if the hands themselves were emitting a subtle consequence around the room. "You see?"

As nice as Matsuda's analogies were, I wasn't sure just how far his points could go. He made poetic comparisons, though. Almost as poetic as my own aphorism, developed in a sophomore Philosophy class: *God's Dog is Dogs' God* . . .

"Japanese people," said Matsuda, "like to be in a group. They like to be close." He interlocked his fingers. "They like to know they are thinking together. We have another expression. *Shudan Ishiki*, the thinking of the group. But America has many more creative, free-thinkers."

I shivered. Perhaps Matsuda truly did have deep knowledge about international relations and, astoundingly, he was sharing it with me—being self-evaluative, even mildly self-deprecating. I felt privileged to be allowed into this sphere.

"Japan is where the normal man fits in best," said Matsuda. "I think we do not have so many first geniuses here. But we have many men who work perfectly. People who are exactly suited."

Matsuda was gazing more intently at me now. Why was he being so frank? His revelations were almost eerie—like strange, truthful words echoing from within the walls of a palace; or revelations of a dead priest . . . My hands were clammy. Was all of this real? Was it just a trick? Could Matsuda just be saying these things to test my reaction? Or thinking he ought to say them? He was taking the opportunity to communicate honestly with an American, right?

But now Matsuda had shut his eyes completely! I felt a nervous, racing pulse. My forehead twitched, and a tingling sensation ran back along the parietal ridge of my skull—Was I being intuitively probed by Matsuda? Could the Japanese have developed their intuition and telepathy, the *unused* 90% of the brain, more than Westerners? In THE JAPANESE BRAIN, a book by a Japanese scientist, it was asserted that Japanese brains function differently than other races' brains. The book was a best-seller—in Japan.

I tried to create a mental defense, in case I was being telepathically probed. I forced myself to imagine that I was snorkeling under the ocean water, seeing schools of fish and rocks and eels. I concentrated more to increase this defense, mentally transporting myself back into the experience of snorkeling too close to *Bird Rock* in Laguna Beach during seal mating season. The male seals had jumped off the rocks to scare me off, swimming through my legs and up to my face, gnashing their teeth . . . Now I could almost taste the brine of the salt water and smell the freshness of the ionized beach air. I focused even more: Sunlight filtered through the top of the sea water, bubbles of carbon dioxide rose to the surface; I was swimming like a dolphin, kicking both of my feet together, mirroring the motion of its tail . . .

"Are you alright?" Matsuda broke my trance. He had a quizzical look now, with one eye half shut.

"Oh—yes, I was just . . . thinking, for a moment."

"I was saying that I have told our New Products Division that perhaps our thinkers should go to America to learn to be creative— What do you think? Is that a good idea?" His tone had gotten sharper.

I had to answer. My thoughts flashed. "Perhaps . . . But the beauty of thinking is, is that you can do it anywhere, ne?" right?

Matsuda laughed, and his expression softened. We laughed together. This was not a humor based on inconsistency or derision. It was a different kind of humor, based on profundity, appropriateness, essence—or perhaps subtle evasiveness.

Matsuda continued. "There are many types of creativity in business. There are <u>three</u> types. First, there is Theory—the invention of a thing; second, there is Product Design; and third—third, is Marketing." He gave a firm nod. "America is very strong in Theory but lacks numbers Two and Three . . . Japan is very strong in these—in making products and selling them."

I tried to interject softly. "Yes, but—"

The smile had left Matsuda's face, and he kept talking, right over top of me. "In America, much of your new technology is linked with the military."

"Also, we have some university—"

Matsuda interrupted again. "This military focus can be limiting."

Indeed, Matsuda had the sophistication that I had surmised. He had the grace that I admired. But he would speak only about his side of the subject, his own opinions. He didn't have the intellectual flexibility—or the interest—to listen to my opinions. This was a one-sided transmission of ideas, not a true multi-dimensional analysis.

"Like a *GO* game," Matsuda continued, "With the first stone, Japan has learned to go for long-term results. American business must demonstrate profit to stockholders, so it views only the short term, which can also be a problem." Matsuda stared down at his tea and then stared at me. "What do you think of the trade situation? Do you think Japan is an 'unfair trading nation'?"

Was this a real question? Did Matsuda want to hear my side? I squelched my urge to tell the Matsuda what I really thought—after all, I was trying to sell an advertisement, right? I couldn't take any risks. "Sometimes, it can be difficult for one country to see another clearly," I said.

Matsuda nodded enthusiastically. I had scored a point! "Yes. It is just that!" Matsuda kept nodding, "Americans have a different notion about free trade. And they haven't learned our markets. There are always two sides to a truth."

"That is the nature of truth."

Then Matsuda gave me a warm concurring smile as if I were a colleague with whom he had been working for twenty years, and together we had just made a wonderful breakthrough.

But l hadn't said what I knew to be the case. I didn't tell the *real* truth—exposed in a recent *Gai-jin's* book, THE ENIGMA OF JAPANESE POWER: Japan was a closed and protected market. There wasn't free trade. Government-endorsed cartels fixed prices and *keiretsu* combines strangled new suppliers. Complex distribution systems made it almost impossible to get out any new foreign products, and "safety" requirements held up foreign goods for years while they were being "tested"—when, in fact, the time was used to copy the new product and make Japanese versions. And since there was no price competition from the foreign products, Japanese companies could compete on the basis of quality alone. They could sell their goods at top prices at home, which gave them enough extra money to sell them at cutthroat prices abroad . . . No, I didn't say any of these things, although I wondered how Matusda would respond. Instead, I opened my briefcase. "I would like to show you our publication, <u>Tokyo Time</u> . . .”

"Yes, please. I will help you, anyway I can," he said. But his eyes were distant. He had a funny half-smile, and he began to chuckle. "*Boko wa tada no furui koishi da nagasarette nameraka ni natta.* I am an old pebble, washed down and smooth," he said. And then he was laughing, chest shaking as the humor overcame him. He fought to regain composure.

I went through the <u>Tokyo Time</u> demonstration. Matsuda said he would "evaluate" the publication. Somehow, I didn't have much hope. But I pretended.

Outside, the mist was so heavy that I could feel it on my tongue. Soon it started to rain—oozing oily drops—and umbrella-less, I ducked into a Wendy's Hamburgers to wait it out. Dammit, I should have paid more attention to the weather. Inside the train station, the icy air conditioning strafed my wet jackets and pants. I felt a chill coming on and hoped it wouldn't get worse. Then I sneezed, a textbook sneeze that tickles and itches and comes from the stomach and makes your shoulders twitch. Of course, I covered my mouth, but nearby Japanese looked up at me as if I should be quarantined—or at least be wearing one of the surgical masks to prevent my germs from spreading across their nation.

Back in the subway station, I stared down at the immaculate floors—perfectly free of trash or mounds of stuck chewing gum. Then I followed the orange Ginza line painted on the wall. Down a long windowless corridor, I marched, where the air was hotter, but the light garish. Then I saw it! A Japanese radio station advertisement—a picture of a portable FM radio sitting on a folded pair of Levi's, with the caption: **What's left to admire about America, except blue jeans and great FM stations?** Below was the rhetorical response: **Now there's only blue jeans . . .**

It was a curious and conceited advertisement. A benchmark of post-war historicity, following the spirit of the new Japanese economic mantra, "*Oitsuki Oikuse!*" Catch up and Pass!, and the national perception of "JAPAN INC."—a single monolithic entity, destined for financial supremacy. Of course, the radio ad made no hint of the fact that after World War II—after Pearl Harbor, after the massive fire-bombing of Tokyo, and after the atomic bombs—the U.S. had paid for the rebuilding of Tokyo cities and factories to a point which made them, in many cases, technologically superior to those in the U.S. itself. And for the past forty years, Japan had avoided major military expenses by sheltering under the umbrella of U.S. protection . . .

I looked again at the ad. I knew the real answer to the question, the answer that most of the Japanese couldn't conceive of in their conformance and societal cohesion, in their ceaseless hours at work to beat America. Goddamn it! What was left to admire about America? Individuality, Freedom, Self-Actualization, Privacy, and Second Chances . . . Respect for Creativity, Free Expression, Opportunity, Diversity, and Free Thought! These ideals were all left to admire. And in large part, they were still present.

I plotted how it might be possible to disfigure the radio advertisements. If I snuck in at night, just after the last trains, could I graffiti the ads? Did they have cameras in the halls? How could I find out? They must have station plans or blueprints somewhere. Maybe I could call Tokyo English Information—they were so damn efficient. They could help me plot the crime.

Outside the station, the rain soaked the streets. But in the far corner of the subway entrance was a men's clothing store. Unfortunately, it was sold out of umbrellas. So I decided to buy a hat. "A hat is like a cover on your chimney," my old crew coach used to say on the cold early-morning rows. "Cover the smokestack and keep the heat in." Of course, following that analogy, smoke would also asphyxiate the wearer, but this part of the theory was never explored. I would buy a cover for my chimney. I would keep the heat in, the metabolic and intellectual heat.

Inside the clothing store, there was a veritable fantasy house of choices: pith helmets, sailor's hats, homburgs, fedoras, Stetsons, stovepipes, even coonskins—a thousand possibilities. I took my time selecting, enjoying the free range of choices, the warmth of the shop, the crystal-clear mirrors at face height in which you could check the fit exactly. I had never seen Japanese wearing hats such as these . . . Was this a costume store? Was it for parties? For show? Just for foreigners? I glanced at my watch: 11:30 a.m. . . . . I was supposed to get back to the office by 1:00 p.m. So I quickly chose a sporty, crushable man's hat with a narrow brim. It was an inspector's-type hat, khaki-colored with a buckle. Yes, it was a good hat indeed, with a vintage panache. And it did keep my head warmer.

I was so proud of the hat that I wore it into the office and hesitated for a moment before pulling it off. Then the cold air from the AC chilled my head again. I wanted to keep the hat on inside—but that wouldn't go over too well, so I set the perfectly fitting chapeau on my desk and tried to imagine it on top of my head again. Perhaps the power of this visualization would engender warmth. Only then did I see Hamaguchi, leaning against his doorway, a golf club held in his hand like a riding crop. "Ummm, you bought a hat," he said.

"Nice hat," said Vanessa.

"That ees a very interesting hat," said Hamaguchi.

"Thanks," I said, and smoothed out the crown so there was an exact crease. On the scratched glass top of my desk, the brim had left a dark wet circle. I took out my briefcase and got ready to go home, collecting everything I needed for the next day's appointments, organizing samples—making sure I had enough pens.

Then Max walked in, glanced at the wet hat, and sat down. With a bellow, Hamaguchi called him into the back office. I stood up and put on my hat. Now dashing and suave, I was prepared for any elements or adversity. It was true that a man needs a good hat. Why had hats fallen out of fashion? I stopped for a minute in the hall, using the reflection in the mirror to adjust the brim. Then Max rushed in. His eyes fixed on the hat like a target. He walked up next to me and stood there, too close. I stepped back.

"You must not wear this hat," said Max. "It ees not a businessman's hat."

A flash of anger jolted through my chest and ran down my arms. I tried to speak calmly. "I don't care if it's not a businessman's hat. I only wear it outside, so I don't get sick"—which I realized was not entirely true, since I had it on inside the hall just then and perhaps had foolishly worn it into the office.

"That is not a traditional hat, said Max. "People will laugh at you. It looks like a bum's hat."

"Let them laugh. I know I'm not a bum. I just don't want to get sick, that's all."

Then Max played his trump card: "*Shachou* told me to tell you not to wear thees hat."

My forehead burned. "Well, he's not the arbiter of fashion! He wears stupid shirts and goon suits that even Liberace wouldn't be caught dead in. He wears jackets with exposed penile areas, for Chrissake."

Max nodded, at first pompously, then consolingly. "Yes, he does wear different suits. He wants to be an individual, but he wants his company to be traditional. You don't want people to laugh at you, do you?"

I didn't care if they laughed. They laughed whether or not I wore a hat. But to a Japanese person, this threat of laughter must be a devastating promise of humiliation. Max walked closer and touched my shoulder. I froze.

"Now you are manager for a Japanese company." His tone was stern. "You are a company representative. This is much more important than with an American company. The welfare, the image of the company comes first." He nodded, proud of his sermon. "You must be a professional—and always look your best."

"Even when I'm on the toilet?" I shot back.

Max pursed his lips, and his eyes narrowed. The small space of air between us was hot and dense. Max shook his head. "People will think you are a bum," he said again, and walked back into the office.

I tilted up the back of the hat, so the front brim slid forward and down over my forehead in a rakish angle, a Cuban drug runner's braggadocio, a pimp's lid. A series of images of men in hats streamed before me: Frank Sinatra, with his rat-pack chic; Patrick MacNee from *The Avengers* TV show—always dapper and prepared; the G-Men from the 1930's, ready for any entanglement and irresistible to women—Marlene Dietrich, Jean Harlow, Heddy Lamar . . .

Max wasn't going to pressure me into anything. And dammit, Hamaguchi could tell me himself if he had something to say! Max wasn't my boss. I was a manager, now. I made it on my own, in my own way. It didn't matter that in Japan, success was measured in terms of conformity and cohesion. In the U.S.—and I was still an American—originality and individuality were a success in themselves.

The rain seemed to have lessened. I was just about to open the door to step outside, when Max came into the hall again. I glanced at him but said nothing. He reached into his front pocket and pulled out a gold tube that looked like it contained lipstick. "Hey, Buddy! Look!" he said in an oddly excited tone. "I got you a present because you are manager now!"

I felt vaguely nauseous.

"Open eet!" said Max. "You must see!" He put an arm around my shoulders, a heavy arm.

"What is it?"

He handed me the tube. I tore off the gold foil wrapping, heedless of the intricate embossing. Inside was a gold plastic cylinder with a cover, and inside that a smaller tan-colored tube with a domed cap on one end. On the other end, my name was spelled out in *katakana*. It was a *hanko,* a traditional Japanese stamp to sign a document. I had my own *hanko* now. "Thank you very much, Max." I smiled and slid the hanko into my pocket.

"Aren't you happy?" asked Max, "I thought you'd go crazy."

"Yes," I said. "Thank you. I am happy. It's great. I guess I really made it now. I am a success." This time I forced some energy into my smile, pulling back my lips, although the smile felt frozen on my face.

"Boy, I thought you would run to stamp everything—to stamp thees and stamp that. You're not even happy about it!"

"I am happy," I protested. Then, I felt the heat under my collar, the pinpricks in my neck. "I'm ecstatic. I'm joyful—I'm in rapture . . ." And then I was sorry when Max's eyes turned cold, hard as steel. Without another word, he walked away.

I felt the flush of shame in my cheeks. Perhaps also the flush of fever. I was dizzy and queasy and just stood there, immobile, staring out the window, trying to find the energy to move.

"It haz more energy, deep inside . . ." That's what my old college biology professor had said. She was a hefty Austrian woman who assigned the class an experiment: Different weight stacks of washers were taped to the backs of snails. The goal was to determine the absolute maximum weight that each snail could carry before it died of stress—or simply gave up. When the snails stopped moving, we were instructed to tap their backs with metal prods to scare them and muster the very last energy left in their viscous bodies.

I put a hand on my forehead and felt the burning heat. I did have a fever. And my wet jacket felt heavy and cold on my shoulders. I had to conserve energy. I couldn't give in.

Outside, the rain had stopped, but the air was still damp. I walked slowly to the subway station, avoiding puddles. Near the entrance, I saw the sway of long red hair and wondered if I was hallucinating—it was Lizzie! But I heard she left Tokyo . . . Had she come back? She spotted me, veered to the side, and then seemed to decide to keep walking toward me.

"Hi, stranger," I said.

Lizzie gave a slight smile.

"I thought you just packed up and left."

"We moved. Stanton gave us a flat in *Minato*." Her pronunciation rhymed with *to-mah-to*.

"Lucky you. You might have said goodbye."

She glanced down. "I know. I acted terribly."

"Well, you were upset."

Her eyes widened and teared up. Then she blinked quickly a few times, and the tears were gone.

"Want to go for a drink?" I asked.

"No thanks. I hate Japanese bars."

"There's a half bottle of whisky in my room . . ." It was a weak try, but it was a try.

She shook her head. "Sorry."

"We could watch that Japanese TV you love so much."

Now her eyes were distant. "You *can't* . . ." she said.

"What do you mean?"

"*You can't go home again.*"

"That's just an expression. It's not the truth."

"It's from an <u>American</u> author," she said defiantly.

"Well, even Americans get things wrong sometimes. You can go home again—as long as you have a key to the door . . ."

"See you around." She turned and walked away.

I stood immobile. My throat hurt. I watched Lizzie's long, red hair disappear into the past.

XII. N-10

Nigel, the Britisher, liked British rock. He liked it loud. Sunday night at ten-thirty p.m. in Sanjo Ryokan, the music from Nigel's room across the hall was far too loud again. Pink Floyd—*Dogs* . . . Pulsing, throbbing bass. Stinging guitar. Crashing percussion. I lay in bed and tugged the pillow over my face, then wrapped it around my ears. I pulled the comforter over my head, but that didn't help much. I rolled onto my stomach, then flopped onto my back. Finally, I gave up and stumbled into the hall. The music was deafening.

Nigel himself opened the door to his room and peered out. Face flushed, a half-full bottle of Kirin beer in his hand, he grinned at me. Long, stringy hair fell over his eyes. "Oh, hello there. What are you doing up, mate? Where's your fussy English girlfriend?" he shouted.

"We broke up."

"Easy come easy go, eh what? Listen, come have a beer with us. Claude's in there. Do you know him? Ace, too. You look like you could use a beer actually. Come in whenever you'd like."

"Thanks," I said, nodding and trying to look interested. "I'll be there in a few minutes." But I wasn't at all sure I would.

"Right-o." Nigel gulped his beer and ducked back into his room. Someone turned up the music volume even more. I closed my door and automatically lay back down on the futon. Then I jerked to my feet and stood up. The floor was vibrating. I paced back and forth along a five-foot stretch of tatami mat, uncertain just what to do. But there wasn't much choice. The din of the music made its own demand. So I headed out into the hall and knocked on Nigel's door.

Inside, Nigel's room was hot, as well as unbearably loud. Claude, a black man from Canada, sat next to a large stereo speaker. Despite the volume, Claude's ear was pressed against the grill, and his hand rested on an equalizer, the top piece of equipment in a silver rack of amps, pre-amps, monitors, and various other controls. Ace sat on a lime green leather couch. God knows where Nigel had found such a couch in Tokyo. It seemed brand new. In one corner of the room hung another speaker, cube-shaped with chrome bindings. It looked interplanetary and extremely expensive. Ace saw me staring at the speaker in the corner. "That's the *subwoofer,*" he explained, and took a big sip of beer. "It barks in rhythm. Wanna hear it?"

I shook my head no, but Ace didn't notice. Claude was pouring some of his Molson beer into Ace's empty beer mug. "Take the Canadian challenge," said Claude. "Once you go Canadian, you never go back . . ." He lifted his bottle higher, and a stream of beer gushed forth.

"Watch the couch, you brute!" said Nigel pleasantly. But he didn't seem to care. He turned to me. "Where's your beer, mate? Must drink at least two beers per hour to stay in this room. By order of the queen."

Unbelievably, Nigel turned up the stereo volume all the way. Now the sound was truly ear-splitting. The door and window panes shook. The equalizer display flashed bright red. Nigel handed me two Sapporo beers. Then he produced an opener with a handle that appeared to be made from a deer antler and removed the bottle caps. I took a long gulp. Then another. I had forgotten how good a beer tasted. How fine it was to drink with friends and forget about stress. Somehow, even the music seemed more tolerable.

I raised both my beers in a toast. "To the queen," I said, but no one was paying attention. So I drank by myself, finished the first bottle, and felt the pull of alcohol in my cheeks.

"Hey, where's your girlfriend? That redhead?" yelled Ace.

I realized, with a pang of remorse, that Lizzie must have been a subject of romantic attention. "We broke up," I yelled back. "It wasn't working out."

Ace opened his mouth and began to talk, but I couldn't hear him at all. My expression must have indicated this because he walked over to the stereo rack and turned down the volume. "There's only one thing to do," he said.

"What's that?"

"Drink more beer."

But there wasn't any more beer—a discovery which shocked everyone. Ace appeared flabbergasted. His chin dropped, so his mouth formed an open "O" and hung that way for several minutes. Claude crawled on the floor and lay his cheek against the carpet, peering under the couch to see if any bottles had rolled beneath it. Nigel turned off the stereo completely so that we could concentrate on our search. In the end, all possibilities of hidden beer were exhausted.

Claude had even rummaged through Nigel's sock drawer and closet, in case Nigel had forgotten where he kept the beer. Nigel didn't stop him. He just sat on top of an old chest and slurped down the rest of his own beer, which was still half full.

"Listen," said Nigel, "We ought to go to a bar. I know a few places in Roppongi where all the birds are. I'll buy first round."

Claude raised one eyebrow but said nothing. Ace looked tired and rubbed his mouth. I knew my expression was blank and stoic, trained from many Japanese business appointments.

"I'll even pay for the taxi," said Nigel.

"Okay, you sold me," said Ace.

"Yeah," Claude nodded, and stomped his foot.

And I had to agree.

In Roppongi, the nightclub "Safari Sam's" *(Sa-fa-ri Sa-mu-so)* had a huge fiberglass bull elephant skull hanging over the door. The bar was jam-packed with foreigners and Japanese, mostly Japanese girls. There were also a few salarymen who probably just wanted to practice their English.

We fought our way toward the door, jostling through the crowd which bulged out of the doors and into the street. Nigel went first, saying *"Excuse us, please"* to the girls and *"Watch it!"* to the men.

Claude went in second. When a businessman scowled at him, Claude shouted, much to my surprise, *"KUROFUNE TORAI! KUROFUNE TORAI!* **THE BLACK SHIPS ARE COM-ING**!"—which was the call to arms for Japanese in the 1800's when Commodore Perry's coal-powered ships, cannons loaded, belching thick smoke, blustered their way into Japanese waters. Perry had demanded that Japan open its ports to free trade or face destruction.

"KUROFUNE TORAI!" yelled Claude again and capped it off with a wide-cheeked grin. The Japanese men were impassive, as if immobilized by a stun gun. But the girls looked on with interest.

Eventually, we made it to the bar, and true to his word, Nigel ordered us beers. But he seemed to know the bartender, another Britisher, and I never saw Nigel actually pay. Then I smelled perfume and felt a soft leg push against my own. I turned to see a cute short-haired Japanese girl in a red sweatshirt with "Beaver Team Choo-Choo" printed across the chest. She pressed up to the bar and waited politely for the bartender to notice her—which would probably be a while, as he was mobbed with screaming Americans, singing Australians, toasting New Zealanders, smirking British, troating Germans, and legions of other Japanese girls, most incredibly well-dressed.

"Ano, tokidoki nagaku machi masu yo," Sometimes it's a long wait, I said to the Beaver Team girl. I used the colloquial opener *"Ano,"* followed by a short grunt. Spoken Japanese was mostly a combination of appropriate noises, grunts, and cadences, I had come to realize. *"Shimboshitte machimashoo,"* We must be patient.

The girl gave me a perky, quivering smile for a moment. Then she glanced away.

Ace tapped me on the shoulder. "Listen, Bud. Speak <u>English</u>. That's what turns them on. And use a lot of slang. They want to know Americans—not weird Japanophiles."

I felt a flush of embarrassment. Good thing the bar was dark. Then Nigel fought his way through the crowd. He was reaching in and out of the pockets of his leather jacket, tugging at the zippers and patting his trouser pockets. His lips twisted in a confused half-smile. "BLOODY HELL!" he shouted.

"What is it?" asked Ace.

"Bullocks!" cursed Nigel. "I lost me damn . . ." He looked up wide-eyed as if for consolation. Then his gaze landed on me, where it stayed. "Listen, could you possibly do me a fave? I mean, I hate to ask right in the middle of the fun and all, but . . ."

"That's all right," I said.

Nigel's expression turned sheepish. He lowered his eyes for a moment. "You see, the thing is, I lost my key. I've a locker at Ikebukuro station. You speak a bit of Japanese, right? Maybe you could come along and help me explain it to them?"

"When did you rent it?" I asked.

"Just the other day."

"Okay, it shouldn't be too difficult. Let's go."

We shook hands with Ace and Claude, sliced through the crowd, and forced our way out into the patchy clouds of the evening.

The wide steps down into Ikebukuro station were slippery, spotted with oil and dirt from the gutter. Side by side, Nigel and I walked through the beige and gray corridors, mostly empty this time of night. I inquired at the guard booth, and we were politely directed down another curved hallway to a small office in the back. I explained the situation to the clerks. We were asked to pay for the lost key, which seemed reasonable. I waited for Nigel to pay. He apologized and said he didn't have any more cash, so I paid for him. It wasn't much, only a thousand yen, about eight bucks. Then, with the station attendant leading the way, we walked back down the empty hall towards the lockers. But Nigel was walking too fast. He had to keep slowing down so as not to get ahead of the attendant.

We found the locker, N-10, and the guard jiggled his chain of keys—a hundred keys at least, clanking and shimmering. He had to try a lot of them. I leaned against the wall. I was tired now, and tomorrow I had to work . . . I glanced at Nigel, whose chin was trembling. A tendon bulged in the side of his neck, and sweat shone off his brow, which seemed odd. It wasn't that hot in the evening.

The next few seconds were a blur. The guard found the right key and squeaked open the locker. Then Nigel was shoving in next to him, wrenching out a big duffel bag—frantically tearing at the handles and yanking the bag out. Two hands on the bag, shoulder-driving the guard, Nigel was off—running like hell down the corridor, skidding into another hall, leaving only the sound of his footsteps behind.

I shuddered. I glanced at the guard and the office down the hall. Then I was running, too. The guard was trotting behind me, trying to catch up. *"TOMME!* **STOP! YOU MUST WAIT!"** he yelled.

But I was too fast. I turned down a long hall—sprinting past ticket booths and drink machines. I hoped I was heading for an exit. My ears pounded. My legs stretched out, and my strides lengthened. I skimmed through the halls like a speed boat. There! A steel door. It was unlocked! And I was out—dodging an old woman on the sidewalk, dashing behind a statue, racing across the street like a madman, cutting a jagged route through the taxis. Gasping, I halted for a moment to check and make sure no one was following me. It seemed safe for now. But I decided to walk so as not to attract attention. I took slow, steady steps. Careful steps. Strolling down the street like a good foreign visitor. Pacing leisurely—keeping my head down . . . Eventually, I made it back to Sanjo.

Nigel had set me up! He must have had drugs in that bag. I would have been sent to jail for life—throw away the key! Maybe Nigel had even stolen the bag from some other drug runner. He had used me like a piece of stinking fish bait! He even made me pay the fine for the bag. I would have been accused, jailed, and convicted—faster than a blink. And God knows what would have happened to me in the Japanese prisons.

I wanted to curse. I wanted to kick or to spit. Who could you trust? Was I just stupid and naive? The fact was that you couldn't trust anybody. You could only trust yourself. All alone. Autonomous. This was a lesson that, somehow, seemed impossible to learn.

Then I was walking past a liquor machine, and because it seemed like the right thing to do, I bought a bottle of Scotch. I leaned back my head, peering up at a clear patch of sky and a hovering moon. I downed the bottle—pouring the liquor into my mouth, gulping for air, then sucking down some more. I finished the whole damn thing.

I staggered back to Sanjo, through streets now wet with dew. In the entryway, I closed my eyes which burned from the grime of the city. I hauled myself upstairs. Then there were footsteps behind me. Two sets of steps. My chest tightened. My ears roared. My hands were hot. I didn't want to look, didn't want to know. But then I had to. I turned . . .

It was Nigel. He stood next to a mulatto-looking, quasi-Asian whom I had never seen before. Nigel was all friendly then—a man good at controlling his emotions, practiced at managing people. "Hey, we make a good team, eh? Like clockwork," he said, and took a step forward, the false smile still frozen on his face. "Well, we—"

"**GO TO HELL!**" I spat out. The words were hot bile in my throat. "You—just, go to hell." I looked away and fought to get the key in my door lock. I heard Nigel working his own key in his door. Then he called out my name . . . I would have ignored him. I wouldn't have turned, except that there was a new tone in his voice now, a steely rasp of honesty. I faced him and stared into his beady eyes.

"It was ten million yen, and I took a fucking chance," said Nigel.

That was it. The cold truth.

Nigel went into his room and slammed the door behind him. The hall closed in on me. A moldy odor stung my nostrils. I reached out a hand, a shaking hand, for my door handle.

I was tired.

I was tired, bitter, and old.

XIII. THOUGHTS FROM THE HEART

In the morning, as I sat at my desk at the office, a Japanese newspaper was thrust in front of me. I looked up, and there stood Max, holding out the newspaper with one stiff arm. His eyes were cold, but he had a taut smile. He pointed at one of the kanji in the headline. "What does this one mean?"

The strokes of the kanji had a dynamic triangular bottom and four smaller squarish shapes above. The bottom looked vaguely like a capital "A," with a capital "E" above it, to the right: "AE!" This was the pneumonic device I had developed for the kanji—the shouting sound of a karate *kiai* which accompanies a punch or a kick. "Attack," I said. "That's the kanji for *Attack*."

I read the rest of the headline: **Japan Attacks and Captures Rockefeller Center**! My feet went cold. Such military references were standard in Japanese descriptions of international economic developments, and "capture" meant "buying," but the war-like references conjured images of guns, bombs, tanks, and carnage . . . The cry of victory was humiliating, even as I tried to distance myself.

"You'd better be careful," said Max. "They'll buy the whole U.S.A." Now he was smirking and leaning forward to look more closely at my expression.

I tried to keep my face impassive.

"Japan almost owns the whole America now, don't they? They want to teach America a lesson."

I felt the blood in my gums. "I don't think that's accurate, Max. It's not accurate at all. Japanese holdings in America are only about half of British and Dutch holdings."

"Well, now Japan is gaining. Rockefeller Center! Isn't that where the governor lives?"

"It's not the governor's. It's a commercial place."

Max was grinning now, showing yellowish, nicotine-stained teeth. I could smell his odor of cigarettes and spicy pork from the "secret restaurant." Yes, Max was taunting me. Perhaps his Arab heritage led to an antagonism towards America, and he enjoyed Japan's forays against us. Maybe he just wanted to get back at me . . .

Hamaguchi waddled in, and Max immediately went to show him the newspaper, "*Shachou! Shachou!*" Max panted, "Did you hear? Japan just bought Rockefeller Center of America!"

I stared down at my desk. My neck burned. My collar was too tight. I hoped I wasn't blushing. Through my searing ears, I heard Hamaguchi's low voice. "Yes," he said. "Very interesting." He went into his office and shut the door, leaving Max standing in front of it, holding the wrinkled newspaper.

I took a deep breath. I was grateful that Hamaguchi had the sense, just this once, to shut the hell up. It was a little thing—a mere civility anywhere else, but I took it as a favor. Perhaps one day I would pay Hamaguchi back, repay the debt of *On* that any favor prescribed. Perhaps I wouldn't.

That evening after work, walking to the subway station, I glanced at a store window and caught sight of my image on the glass: wrinkled khaki pants, oversize white pinpoint cotton oxford shirt, striped regimental tie blowing casually—then with a gust of wind wagging flagrantly around my ears. For some reason, my hair stood almost straight up. I tried to pat down the hair, but it sprung up again like wire bristles. So I tucked the sideburns behind my ears. In the reflection, I noticed that the back of my hair reached well past my collar. It was too long. And far too long by Tokyo standards . . .

It had been many months since my last haircut, maybe almost a year. The last one was in California, a week before my flight to Japan. I had asked for it extra short, to buy me a lot of time before I needed another cut. Over the last few months, as the hair got longer and longer, I had just slicked back the sides with gel. But now, the hair was definitely past the stage of "stylishly long." It was out of control. And by any standard, I looked—well, sloppy.

Fortunately, on the corner at the intersection was a barbershop. It was replete with the rolling red, white, and blue striped barbershop pole, a plexiglass cylinder—the worldwide symbol of men's coiffure. As I had learned in a History class, the barbershop colors derived from "medical" *bloodletting* in medieval times, when it was thought that "bad blood" caused illness. At first the clergy had performed the bloodletting, but then they were forbidden to do so, and it was left to the barbers—who advertised their skill with colors on the pole. Red, of course, represented Blood. And white represented Bandages. The blue was added in America, as a show of patriotism. Curiously, this Japanese pole had the blue color as well—not just red and white stripes like on English barber poles. Apparently, this shop preferred an *American* barber pole, which I took as a positive sign.

I opened the flimsy door to the shop, bowing to the three barbers. I spotted a price chart on the wall, written in katakana. You could get a "*Shian-po Katto*" for 3100 yen, about $22, or you could get a plain "*Katto*" for 1675 yen. I would just get the plain cut. No need for extravagances. Besides, I didn't want these guys touching me for a long time. Then I looked up—and noticed that two of the barbers were in fact female . . . Well, that didn't change things much. All I needed was a plain cut.

I took a seat at the open end of an old red vinyl-covered bench, behind three Japanese men. I noticed, without much surprise, how the man next to me, with a slight purse of his lips, moved to sit as far away from me as possible. But then the man at the far end of the line was called to the barber chair, and each person on the bench scooted down one seat. There was a tidy order as to which patron would be called next.

I studied the three barbers. I decided to give myself an intuition test, or perhaps a judgment test: There was one pretty female barber, one older female barber (who kept glancing surreptitiously at me), and one balding, overweight male barber who held his tonsorial tools like conductor's batons. I closed my eyes and tried to visualize myself sitting in the pretty barber's chair, a girl who didn't seem shy about pressing her chest against a man's shoulders, shoring and cushioning him . . . Visualization was said to be a path to *Actualization*. Then I tried to determine exactly how much hair each barber had left to cut on the present clients—which barber had the most work left. Per my calculations, the pretty one had the client with the longest hair, and thus the other two barbers would be done first. Since there were two Japanese men ahead of me, in turn, one would go to the male barber, the other to the old female barber. And I would get the pretty female barber. Yes, it was destiny! Destiny hypothesized by intuition and analysis and actualized by Visualization—with both the left and right side of a *Gai-jin's* brain.

On the table in front of the bench was a stack of *manga,* obscene comic books. I picked one up and opened it. I couldn't read all of the kanji, but the cartoon involved the gang rape of schoolgirls by thugs, who were unmistakably misfits because of their long hair, unshaven faces, and long sideburns. On the last page, in jail, all the thugs were crying—and one screaming—with remorse over their acts and offering admissions of their insanity. But in the final frame, as a result of a faulty Korean-made lock (its country of manufacture unambiguously stamped), all of the villainous thugs escaped, no doubt to commit more heinous crimes in the next issue . . . I flipped to the back of the manga, where one could buy mail-order condoms in two sizes: "Kimino"—small tannish rubbers, and "Maxx" big black rubbers. Someone's fingerprint, in whitish lines of skin oil, covered the ad photo of the "Maxx."

In turn, both men in front of me were summoned to a barber chair, and I moved to the end of the bench—the position where I definitely would be called next into a chair. Trying to determine which barber would finish first, I watched the haircuts in progress as if I were watching the changing odds on horses flashing on a video screen at the racetrack. My heart beat. Was my logic correct? Was my intuition working? Would my Visualization succeed? Would the pretty female barber finish with her client and beckon to me soon?

The bald barber started brushing the hair off his client's shoulders. Dammit! I wanted the young female barber to finish first and call to me. But then the bald barber hesitated—and I was still in the running! He was just preparing to shave his client's chin with an electric razor . . . And suddenly, excitedly, I heard a voice in my head, the monotonous breathless murmur of a track announcer: *And in the first of fat barber, client receives shave on the head. Rounding the back, breasts pushing in, bringing up the rear with a nose in the stretch, pulling ahead . . ."*

The client got up from the pretty barber's chair. YES! I almost jumped up from the bench in victory, with a vivid recollection of the time I won at Santa Anita. I flexed my chest muscles. I was ready. *Need Hair Katto Purease,* I would say.

The barber girl glanced at me sitting on the bench and blinked several times. She seemed to tremble and began arranging her cutting tools in perfect position on a side table. *Oh, come on . . .* The girl took a second glance at me, and then decided it was time to sweep the floor, with long elaborate strokes; then with slow, circling strokes around the chrome-plated chair base. Another client came into the barbershop, hesitated for a moment, and sat down right beside me, which made me feel a little better—even though this was probably the rule, so space was available for the most customers to wait. But then the bald barber finished with his client and walked over to me. "*Hai!*" Yes, he said loudly. And blinked four times.

"*Katto, onegai shimasu,*" A cut, please, I said, and stood up. I glanced over at the pretty barber, who had immediately called up the next Japanese client.

The male barber picked up a heavy pair of shears, opening and closing the blades in a rapid motion, like a deranged killer crab. He motioned me into a chair, and I sat down. He leaned forward. I leaned back. He brought the shears towards my head. Wasn't he even going to ask how I wanted my hair cut? Did everybody get the same haircut in Japan? "*Chotto matte, ne,*" Just a minute, I said. "*Koko ni zempo, nagai,*" Here, in the front, long. I indicated the length down to the bridge of my nose. "*Sobu, mijikai,*" The side, short. I made a line above my ears. "*Ushito, marui taipu katto,*" In the back, a circular-type cut.

"*Hai,*" Yes, said the barber again, uncertainly, as if I just commanded him to plant a tree upside down, a task which he was very hesitant to accomplish but would perform out of duty.

Then the cut started.

At first, in the wall mirrors on both sides of the room, I carefully watched the gleaming shears, ready to twist my head if they got too near my eyes—or stop the barber if he was cutting too much. But in an odd relinquishment to fate, I decided just to close my eyes and allow the barber to do his job. He didn't seem interested in any blood-letting . . . And even if he messed up my hair, it would grow back, right? Plus, I would have a Japanese style *Katto.* Would that make me fit in better?

As the barber worked, I felt the hair fall down on my neck and catch on my eyelashes. I could tell some clusters of hair had dropped onto my shoulders. Then I felt the barber applying warm foam to the back of my head, and I opened my eyes to see his pudgy fingers massaging shampoo into my hair—but I had told him I only wanted a *Katto!* I didn't even know if I had the 3100 yen for a *Shian-po Katto!* But it was too late now. I guess I could always take the emergency money out of my shoe.

The barber swiveled my chair around, and for a minute, I saw my lathered head in the mirror—foamed hair, flushed forehead, bulging vein on my left temple. I glimpsed the barber standing behind me. He picked up a seven-inch straight razor and gazed down at my neck, stone-faced, like a veterinarian reticent to scrape the crusted skin off a dirty mole rat . . .

The barber began to press down on the back of my shoulders, pushing my head toward a barf-colored sink with a neck opening. He pushed harder. I realized that he wanted me to put my head face-down in the sink! What kind of shitty hair wash with this? I didn't see any Japanese getting a face-down hair-wash . . . Silently, I fumed. I considered jumping out of the chair and dashing away, and then I saw the blade of the straight razor dangerously near my neck.

I took a deep breath, closed my eyes, and lowered my face down into the sink water, accidentally inhaling some shampoo foam. Curiously, I felt myself at a pinpoint of History, a point infinitely more expansive than the pressure of the man's hand on my shoulders—a culminating point which reverberated a fifty-year chain of events: the Japanese Bombing of Pearl Harbor; the massively destructive American Firebombing of Tokyo; the brutal Mistreatment by the Japanese of American P.O.W.'s in the Bataan Death March and Prison Camps; the horrific American Atomic Bombs Dropped on Hiroshima and Nagasaki . . . In a historical arc, all of these events coalesced in my mind, and I wondered if—consciously or unconsciously—the barber was aware of them as well . . .

The sink water was warm and perfumed. I snorted out my nose and tried to block the water from entering my nostrils as best I could. Was this the way all Japanese got their hair washed at the barber? Or was this only a special treatment for me? Was this The American's Shian-po Katto?

It wasn't so bad at first. I tried to comfort myself by thinking, *When in Japan, do like the Japanese.* But then the sink began to fill up, and I could feel the gelled shampoo blobs and cut bunches of hair against my cheek, in my ears, and in my nose . . . I thought I heard my barber laughing. I almost inhaled some more foam, then snorted it out again. The drain made a horrible sucking noise and the water rushed out, giving me just enough time for a few gasps until the sink filled up again. Shampoo clung to my lip. If I tried to lick it off, would all the dirty water rush in my mouth? How often did they clean these sinks? How many clients went through this? Was I the only one?

I turned my head and opened my right eye for a moment. I could see the barber's hands sterilizing the blade of the straight razor with a bottle of alcohol and a white cloth. I tried to stay perfectly still. I didn't want the razor to slip. In a nervous twitch, my foot jerked to the side, and I felt I was about to lose bladder control . . . Again, I almost jumped out of the chair, erupting into a scream of protest, wiping the foam from my face, spitting the dirty water out of my mouth—but then the straight razor was on the back of my neck. I held my breath . . . The metal was curiously cold against my skin as the scraping began. *Scrape, scrape, scrape* on the left. *Scrape, scrape, scrape* in the middle. *Scrape, scrape, scrape* on the right . . . Just relax, I told myself. REEEE-LAXXX. Everything's Okay. Everything will be all right . . . And I could only hope.

The barber squeezed some lotion out of a bottle and applied it to my neck. It burned. Then he wiped my neck with a warm rag. And took a step back. And waited.

The haircut was over.

I was trembling. My entire body was perspiring the way it did during eye-lid surgery. I sat up. The barber was staring at me expectantly. Then I managed to stand. I trembled and brushed some hair off my pants.

"*San sen, hyako en,*" Three thousand one hundred yen, said the barber, as he washed his hands in the sink and scrubbed them with a gritty gray soap.

I shook my head, but the older female barber had heard him too, and she shrieked a nasal condemnation. She told him she heard me ask for the "*Katto,*" NOT the "*Shian-po Katto,*" he had administered.

I nodded solemnly, verifying the truth of her shrieks. The price was reduced to 1675 yen, which I paid. At least they were honest—or one barber was.

Still shaky, I walked out of the shop without even glancing back at the pretty barber. I didn't want to know if she was laughing at me.

A block down the street, I stopped by a store window to check my reflection and see how bad the haircut was. It was actually okay. Not bad for a bowl-cut. A water gash . . . A dirty shampoo slurp . . . I couldn't see how the hair was cut in the back. But if it was too short or uneven, the hair would grow. Hair overcomes adversity and grows back. That is its true beauty.

¥

It was getting dark. I kept walking toward the subway station. My legs were heavy and stiff. I spit out some saliva to try and get rid of the chemical shampoo taste in my mouth. I didn't even check to see if anyone gave me a dirty look for spitting . . . There was tension in the soles of my feet and a knot in my left calf. I walked exactly in step with the man in front of me. I was one more salaryman in a long line trudging home. Then I glanced at the faces of the other men. No one seemed to be upset. No one was fighting. They were tired, bored, or drunk workers—but they were not rebels. They were resigned and acceptant with the spirit of *akirame,* resignation without despair, the belief that all events occur naturally and to fight them is anathema. I looked at the men again. In their glazed eyes was a certain pride. They had served a long day for the glory of their country, as it should be.

Had I lost my self-respect? Had I given up? Had I failed to sufficiently defend my country against the "attack" at Rockefeller Center? Could I ever forgive myself for allowing the barber to push my face into the sink? Should I have bolted from the chair and risked the razor blade slicing my neck? A knot of guilt twisted in my abdomen. Suddenly, I was taken by the vivid image of dark red blood spurting out of a deep razor gash below my jaw, the blood gushing and pooling into my white shirt, and khaki pants . . . Was this vision proof I had done the right thing? I didn't know. And I had a bad headache. It was all too much to ponder anymore. My daily reward—for success or failure—awaited me in my room. A soft pillow on a futon bed, a closing of eyes, a fitful night's sleep, and a forgetting . . . But these days, no matter how much I slept, I always seemed to be exhausted.

I gazed down at the sidewalk and let the evening sounds wash over me—the whoosh of taxis and clicks of pedestrian heels, the synthesized electronic tunes at the crosswalks. I blinked at the glaring light from a Pachinko parlor. The players' bodies were hunched over as they stared relentlessly into the machines, portals away from quotidian life, leading to an oblivion of mechanized Zen enchantment.

As I got closer, it was much less the light than the intense machine-gun ricochet of clattering metal Pachinko balls which was penetrating—thousands of dime-sized steel ball bearings, colliding and banging against millions of pins and bumpers in scores of machines, at intense volume. Together with the flashing LED's and frenetic computerized sounds, the Pachinko parlor seemed almost a huge electronic being—or an audio-visual view of its innards: circuit boards and synapses . . .

I turned up an alleyway, a shortcut to Meiji Dori Avenue, and was surprised to hear the yells of an old man. Then I spotted him, leaning against a building. He had a wrinkled suit, disheveled hair, and a face flushed from liquor. He yelled again, and the words reverberated off the buildings' windows. His drunk voice pierced the back alleys. "*OT NOUNU BAKU!*" **ALL MEN ARE FOOLS!** The man screamed, "*OT NOUNU BAKU!*" Whether due to intoxication or not, there was something refreshing about these words and their counterpoint to societal cohesion. Was alcohol the key to freedom here?

I looked again at the streets, and buildings, and lights, and suddenly they felt all too surreal, all too artificial, as if I had injected myself into a cartoonish dream. The years I had spent studying Japanese language and the culture, the thousands of hours, felt like an aberration, a spike in the line of a graph, a discrepancy in mind and body. The too-closely shaved back of my neck burned. And suddenly, the questions loomed: *Why had I brought myself here?* There was a long series of answers to that: Expanding my horizons, Gaining new insights, Learning about another culture . . . I didn't need to ruminate about them. Then another question: *Why did I continue here?* That led to a blank. I searched my mind but couldn't seem to come up with a satisfactory answer. Certainly nothing convincing. The mere posing of the question seemed to provide its own answer: *There was no reason to stay.*

Everything had become stressful. Everything had become a hassle. I couldn't take it anymore. I had fulfilled my quest. There was no more joy of discovery. I had given Tokyo more than a chance—I'd been a martyr . . .

I recalled the day when I first arrived and found a room at Sanjo boarding house. A juggler from New Zealand with uncanny green eyes was moving out. His suitcase had opened accidentally—and a red rubber ball dropped and bounced on the sidewalk. I handed it back to him and asked why he was leaving Tokyo. A taxi pulled up, and the juggler gave one answer before he got in. He spoke one sentence: "When you start to hate it, get out fast . . ." It was a curious statement at the time, but now I understood what it really meant. There came a point when you can't keep fighting an oppressive situation, when you just have to extract yourself from it. And the time had come.

It was over. It was time to leave. It was time to go home.

What would I do when I returned to California? Anything! Anything I wanted—play music; learn to surf; train to climb mountains; study marine biology; fly hang-gliders; go to Art school—anything at all to make life interesting. To live, not to merely exist.

The soundness of my decision resonated through my body. This was a gut feeling. I allowed myself a Japanese term to describe it: *Haragai*. Making decisions on the basis of gut-level sensations.

I glanced at the McDonald's across the street. And at the Seven-Eleven store (*Se-be-nu E-re-be-nu*) next to it. And the KFC Kentucky Fried Chicken down the block . . . The mysterious, glorious old Japan did not exist here. I had gained a philosophical understanding of Tokyo, just as I had gained the scar on my elbow from my bicycle crash. Now I understood the advice of early writers on Japan, the words which I had originally dismissed as excessively ethnocentric: If you try to be more than just a guest in Japan, if you try to truly become a member of society, you will be psychologically crushed, forever yearning, hoping—forever denied. I laughed out loud, a hollow scoff of a laugh. The Japanese had the exact phrase to describe this condition as well: *Kagokare* - Yearning for that which is innately unattainable.

What would Hamaguchi say when I told him I was leaving? Would he be furious that his top-selling new manager just quit? So what . . . And Max? Too bad . . . They would survive together. Like birds of a feather. I had to **LEAVE**. The writing was on the wall. The decision was made. Or—in a new Japanese aphorism that I just invented: *Tamago wa mo hira nabe no naka da.* "The egg is in the frying pan already." It could not be put back inside the shell.

When I awoke the next morning, I threw off the dirty cotton comforter and jumped up with a martial arts champion's "feet of living motion." I jerked on my clothes and rushed outside to experience the freedom of my decision, to feel the fortuitous winds of departure.

The street in front of Sanjo seemed smaller than before, on a tiny scale—as if I were surveying it from a hot air balloon or looking through binoculars—as if I had taken off my rose-colored magnifying glasses. It was garbage day, and on every corner, old rubbish lay in piles: a stroller, a broken crystal sphere, a couch, a lamp, hundreds of intact yet un-recycled beer bottles, and scores of identically-sized small white garbage bags, each tied with a perfect bow.

I jogged back to my room, took a fast shower, put on my suit, and grabbed my briefcase. I decided to take a taxi to work—why the hell not? I deserved it. A break from the subway crowds. A gift to myself. As if in confirmation of this good judgment, the first taxi I signaled stopped, and the driver gave me only a quizzical look, not even an insolent blink, as I settled into the back seat, feeling my wet shirt stick to the vinyl seat cover. Trickles of water from my wet hair ran down my neck.

I had a big day ahead, a momentous day of formal notification. I would just say it straight out—no hemming and hawing, just be frank: "There's been a family emergency," I would say. "My grand-father is ill. I have to go back to America immediately." Of course, I wouldn't say the truth—that life in Tokyo made me sick. That Japa-nese arrogance pissed me off . . . No, I would just end it in the Japanese way—give an excuse. Save face. Avoid conflict . . . What could Hamaguchi do? Not much.

I wanted to go into Hamaguchi's office first thing. But I stopped to buy a cup of coffee—three dollars for a small cup. I needed the caffeine boost before the argument—would there be an argument? It didn't matter . . . What about proper notice? Should I give thirty days' notice? That was the customary practice in Japan . . . Did I have to give *any* notice? Would that be best for me? Probably . . . But I decided to give two weeks' notice to ease the company's transition. In America, two weeks' notice was standard. Did Hamaguchi deserve even that much? No . . . But then, in the back of my mind, dimly, as if lit by a flickering candle, I remembered that he had let go of the issue of Japan's purchase of Rockefeller Center and saved me from more embarrassment . . . Okay, I would give proper notice. But only two-weeks, though—American-style.

So now there were only two weeks left.

I pictured just walking into Hamaguchi's office right away, making my statement and getting the whole thing over with, quick and pre-cise as a stiletto blade. But when I arrived at work, I realized that it was absurd, even weird, that I hadn't considered the possibility—the overwhelming probability—that Hamaguchi wouldn't be in yet. He rarely came in before noon. And of course, he wasn't there. Nor was Max. Vanessa sat at her desk, dark weary bags under her eyes. Half-heartedly, she tried to disguise the tiredness with dabs of rouge and concealer from her compact that she held close to her mouth. The mirror steamed up, and she wiped it with her sleeve.

Of course, Tanaka was at his desk working busily, scarcely looking up. Surprisingly, Paul was in too, with his huge feet up on his desk. He was leaning far back in his chair as he gossiped into the phone and doodled Snoopies on his notebook, absently allowing a trail of drool out of the corner of his mouth. Soon he slurped it up. Consciously, I tried to think kind thoughts about Paul—that he was a good sort at heart, just goofy, but basically friendly. I tried not to feel annoyed or irritated with him. After all, I needed as many allies as I could find. Then Paul blew his nose in a trumpeting snort which sounded more goose-like than human.

Quietly, I sat down at my desk and gazed around the office in a parting glance, committing the image to memory, like a last look at a home which has just been sold.

There was the sound of the office door opening and then a grunt in the hallway. Hamaguchi had arrived. He poked his fat head through the doorway and looked around the room as if he had caught the entire staff secretly sleeping. But ultimately, he seemed to decide that all was well enough, and strutted into his private back office. I heard him sit down in his chair and let out another grunt. Thank God I only had a few more weeks of grunting to endure.

I gave Hamaguchi five minutes to settle in before I went to tell him. There was a sick weight in my stomach, but I ignored it. "I'm sorry, *Shachou*, I have some bad news," I said.

"Oh?" Hamaguchi's lips pulled back in a chubby smirk.

"I have to go back to America. My grandfather is sick," I said flatly. "I have to give you my two-weeks' notice. I'm sorry."

First, Hamaguchi smiled. Then he frowned. Then he sat back in his chair and gave me a blank look for a long moment. "How sick ees he?"

I forced a grave expression and shook my head. "He's pretty sick. The doctor isn't sure how long . . ." I let my voice trail off and looked down at the dirty carpet.

But Hamaguchi pressed on, dense and rude. "Do you think he will die?" he asked in a loud voice.

The blood rushed in my ears—What a nerve to ask a question like that! What an ass. Then another possibility dawned: Did Hamaguchi see through my plan? Did he know I was lying?

Now Hamaguchi was shouting, bellowing questions, "Why can't thees grandfather get someone else? How sick ees he? Is he going to die?" he repeated. His eyes were narrowed and beady.

I was silent. Such rudeness deserved no response. But soon, Hamaguchi was barking commands, obviously upset, frantic that his top salesman was leaving "You must make a list, a beeg list of all your appointments," he hollered. "And you must show all your appointments to, to Paul—" He thrust out his arms in a clumsy gesture.

"There's no need to raise your voice," I said.

"What?"

"I can hear well. There's no need for shouting," I continued with a condescending tone. I stood straighter, dominant, superior, looking down at my selfish, greedy boss. He was lost—only able to express raw negative emotion in the face of crisis, unable to maintain control.

Hamaguchi's cheeks were red. Perspiration gathered on his forehead. If he had lost his cool, in Japan, he had lost the game. Unfortunately, his face showed no real signs of vanquish.

"This ees what you must do," said Hamaguchi—but then the telephone rang in a loud startling burst. "*MOSHI-MOSHI*!" **HELLO!**, Hamaguchi yelled into the phone. Then he slammed the receiver down when no one seemed to answer. He turned back to me, even angrier now, brows arched in a jagged, furry V-shape. "Make a leest of all your ad possibilities. You must take Paul along with you to all appointments. He will take over your accounts." Hamaguchi took a deep snorting breath through his nose. He stared at me. "You know, Japanese system ees much different than American business, where you change jobs like . . . *gypsies*."

The muscles in my chest tensed. "Didn't you change jobs?" I countered. "You said you quit your job with *Japan Economic News*. You told us that before."

Hamaguchi looked as if he had just been informed there was piss mixed into his soup. "That was different," he said quickly. His face drained of color. "I always wanted to start my own company."

"Yes," I said. "And I always wanted to help my family if they needed me."

"Make your leest!" ordered Hamaguchi. He thrust out his bottom lip. The epicanthic folds of his eyes tightened. His neck was red and erythmic. He glowered at his desk.

But I stood there for several seconds, staring down at him like a lion that has just felled a tusky boar. Then I walked out. My hands tingled. My eyes burned. I stood up straighter and glanced around the room. Everything seemed slightly out of focus. I realized that Paul had left. It took me a moment to catch a view of Vanessa watching me. Her eyebrows were raised, and her nose twitched like that of a cat startled from a nap, unnerved by the nearby hostility—probably almost an incandescent red glow—from inside Hamaguchi's office.

I sat down at my desk, opened my phonebook, and pretended to work. I was good at that.

Then Paul came back to the office. I motioned him toward me. "Paul, I have to tell you something,"

He looked curious, alert to the new tone of sincerity in my voice.

"I just quit," I said with a little laugh. "I'm going back to America. My grandfather is sick."

"What? You mean you're givin' up your job? Your contracts an' everythin'?"

"Yes. And you're getting them. All the contracts—they're yours."

Paul was dumbstruck, amazed as a little boy at Disneyland. There was a look of raw pleasure on his face. "Even Nissan? I get Nissan?"

"Yes." I nodded dramatically.

"Well, Thanks—Thank you," Paul gushed. "Gollee . . ." He smiled and rubbed his ear.

Then Hamaguchi burst into the main office. Haughty and smug, he stood in front of the doorway to his office, surveying the staff. Then he called across the room, "PAUL, COME INTO MY OFFICE. I HAVE BEEG ANNOUNCEMENT TO—"

"1 told him already," I interrupted. "I told him all about it." Then I tried not to laugh at the utter surprise on Hamaguchi's face, astonishment which widened his eyes and dropped his jaw, so his mouth hung open.

"Umph," said Hamaguchi. And he was quiet for a moment—that shut him up. Eventually, he thought of something to say. "When is your next appointment?" he asked me.

"Monday, at—"

"Where is your meeting?

"At Restaurant Karina."

"Paul, you must go with him. Okay—I am very busy now." He turned away.

A few minutes later, Max came in, and immediately Hamaguchi

yelled out at him to come into the back office. It wasn't hard to figure out exactly who would be the topic of conversation in their meeting.

Soon Max emerged, a resigned yet controlled expression on his face, like that of a young doctor aware of a serious condition in his patient but confident of his ability to cure it. He walked over to my desk. "I heard the news," he said flatly.

I nodded.

"Come, we must talk," said Max, and strode away.

I stood up and followed him. I didn't want to talk, or listen, but there seemed no better course of action. We walked down the stairs and outside into the little street next to our building. It curved toward the cemetery and the park. "You are making beeg mistake," said Max, without looking up at me. He shoved his hands into his pockets.

I was prepared for this—the answer was easy. "My grandfather is sick. I have to leave," I lied. I was a bad liar, particularly when I had to keep a straight face. But if I couched the lie in false earnestness, I could be more convincing. So I wrinkled my brow, clenched my jaw, and tried to look troubled.

Max turned to me with a distant look on his face. "A man's real happiness ees knowing that he uses same toilet as his sons . . . And his grandsons will use it too, you know?"

My skepticism about the analogy must have been pretty evident because Max added a quick follow-up. "You could make a new life here and start a family, just like me."

I shook my head weakly, as if Max's suggestion were tempting, but impossible—since destiny itself stood in my path.

Max spoke faster now. His words had an artificiality to them, and I recognized the tone. It was the tone he used to sell his clients into an advertising contract, a prideful yet beseeching tone, a soft/hard sell. "You know, now Japan has all the money. Japan is land of twenty-first century. Even they have better technological than America. Why do you want to go back?"

"I told you."

Max stopped walking. He spoke louder. He was a salesman who must drive his point home, who must bring back the deal for his boss; who would not take *No* for an answer. "Just look," said Max, "The Japanese planes—what is it the FSX?—even the planes are faster. Soon they will take over America even."

"You're wrong!" I said. Of course, Max was bending the topic to skew the argument in his favor. No longer were we talking about why I should stay in Japan. Max had shifted to argue that Japan was dominant over the U.S.

And he kept on. "Just look at the banking industry. In 1979, most of big banks were owned by United States. Now, in 1989, no American bank is even een top twenty—and <u>fifteen</u> Japanese banks are on top!" He paused to let this sink in. Then he laughed and continued mercilessly. "Even your last president, Meester Ray-gan, even he is paid beeg money to make speech in Japan. Even he is EMPLOYEE of Japan!"

I shivered.

"THEY'RE GOING TO BUY YOU OUT!"

"It's not a question of Japan's artificially-inflated economy, Max." I spoke rapidly, in flurries of words, "It's a question of raw materials, supplies, and military MIGHT"—I hit this last word hard. "It's a question of international relations, of political interest in the conditions of other countries, for more than superficial public relations purposes."

Max took a step back and stood with his legs planted widely in the street. He thrust out his pointed chin. "You don't leesten to anybody, do you? "

"I listen to myself," I shot back. "I have certain beliefs and values that I follow."

"You are letting down the company—we were depending on you." I saw the extent that Japan had penetrated him, skewing his perceptions, changing his allegiances, like a bleeding orange wash seeping into his white shirts.

"My family is depending on me," I affirmed. "And I'm depending on myself," I said coldly.

"Americans are always so selfish!" Max was angry now. His in-group was disintegrating, and he was failing at his mission for the boss. "Americans are self-centered," he continued.

Dammit! Max wasn't going to talk about Americans that way! I felt the jolt of adrenaline in my chest. "Yes, Americans are individuals—you're right! We're not willing to sacrifice our whole lives to slave away in companies and never see our families. Americans want individual satisfaction. They want self-actualization—" I was pretty sure Max didn't know the term, but I didn't care. "Americans use their own minds. It's a free society. It's a free market. It's not an artificially prescribed economy like Japan. It's not a rigid, controlled hell!" And with that, I stopped. I had said enough.

There was silence, hard silence, for a while. Only the rush of distant cars and crunch of gravel somewhere beyond the fence line. "You're making a beeg mistake," Max said again. "You know that, though." Suddenly, he changed tactics and spoke in a lower voice, almost confidentially, "You can be a beeg success here. Talk to *Shachou*. Maybe he'll change his mind," he added, as if it were Hamaguchi who had made the decision in the first place, not me.

"I'm not interested in the kind of success that occurs here. Sorry," I scoffed and walked away.

Max's footsteps quickened as he tried to catch up. I walked faster. But then Max was beside me, the tension separating us like an icy wall. Max pushed through it and lay a hand on my shoulder. The fingers on my right hand started to curl into a fist, but I extended them again.

"Leesten," said Max. "Leesten to me. Good friends always argue, right?" He blinked a couple of times. "There ees a word. A Japanese word, *Ishin Denshin*. It means 'Thoughts from the Heart.' Japanese think it is special term only for Japanese. But it is also good word for foreigners." He looked up. His coal-black irises—intense as those of a bird of prey—peered right into my eyes. "We are foreigners. We must stick together."

I didn't answer.

Max let out a heavy breath, almost a whistle. He spoke again, forcing some levity into his voice which made his accented words screech a bit. "Leesten—we should go for a drink, eh buddy? Or go to play some pool. That ees what buddies do."

"Yeah."

"I will pay," said Max.

"No, I can't let you do that."

Max reached out a hand to touch my shoulder again, and then seemed to think better of it. His arm fell back to his side. "Hey, we're buddies—remember?"

I didn't answer.

Then Max walked away.

Alone and detached, I stalked the avenues for a while until my pulse slowed down, until my breaths were long and relaxed again. I gazed at the office buildings, and up at the pale cloudless sky. I glanced around to look for trees, or bushes, or flowers—but there weren't any. So I turned up a new street, then ambled back down again, and eventually—since I didn't know where else to go—I returned to the office.

Tanaka looked up at me when I came in. He stared openly, strangely, as if viewing me for the first time. I sat at my desk and felt Tanaka's gaze on my back. I could feel his new demeanor. His entire axis toward me had changed. No longer was I *Nakuma*, an "inside person"; now I was *Tanin*, "outside of the group"—far outside, in my case.

But it didn't matter. I knew the truth. God knows I had found out the truth. A foreigner would never fit into Tokyo—not without demeaning himself, skewing his perceptions, and changing his allegiances—not without losing himself . . .

XIV. HONORABLE CRAB

The twenty-three-story twin towers of *Aoyama I-Chome* cast two dark shadows over the sidewalk. They were long thin shadows—legs of a spindly, emaciated giant. I could feel the perspiration on my back. Paul hurried his steps until he was walking beside me. He wiped his ear using a napkin with little gold arches that he must have saved from lunch at McDonald's. Then he moved the napkin to his neck and rubbed harder. Tiny flakes of napkin fell onto the back of his suit collar and lay there like dandruff. I didn't say anything. The air was cooler in the shade. I straightened my tie and checked my briefcase to make sure I had brought the advertising contract papers. Yes, I had remembered.

"Hey, we almos' there?" Paul's Mississippi twang silenced two women in turquoise-patterned silk kimonos who passed us, at the greatest possible distance, on the sidewalk. Paul made a loud grunting noise—and a werewolf's groan—from deep in his throat. One of the women shuddered. Her kimono sash trembled, and she hurried away.

"What was that noise, Paul?"

He grinned but didn't answer.

I could see inside the woman's cart. She had bought some of the dried red squid, veiny with bulging black eyes, that were sold at the market. Packaged in clear plastic, the squid looked like fishing lures or disgusting rubber toys. I had considered buying a number of these veined squid myself before leaving Tokyo—as gag Christmas presents for friends. "Did you bring your business cards?" I asked. "Remember, just let me do the talking."

Paul shrugged. "You're the boss."

Perhaps since I had just given my two-weeks notice at work, Paul was a little sorry to see me go. I was just about to tell him about the napkin flakes on his collar, but then his tone became smug. He pursed his lips. "Remember, *Shachou* said I get the commission."

The heat flared in my temples. "Sure, you get the contract. I couldn't care less. When I'm home lying on the beach in Malibu, it won't make any difference to me if you have one contract or a hundred. Ono's a nice guy, and I just don't want him to get offended that you're taking over."

"You think I'll offend him?"

"Frankly, you might. Just let me do the talking."

Paul didn't answer. But when we reached the entrance to the Aoyoma towers, I noticed with some satisfaction that he waited for me to enter first. He stood aside at the top of the stairs like a polite cub scout and walked slower to let me go first through the automated doors.

Restaurant Karina was in section B-2. Even though I had been there before, the underground entry level was a maze of hallways and elevators. For a moment, I was disoriented—dizzy, really. I glanced around to try and get my bearings. It was mid-afternoon, so most of the businessmen who thronged the corridors during lunch and after work were up in their offices. The halls seemed stark and hollow.

We walked into the mezzanine. On the left was a tiny bakery, hardly bigger than a closet. There were no customers. The attendant, a nubile high-school-aged girl, was not gabbing on the phone. She was not reading fashion magazines. She was rearranging the rows of pastries behind the glass. Using two sets of tongs, snapping and flexing them like some divine crustacean—Aphrodite of the Sea. She lined up the pastries with meticulous precision. The rows already looked perfect, but the girl found minute problems with each and painstakingly corrected them in adjustments to the millimeter, to the micron.

On the right was a hairstyling salon where a fat businessman was getting a shampoo. The man's chair was reclined, almost horizontal. The female attendant began to wash his hair with her hands. Soap foam wet her blouse as she massaged his scalp. She leaned over, and her breasts pressed against the man's face. His eyes were closed. His head bobbed slightly with the rhythm of the woman's fingers. A vein stood out on his forehead, and he flexed his plump thighs.

"Good thing he's got that newspaper over his lap," Paul observed. He stopped and turned toward me. "Which way now?"

"I think it's down here."

"I thought you'd been here before . . ."

I didn't answer. Then I recognized a bar down the hall and started towards it. Next to the bar, behind teakwood lattice and lace curtains, was *Restaurant Karina*.

In the entrance, there were maroon velvet couches, black end tables, and triangular brass lamps emitting a faint light. At the reservation desk, bathed in the strangely luminous glow of an old clock, a woman sat hunched over some papers. She glanced up once when we entered, then looked back down to her work and ignored us. I stood there and waited for some further acknowledgment from the woman. Maybe she was testing us. Trying our patience . . . So when Paul started forward, I held out a hand in a quick motion that he should wait. But after several minutes, the woman still hadn't glanced up again.

She opened a drawer and took out a wooden abacus-like device, a Japanese calculator with disks that slid on metal pegs. In Japanese class years ago, I had learned the name of this thing. Now I had forgotten it. In a few weeks, the old calculator would be the farthest thing from my mind.

Soon it was clear that the woman had no intention of speaking with us. This was not a shy hesitation. It was not a test. It was a flagrant refusal to talk with foreigners. Heat flashed in my neck. I took a deep breath and approached the desk. The woman's fingers moved swiftly over the calculator disks as if they were keys on a musical instrument. She slid the counters back and forth so quickly that the motion was a blur. Despite my annoyance, I was fascinated by the fluid motion of her hands and drawn irresistibly to the clicking and stacking and counting. To use this kind of calculator took years of practice and special lessons. It made a rhythmic sound.

The woman's lips were moving as she murmured her numbers. I waited until the woman's lips were at rest. I kept silent until she had jotted down a few *kanji*. Then I spoke softly in my most polite Japanese. Last week, I had read that Japanese people felt most Westerners spoke too loudly. I might as well end my Tokyo job in a sizzle, a sparkle of Japanese expertise. "*Sumimasen, Ono-san to no appointo arimasu,*" Excuse me. We have an appointment with Ono-san, I said.

Slowly the woman raised her head. Her eyes met mine, locking there. She spoke a single word then, over-emphasizing the syllables, almost savoring them. "*I-ma-sen.*"—Not here.

I felt the indignation swelling in my throat. Just then, with the timing of a savior, Ono walked into the room. His face was flushed, and he was laughing. Even five feet away, I could smell the liquor on his breath. Like last time, Ono was wearing not a suit, but a silk shirt with pleated trousers. He sobered his expression. "I am sorry you had to wait," said Ono.

"Oh, not at all. We were just enjoying how peaceful your waiting area is." I made sure to glance around the room appreciatively, without looking at the grumpy old hostess.

"Thank you." Ono exhaled and bent his head forward. When he glanced up, his expression was clearer, like a sinner after penance. He seemed reassured that I knew these subtleties of Japanese business etiquette, that I wasn't a pushy foreigner.

"Please allow me to introduce my associate, Mr. Bass," I said. In a clumsy swing of his torso, Paul bowed. Then he reached into his pocket for a business card which he held out casually with one hand. "Two hands," I said. Even if Ono heard, he wouldn't understand English spoken this rapidly. Without changing his expression, Paul corrected himself and held the card in the honorific way: between both sets of thumb and forefingers, with the printing facing Ono.

Ono studied the card like a puzzle. He made a soft lingering grunt. "Bassu-san?" Brow wrinkled, almost confused, he patted his pockets. Then he bowed again. "I am sorry. I have no more cards."

Paul grinned. "Oh, that's okay. I run out myself a lot. Especially you must be very busy." Paul's voice sounded loud and coarse in the narrow entrance way, and I wondered whether the Japanese were right about Western speech. But then, in rushed a giggling girl in her early twenties—one hand clamped over her mouth. She froze for a moment in front of the entrance door when she saw us all, and her eyes widened. A clinging black dress showed off her body. She wore a pearl necklace and matching pearl rings. She breathed rapidly as if out of breath, and her breasts rose with each inhalation. A crimson glow shone on her face and neck. I didn't think she was Japanese, but couldn't tell where she was from.

"Ono-san!" she tittered and swatted Ono's shoulder, wriggling her hips and bending into him. He whispered to her. I could only catch a few of the words, something about "waiting" and "men." Then Ono and the girl laughed together like high school sweethearts, gazing into each other's eyes. For a few seconds, they seemed to forget that anyone else was in the room.

Finally, Ono introduced her. "This is Lee-san," he said. "She is my teacher." He stuck out his tongue and held it softly between his teeth. Lee began to introduce herself in Japanese, but Ono interrupted. "No. You must practice English." He gave a sovereign nod, and Lee pouted, which made her even more attractive. Three men were all watching her, and she knew it.

"*Haro purease.*" She squared her shoulders, held out a bejeweled little hand, and trembled a bit as she tried to keep a straight face. Ono fell forward in a fit of alcoholic mirth. His belly shook. When he looked up, his eyes were watering.

Paul took Lee's hand. "Hi. My name is Bass. You know, like the fish."

"*Fishu?*" She didn't understand, and Paul repeated himself, over-enunciating each syllable as if he were speaking to a child with a hearing problem.

"It-sa fish . . ." He waved his hand side to side, as if to show his fingers swimming though water. Then he opened and closed his mouth like fish lips until Lee got the idea.

"Meester Feeshu?" she asked.

Ono sputtered so hard, noises themselves almost ichthyic, that he had to sit down. Lee looked back and forth helplessly. *"Nani? Nani?"* Soon she gave up and sat on the couch, too.

With a long appraising look that started at Paul's feet, hovered at his belt line, and worked its way up, Ono gazed at Paul. Then Ono spoke slowly, "Meester Fishu, you would like to sit next to Meesus Fishu?" He smiled like a patronizing professor. "After we drink, you can be her *meester.*" Paul and I glanced at each other—Ono must be too drunk to know what he meant. Then Ono jumped to his feet. "Nakamura-san!" he barked at the woman at the desk.

"Hai!" She snapped to alertness, hands clasped in front of her, ready to receive a command.

"Bring the special bottle and one beer!" Ono used the loud, slurred, slightly exasperated tone, which was the signature of a dom-inant Japanese male. The woman rushed away to do his bidding.

We walked through more lace curtains, a spider web of strands, into a spacious dining room. Shining wood paneling covered the walls. Above the tables were large brass plaques etched with scenes of taloned dragons, chattering monkeys, huge insects, and many, many fish. At Ono's prodding gesture, we moved over to a booth where—with two hands on her shoulders as if she were blind—Ono pushed Lee toward Paul. "Meester and Meesus Fish must sit to-gether!"

But when he saw them standing side by side (Lee's pretty head barely reached Paul's chest), he changed his mind. "No, I will sit with Meesus Fish!" He grasped Lee by the arm, guided her into the other side of the booth, and slid in next to her, very close, almost on her lap.

"You have a very beautiful restaurant," said Paul.

Ono nodded several times but kept peering around the room as if his mind were on something else. "Drink!" he shouted. "My mouth is thirsty. Do you like to drink?"

Paul answered first. "Yeah, especially when it's hot outside, a beer tastes real good."

"Yes, it is good to drink when it is hot." Ono laughed. "It is good to drink when it is hot, and good to drink when you are hot!" Suddenly Lee made a squeaking sound, a mink's cry, and jumped in her seat. Ono must have touched her under the table because she gaped up at him, clamping her mouth closed and quivering. "Lee's seat is very hot, you don't think?" asked Ono.

I forced a chuckle, dry and feeble in my throat—it made me cough. A waiter, white-coated and expressionless as a funeral parlor attendant, brought over our drinks. From the special bottle, Ono poured us all some brown liquor which he called "*gado.*" After a small sip, I could only classify it as brackish sherry. Ono himself just drank beer. "It is good to drink in the day!" he said.

I rolled the bitter *gado* around on my tongue. It wasn't polite to bring up business right away, but I just wanted to get back to the office and waste the rest of the afternoon reading the paper.

Ono was looking at me now. His brows were knit, and chin creased. "Do you like thee special drink?"

"Yes, it's interesting, like a fine sherry," I said.

"I don't like it," said Ono. "I prefer beer. Would you like a beer?"

But it was a trap. When I agreed to beer, Ono had me in a corner. "If you really liked the special *gado*, you would want more—not beer . . ." He snickered. And blinked.

"I like to alternate this special sherry with beer. It is better for taste," I replied. I knew this sounded ridiculous but didn't care. I just tried to keep an earnest look. Then Ono seemed to have totally forgotten about the matter. He was staring at Lee's neck.

"She is very pretty, yes?" asked Ono. Paul and I nodded. Lee looked down at the table, blushing and shaking her head. Maybe she understood more English than she let on. "What do you think her most pretty part is?" asked Ono.

"Well, I think overall she is very—"

Ono wasn't listening to me. "Do you think it is here? Or here?"

He gestured first to Lee's face, then to her breasts. Lee's blush darkened. She tensed her shoulders, took a small drink, and sat perfectly still.

"Lee-san is my teacher. In the day, she is my Chinese teacher. And at night . . ." His voice trailed off. "Lee-san is not talking now. I think she is hungry. Perhaps she would like to eat a fish?" But the humor of this train of jokes had dissipated even for Ono, so he shouted at the waiter, *"O-Kani!"* Lee smiled and covered her mouth again. "These crabs are her favorite," explained Ono. Suddenly his expression became very serious. "They are a delicacy. We call them 'Shanghai Crabs.'"

With the quick resolve of a seasoned businessman, I took the contract out of my briefcase. Now was a good time, I knew it. "Mr. Ono, we have prepared the contract for your advertisement. I know there are many foreigners who would also be very interested in these delicious Shanghai crabs."

"They are too expensive for the foreigner," said Ono flatly.

But I continued. I knew when to press on. "Well, they will be interested in something else then. Please, here is the contract for you to read."

"Yes, yes—Where I should sign?"

Was Ono kidding? Usually, the Japanese wanted to study a contract for weeks before signing it. They would have a compulsory discussion with the "advertising team," or at least read the document slowly and carefully, murmuring and sighing. Ono hadn't even looked at the papers. Perhaps he was very drunk. But then again, in legendary Japanese business practice, the written part of a contract wasn't important, only a token gesture. What was important was the trust and camaraderie of the parties. Ono must really trust me . . . Hah! Just when I was leaving, I had finally mastered the system. Just when I couldn't care less.

Ono burped. He reached into his shirt pocket and dug around in it for a few moments but found nothing. "You have pen?" Instantly, I brought out my pen and clicked it open. *"Doko?* Where?" asked Ono, and I pointed to the line. Paul leaned forward to watch. Already his eyes were glazed from drinking. Then Ono etched in the character strokes of his name in *kanji,* twisting his mouth as he wrote. *"Hai!"* he said finally.

With smooth little fingers, in a graceful clutch—the tender capture of a flower—Lee took the pen from Ono just as he was finished.

"I know this pen!" she said. "Good pen!" I had only paid about three hundred yen for it at the stand on the subway platform, but it did write especially well and had a nice smooth tip. Lee held the pen like a long-lost piece of jewelry, a sapphire broach, clutching it to her breast. "I try to find this pen, *demo* . . ."

"You can have it if you'd like," I said.

Lee rubbed the pen, massaging the glistening metal between her fingers. "Thank you, please," she said and smiled.

Ono frowned. "Nakamura-san! Ball-pen!" he shouted. Then Nakamura scurried out from some alcove in the wall where she must have been hiding. She trotted over and handed Ono a plastic pen. In turn, Ono gave this pen to me, poking my arm with it. "You must have this pen," said Ono. Then he stared at Paul, as if in decision. Finally, he spoke. "Lee-san wants *your* pen."

Paul looked embarrassed. He reached into his coat pocket and patted his pant legs. "I'm sorry. I forgot my pen." He looked relieved when, just then, a waiter wearing heavy gloves brought over a huge silver tray. The tray was covered, but puffs of steam escaped from under the edges, accompanied by the salty piquant smell of the crabs. Lee touched her lips, and her eyes gleamed. The waiter handed us each a small plate, although there didn't seem to be any utensils or chopsticks. On a command from Ono, the waiter hurried off to get something else which I hoped would be forks. Instead, it was four large bottles of beer.

With a flourish, a quick whisk of his hand, Ono pulled off the tray's cover and—through a cloud of steam which moistened my face and fogged up my glasses—I saw ten medium-sized crabs in two perfect rows. They were orange-colored with small red horns and pointed jagged feet. White froth bubbled out of hairline cracks in the shells and oozed around the eye stalks and in between the ridges of the claws. Lee's eyes bulged. Paul let out a low whistle. He loosened his tie and leaned into the table. "Boy, those sure are pretty crabs," he said.

"Yes," said Ono, staring reverently at the platter.

I was reminded of a Japanese tea ceremony where everyone is supposed to offer a compliment about the color of the tea or the beauty of its leaf patterns. Maybe Ono was waiting for me to say something nice about the crabs. "These horned crabs have a very fine aroma," I said.

"Yes. They are a delicacy. I have twenty-five crabs flown in every day. You must eat the brain."

Lee had no comment about the crabs, but her fixation on them was compliment enough. She hadn't taken her eyes from the tray since it arrived. She seemed to have forgotten to blink, and her eyes were moist. Paul looked a little hungry, too. I wondered when the crabs would be served. But Ono had another idea.

"Now, Lee-san must sit with Mr. Bassu. We will watch how they eat together." Ono stood up. Paul glanced at me in wild-eyed alarm. "Mr. Bassu will sit here," said Ono, and slid out of the booth.

"Just go with it, Paul," I said. Then Ono got out of the booth, and Paul stood up beside him, looking very tall and gawky next to the shorter man. Like a dentist securing his patient, Ono put two hands on Paul's shoulder and gently pressed him into the other seat. Lee adjusted herself in the booth then slid closer to Paul.

Ono served each of us crabs, which amounted to grabbing a shell with two sticks he took from a slot on the side of the tray and dropping the crab unceremoniously onto a plate where it spun, wobbled, and finally was still.

The crabs did look attractive, like miniature sculptures on the white plates. Daintily, Lee touched the pincer claws of her crab. Then she lay four fingers on top of the shell and closed her eyes as if she were meditating or maneuvering a Ouija pad. Finally, with her left hand, she held the crab down hard. With her right hand, one-by-one, she ripped off its legs. Juice from inside the crab legs splashed onto Lee's chest and glistened. She didn't seem to mind.

When the legs were off, she slid a finger in the front of the crab near the eye stalks—into what I guessed was its mouth. Using both thumbs, she snapped off the top of the crab's head, lifted the remains of the creature to her lips, and eagerly slurped out some of the yellowish pulp inside. *"Oishii!"* Her eyes sparkled. "Dee-lishus!"

"Yes, it is the brain," said Ono. Lee looked over at Paul, made a soft whimpering noise, and decided to help him with his crab. She broke off its legs, then its head. With her pinky in the yellow goo, she showed him where to suck the brain. Ono watched and trembled, almost transfixed, his knees knocking together under the table.

"I've never had crab like this," said Paul. He swallowed hard. Then, bravely, he took the crab body in two hands and slurped. After a moment, he smiled. Yellow froth clung to his upper lip. "It tastes kinda like egg."

"Yes, it is the brain," Ono repeated, with solemn nods. Lee had moved on to the legs, which she sucked like a straw, despite the jagged edges of shell. This required quite a bit of suction and made some noise. I knew it was polite form to make delectable noises while you ate, so I made a few good loud slurps as I struggled with my own crab. I tried a little leg first, then some brain. It wasn't as bad as I thought. It didn't make my stomach turn—I didn't need to vomit. Actually, the brain did taste like egg yolk.

Curiously, Ono himself didn't eat any of the crabs. He seemed content just to watch us. He sipped his beer slowly and wiped his brow. "When I dive, I like to watch the crabs the most." He pulled back his lips, wiggling and snapping his fingers like a crawling shellfish.

"Oh, you dive?" I asked.

"Of course," said Ono, lifting his nose.

I saw no reason why this should be obvious, but I didn't say anything. I glanced down at my crab, shivered, and drank some beer instead.

"I just returned from Bali," Ono announced. "Lee-san dives too, but I do not allow her to wear the bathing suit. She must be to dive naked!" He started in with another laughing fit.

Lee was still concentrating on her crab legs, pulling and sucking at them. Paul was starting to look very drunk. His eyelids were heavy, and he swayed in his seat. He only caught the word "naked," but brayed along with Ono and gave a prurient, full-toothed grin. Ono shifted in his seat, so he faced Paul directly. "Mr. Bassu, you would like to make the naked dive with Lee-san?"

Paul's nose quivered, rabbit-like. He hesitated and finally spoke, "Well, I don't know. I'm sure that would be very interestin'." He blushed. Lee stared even more intently at her crab. Her fingers were white and water-wrinkled from its juice.

"We must drink first! It is good to drink first!" Ono grabbed for his beer and missed. His hand knocked into the wine bottle instead, and it toppled over with a crash on the silver serving tray. A heavy stream of sooty brown wine gushed across the table and down into Paul's lap. He gasped as the wine hit his pants. With admirable speed, Lee righted the bottle and used her napkin to wipe up the mess. She didn't hesitate to lean over and spend some time sopping up the wine between Paul's legs. As she wiped, Paul developed a thin-lipped guilty smile. Without the slightest hint of apology, Ono bent over the table and peered down at Lee's scrubbing hand. He moaned. "Yes," he said. "It is good to drink first!"

No one spoke for a while. Lee busied herself cleaning up the spill. Paul, a bit groggy, looked at me for some kind of reassurance, like a little boy gazing up at his father. But I betrayed nothing. I nipped at my beer and glanced at my watch, which Ono noticed. "Yes! I forget," said Ono. "What time is it now?"

"Four o'clock," I said. Ono looked uncertain, so I translated, *"Yoji desu."*

"Yoji! Yoji!" Ono's eyebrows shot up in alarm. "Soon, I must leave. But we must drink more!" His face was anxious. "You will come back tonight?"

I didn't want to be rude, but I'd had enough drinking for one day. The gritty *gado* residue coated my teeth yet couldn't disguise the stale aftertaste of the crab. Ono continued, his tone a bit too prompting. "Tonight, we must go to celebrate contract together, yes?"

I understood the real significance of this invitation. Japanese businessmen liked to drink together to cement a deal and show their mutual good feelings. Ono was leveraging the practice to get me to go out. At this point, the deal itself made no difference to me, but Ono was being quite amiable. He was treating me as a true business partner. I looked at Ono's genuine expression. His bloodshot eyes were wide with expectation. He wanted to show his friendship. "Okay," I said, "What time?"

"Eight o'clock. Of course, you must come too, Mr. Bassu. I am sure Lee-san will come also . . ."

Paul snuck a glance at Lee. She had started another crab. "Well, Ah'm not sure," he said. "Ah'll try." The twang in his voice seemed to become more pronounced when he drank.

"Goodu!" said Ono, "I must go." He stood up suddenly, pushing aside his beer. "Tonight, I will see you!" He gave a sly smile and sauntered out of the restaurant, clutching at the tables for balance.

We watched Ono until he had ducked through the lace curtains and disappeared. Then Paul stood up abruptly. His face was ruddy with liquor. A huge brown stain spread over the crotch of his khaki pants and between his thighs. "Well, Miss Lee-san, it sure has been a pleasure," he said. With a twinge of admiration, I saw that Paul managed to be both shy and insinuating at the same time.

"Nisu to meet you," said Lee. She held out her hand, then realized it was covered with crab juice. She reached for a napkin. By the time she extended her hand again, Paul had turned away. I took Lee's

warm, moist hand instead.

"It has been a pleasure," I said gallantly, with a little bow—not a Japanese bow, though—a chivalrous bow of a knight or a musketeer. Then I followed Paul out into the hall. We walked up the steps and into the hot, pallid sun.

I didn't want to be the first one to speak. I would be nonchalant. But after a few minutes, Paul showed no promise of talking. He seemed lost in thought, so I prompted, "Well?"

"Well, what?" Paul scratched his neck and found some of the napkin flakes but held them covertly so I wouldn't see.

"Are you going to *make naked dive* with Lee?" I mimicked Ono's accent.

Paul shook his head. "That Ono sure is a character. I think I'm jest not up to it, though. I feel a bit sick. I might jest have to barf up." He put a big hand over his abdomen, sliding two fingers under his belt.

I stepped quickly and cautiously to the side, just in case. Paul did look a little green, almost seasick. His face was puffy. "Drink some orange juice," I advised. "Or some coffee."

Paul swayed to his right, then recovered. "Are you gonna go with 'em tonight?"

I waited, gauging the answer for dramatic effect. Finally, when Paul looked most interested and even stopped walking, I spoke in a grave, determined voice. "Yes," I said. "I wouldn't miss it. The games are just beginning."

XV. THE FINAL YEN

THIRTEEN HOURS LATER—
SHINJUKU POLICE STATION, 5:46 A.M.

Keys jingled outside the door, and I was jolted awake. Somehow I must have fallen asleep in the tiny room. At first, I was disoriented. Then it came back—the sign, the fire, Ono, the hostess bar . . . A flash of anxiety ran through my body. This wasn't just a bad dream. This was reality. I wanted to turn back time, magically winding back the hands of a clock—or sink down through the linoleum floor and the concrete slab—into a science fiction time-travel tunnel, dilating gravitational fields, flowing back to yesterday afternoon, before this crisis. But of course, I couldn't change things. I couldn't reverse my past. I could only try and cope.

I gazed down at my left leg, exposed through the rip in my trousers. The kneecap and shin were covered in clotted blood, knotted and thick as red licorice. Along the bottom of the knee hung a thick flap of skin, half an inch at least, jagged and white on the bottom. Was that sub-dermal tissue? I shuddered.

More key jangling and scraping noises in the door lock . . . Couldn't they even figure out what key they used to lock me in? Then a pass key slipped in all the way, and the lock ground and turned. The door opened just a crack, revealing the harsh fluorescent light from the outer room. A head and eyes in horn-rimmed glasses peeked around the edge of the door. Then a white-cuffed hand slowly pushed the door open. An officer stepped in. He wore an open-collared uniform shirt and stared at me for a long time without speaking. He gazed briefly at my injured knee, but his expression was blank. Finally, he spoke, *"PASSUPORTO?"*

I took a deep breath. "It's at home. In my room." My head throbbed.

"You must bring it here," the officer commanded. But he stood back and opened the door wider.

I leaned forward. Was it true? Was it a trick? Cautiously, I raised my eyes. "I can leave?"

"Bring passport here," he demanded. "You must bring, passport by three o'clock today. That ees deadline. *Watashitachi wa anata mite imasu*," **We are watching you**.

I knew better than to ask any more questions. I stood up and limped step-by-painful-step out the door and across the outer room. I didn't look at anyone but felt the stares on my back. I peered only at my feet on the gray, pitted floor. Then I checked my direction. Down the hall—yes. To the stairwell—good. Squeezing the banister, hopping from stair to stair on my good leg, I made my slow exit.

Outside, there was a meager hint of daylight. After a few tortuous minutes' walk, I found myself at an empty intersection. A new sawing pain had started in my lower back. I spit, expectorating the stale station smell from my mouth. I rubbed my eyes with the bottom of my untucked shirt. Miraculously, a taxi drove past. I raised an arm to flag it down. Even more miraculously, the driver stopped to pick me up, to take in a bedraggled limping foreigner. Maybe there wasn't much business at this hour. "Ikebukuro station, west exit," I said, in a surprisingly firm voice. I didn't have the energy to attempt to explain the labyrinthine back streets to Sanjo boarding house itself. Besides, I didn't want the cab driver to know where I lived. Soon we were in Ikebukuro. It was daybreak. Flecks of sun shone through the clouds. I got out at the station, paid the driver, and struggled three circuitous blocks on my own to Sanjo. The filthy entryway greeted me like a beacon.

Upstairs, at the hall sink, I turned on the faucets and lifted my knee into the basin to wash the wound. I watched the water turn scarlet, swirl, and rush down the drain. I forced myself to rub the raw bleeding flesh, to pick out the specks of tar and pebbles, to rub away the grime. This hurt a lot, and I clenched my teeth as I scrubbed. I cursed the yakuza bar owner, the police, and especially my friends for abandoning me . . . I tried to force myself to relax, to take deep breaths, to clear my mind of animosity. Then I slammed a hand into the wall. Dammit—I wasn't a martyr! I deserved to be angry! I shut off the faucets. Even my fingers hurt.

Digging through my suitcase, I found two clean handkerchiefs, which I wrapped and tied around my knee. A nasty ache started at the bottom of my neck, and I rubbed the space between my shoulder blades. I remembered a bottle of Tylenol in a side pocket of the suitcase, poured out four tablets, and put them in my mouth. They were old and began to dissolve before I could muster enough saliva to swallow. The bitter acetaminophen burned my tongue. My eyelids hung down as if pulled by gravity, tugged by the center of the earth, drawn down by the Great Spirit which wanted all its creatures to relax, to calm themselves, to sleep . . . I dragged myself onto the futon bed and lay my body there.

I was supposed to leave for work soon. But I could barely move. I needed some sleep, just an hour at least. So I reached to set my alarm for 9:00 a.m. That would get me to the office by 10:30 a.m.—very late, but I didn't care. I pulled the yellowing pillow over my face and hugged it down around my ears.

My arms trembled, but soon my breaths evened out . . .

The buzz of the alarm jabbed like a big-needled injection. I felt a pounding in my sternum. I managed to get up and change into a wrinkled suit. Tucked into the bottom of my toiletry kit, wrapped in a pair of boxer shorts for good luck, I found my passport and stared down at the shiny blue cover with gold-embossed letters: **UNITED STATES OF AMERICA.** A surge of adrenaline pulsed through my arms. I slipped the passport into my pocket and hobbled outside.

At *Mosu-Burger*, the fast-food outlet on the corner, I ordered two coffees and two cups of water. Standing at the counter, right in front of the clerk and a line of astonished Japanese faces, I mixed my coffees and waters together, blending them like decanters from a chemistry class; systematically pouring a bit of coffee into a water glass, some of the mixture back into the coffee, the third mix into the water glass, again and again. I kept blending and pouring with a circular system until I had four glasses of cool coffee-water, easily guzzled—hopefully enough caffeine to get me through the morning. I drank exactly two of the glasses. Then I almost vomited, so I poured the third and fourth coffee-waters into the trash. Somehow I made it to the subway station and found a waiting *Yamanote*-line train. Inside, confined like a captive primate, I pressed my forehead against the window.

When I arrived at the office, the carpet was dotted with dead roaches—tannish-red bodies with jagged legs, desiccated and bent. I walked to my desk and heard the roaches crunch under foot. I didn't want to check to see if they had stuck to the soles of my shoes. I could smell the pesticide, the sickening fart-and-pepper odor which had driven the crazed insects out of the walls, out of their cabinet-back runways and supply-closet nests.

The office girl, Michiko, walked in from the hall. Her shiny black hair was draped over her shoulders. She was wearing her usual ironed jeans and T-shirt. She seemed to be the only other person in the building. Maybe everyone else had been wise enough to flee the stink and insect carcasses. Michiko found a broom and, with an industrious look, began to hunt stray insect bodies and sweep up the remains. Using rake-like strokes to reach under desks and chairs, she soon had a small mound of crumpled bodies and twisted antennae in her dustpan. She carried the pan over to the trash can and dumped it. I could hear the patter of dead insects as they hit the bottom of the metal can. I almost gagged.

I stood up, struggled over to the doorway, and was caught by another wave of fatigue. I leaned my head against the office door. The wood felt cool against my forehead. For a second, I fell asleep just standing there. Then a bolt of pain shot through my leg.

"*Daijobu?* Are you okay?" Michiko's soothing voice caught me off guard. I turned to look at her with what I knew must be a confused glance. I tried to collect myself, to blink away the sting in my eyes and force some coherence into my expression.

She took a step forward, the hurt and wonder in her eyes perhaps a mirror of my own. "Are you okay?" she asked again. Her cheeks trembled, and she looked like she might cry.

I tried to speak in a steady voice. "Just a knee injury, that's all."

She gasped. "*Daijobu?*" She took another step toward me, floating a slender hand in front of her as if she might reach out to touch me. But she didn't. The hand hovered a few inches away. Then, as graceful as a drifting bird, the hand descended to her side.

And so I told her. I didn't lie. I explained the whole story: the drinking and hostess clubs, the broken sign, the abandonment by my friends, the assault, the police station, and the blood—I didn't dwell too long on that, because at the work "*chi,*" blood, her face grew very pale. She didn't speak as I gave my account, but her eyes widened, and she let out a few gasps. "And so I'm supposed to bring back the passport today, if I can walk." Then bravely, I added, "I'm sure I'll be okay."

I looked down at the floor and couldn't help noticing that indeed a dead roach had stuck to the bottom of my shoe. Its half-body—

thorax, abdomen, antennae—protruded from under the sole. I lifted my head to look at Michiko instead, to gaze at her perfect hair, dark eyes, and flawless skin.

She blinked for several moments before speaking. Her words came forth in frustrated little bursts. "I wish—I wish, you could see . . . I wish, you knew . . . ," she said. Her eyes were tearing now, but somehow more distant, as if she were watching the scene from afar. She wrung her hands together, twisting her fingers. "I wish you would have good experience in Japan, and you could remember good experience. And you would tell—tell others about your good impressions."

As much as she wanted to, Michiko couldn't reverse what had happened. Not by hoping as hard as she could. Not by imagining that the events didn't occur. Not even by mustering the faith of a thousand years of Japanese group thinking. There was a saying: *The stain of one Japanese is erased by others.* Michiko yearned to erase the stain of my evening, to heal the bloody gash on my knee. But she couldn't do it. She was doomed to fail. And now her eyes had sunken.

Suddenly she looked up. There was a new glimmer of hope in her eyes. It was a final plea for forgiveness. "Do you like Japan?" she asked.

"Yes," I said. "I have learned many things here." I tried to smile as best I could, to force a sincere smile, although it still felt false on my face. Michiko's expression brightened too, a countenance perhaps as orchestrated as my own. Her mouth looped up at the edges and her forehead relaxed. Then she glanced down again at my knee where I had tied on the handkerchiefs. The fabric swelled around the leg like a swollen tourniquet.

"Your knee, eet is okay?" she asked.

Reluctantly, I gave the knee a bend and felt the deep anginal pain of the wound. I clenched my jaw again so I wouldn't grimace right in front of her. "Yes, maybe," I said. "Maybe it is only a small cut."

But the word *kirikizu*—"cut" sent Michiko into another spasm of an inhalation, and she clasped her hands again. "You should go to doctor," she said. "You should get medical *inten-shun.*"

"Okay," I nodded. But I knew I wouldn't go. I closed my eyes. The fumigation smell seemed weaker now, maybe less intense by the door. I bowed to Michiko as smoothly as I could. Then I staggered out the door.

The going was tough outside. The burning ache in my knee got worse with every step. I found a broken umbrella in a trash can and tried to use it as a cane, but the handle broke off, so I tossed the umbrella into the gutter. I only had a couple more blocks to go. No point in trying to get a taxi. All of the taxis were lined up far ahead. I would just keep hobbling along, dragging my bad foot toward *Ao-yama I-Chome*, the familiar twin towers which made a dark outline against the sky. Deep inside one of the towers was Ono's Restaurant Karina.

I walked unescorted into the main dining room of the restaurant, where the lights were dimmer than I recalled. I could see the brass plaque on the wall closest to me—a giant beetle with beating wings and hairy spurred legs. Then, far down the aisle in a circular corner booth, I saw two men hunched over a table. Their bodies were angled forward as if they had been shot in their backs. I recognized Ono's longish hair dangling over his brow. The crow-like profile of his face was supported by a bent hand and an elbow resting on the table. As I approached, I saw that Ishikawa sat at the table too. His arms were crossed, his fingers were clenched into fists, and his pudgy mouth was set in a scowl.

The men glanced up at me with looks of neither surprise nor expectation—but of resignation, as if the encounter was one they must have but would vastly prefer to decline.

I didn't bow. "Good day," I said.

With a murmur, Ishikawa returned the greeting, and Ono mumbled something. Then he looked away.

"You know, I had some difficulty last night," I began as gently as I could. "After you left, I—"

"I know, I know," Ono interrupted. "We were contacted by police."

"What did the honorable police say?" I asked, without hiding my scorn.

"They are conducting investigation about the sign," answered Ishikawa. "They went to your office this morning. Now they are interviewing hostesses in the bar, and management."

A burst of anger shot through me. I spoke too loudly, then lowered my voice. "THAT MAKES NO SENSE. The girls couldn't have seen anything. They were underground. There were no windows." I spoke faster, "What kind of investigation is this? It's a bogus investigation," I scoffed. "It's a frame-up."

"This cannot be helped," said Ono, with an unsympathetic twitch of his chin. He turned to peer at me as if about to ask a question. Then he hesitated and merely said one word—*"Demo . . ."* But . . . It was a lingering conjunction, an insinuation that hung in the air like a noose.

My stomach burned. I took a step forward to tell them again that the investigation wasn't legal. That we were being set up, that it wasn't fair—but "fair" was a relative term here, as I had learned. So I closed my mouth.

"You didn't do it?" asked Ishikawa. "You didn't break the sign?"

"NO," I said with some force. "I heard it fall, turned around, and saw Ono near it." I realized that I had forgotten to use the polite suffix *"-san,"* but I didn't care. "I saw some sparks and smoke coming from the sign, and there was a fire on the ground. So I stamped it out, and then the manager ran out and blamed me."

Ishikawa hissed. "Maybe you touched sign with your clothing, and you did not know." He nodded as if he were patiently explaining the obvious answer to a juvenile delinquent. I stared at Ono, who turned away and gazed down at his plate of uneaten shrimp and noodles. His hands lay in his lap. His cheeks had fallen. He wouldn't look at me. Clearly, ours had only been a temporary friendship, in business and drinking. When the chips were down, he had abandoned me like an annoying dog left to fend for itself.

I leaned forward to see Ono's face, to catch a glimpse of his eyes. "Did YOU touch the sign?" I asked him. "Did you knock it over?"

Ishikawa shivered at the directness of my questions, but then he also turned to look at Ono and said something in a few muttered syllables that I couldn't understand.

"I don't remember," said Ono. "I don't remember anything." But I thought I saw a faint glint of recognition in Ono's eye, a tiny revelation of shame. Soon it disappeared.

There was silence for a while. Ono toyed with his chopsticks— very rude, I knew. Ishikawa folded his arms again and sat back like a judge presiding at a witch trial. The pain in my leg was fierce, but I didn't want to sit down. I didn't want to sit in the same booth as these guys.

Ishikawa spoke again. "The bar owner wants twelve million, five hundred thousand yen to replace his sign. You cannot pay?"

The blood surged in my temples. I had been found guilty already, even by my friends. Just like the *yakuza* and the police. "No, I can't pay!" I almost shouted. "I wouldn't pay even if I could. The bar manager will pay. For an assault! For a criminal offense. I'm calling the American consulate and the American embassy!" I stomped on the floor with my good, uninjured right foot.

Ishikawa shook his head. He pushed aside his glass and gave me a tight-lipped look of pure mistrust.

Ono frowned. "Bar manager is *yakuza*," he said, as if finally admitting the terrible truth. "He is a <u>fox</u>. A fox . . ." he repeated and screwed up his face into an evil leer like that of the mythologically cruel Japanese fox.

"He will pay," I said, with tremendous confidence, with the certainty of a religious affirmation. The righteousness coursed through my blood. "He will pay for hurting me." I grasped my thigh. "You know, the American government specializes in protecting its citizens," I announced, scanning Ono's and Ishikawa's expressions. They didn't look too convinced, so I spoke louder. "The American Government protects its people. It has a special division for this kind of trouble, for defending its citizens. It's called the, the—" My mind raced, what division? "The CIA!" I declared. And without another word, I turned and left the two men there just as I had found them—hunched and worried, pathetic and treacherous.

Back at the office, everyone else was still out. Even Michiko was gone. Perhaps the pesticide odor had been too much even for her. Inhaling it made my headache even worse, so I tried to take shallow breaths. I had to focus . . . Digging through my briefcase, rifling through advertising samples and candy bar wrappers, I found my map book. The cover was ripped now, but there was a listing of embassies and telephone numbers in the back. Flipping through the pages, running a dirty index finger down the columns, I searched and found the American Embassy—damn right! And there were even subheadings: Visas, Importation, Taxation, Disputes. Hell yes, I had a dispute! With shaking fingers, I dialed the number. "Consulate Department Twelve, Jack Pigott speaking," answered a pure, Midwestern voice.

"Hello!" I said, forcing the quaver out of my tone. "I had some trouble last night," I began. "I need some advice." And I told the story exactly from start to finish—the bar, the sign, the police, my knee, the night in jail. "And, frankly," I concluded, "I'm concerned. I'm very concerned. The *yakuza* are involved, and God knows what they'll do . . ."

"Well," said Pigott, and there was a new timbre in his voice, a smugness which I hadn't heard before. "You know, in any country, there are underworld elements, just like in the United States. But Japan is certainly a functional system. In any society, there are some exceptions, but the Tokyo police department is quite competent and . . ."

I wanted to slam down the phone. What kind of administrative rhetoric was this? I wanted a real answer. I needed real assistance! You'd think they'd have a good old boy at the consulate, ready to help you out. But I forced myself to listen. I had to listen.

". . . And you need to prepare a case, just like in America. You should contact an attorney and have a doctor certify your injuries. Develop medical evidence for your case during the investigation."

Here I cut him off. "—It's not an investigation! Don't you see? They're interviewing people who have no knowledge about the incident. Prostitutes who were underground when the sign fell. And there were no windows. They'll say exactly what the cops and the *yakuza* want to hear. How is that a functional system?"

Pigott waited for a moment before speaking, then continued in a monotone, totally ignoring my outburst. He went on as if he were a tape recording. "And so during the investigation and the booking, you should—"

"The *booking*?" I protested, and the phone dug into my ear. "Will I be put in prison? I didn't even do anything wrong."

Pigott let out an effete whinny of a laugh. "Oh, don't worry," he said. "The police are very thorough. And we'll send someone to visit you in jail, from time to time."

"Well, that's just wonderful." The disgust colored my words like mold on a greeting card. A pressure built in my chest. "Don't forget at dinner . . ." I said.

"Excuse me?" said Pigott.

"AMERICANS EAT WITH A GODDAMN FORK!" And with that, I slammed down the phone.

I took a deep breath and lifted my sweaty hand from the receiver. I had just hung up on my only connection, maybe my only chance. I was completely sapped of energy. I was exhausted, weary, and alone. For a long moment, I sat there immobile, conscious only of my breathing and my heartbeat.

Then I made the decision.

I had to get out! Right away. The police said they were *watching* me, but what did that actually mean? I glanced out the window to check if there was any surveillance. I didn't see anyone—no police cars, no uniformed officers, no binoculars . . . But that didn't prove much. All I knew was that I had to get the hell out of Japan—somehow. I couldn't let myself be put in prison. I had to *escape*. The police obviously didn't expect that, or they wouldn't have let me out. They assumed I would toe the line and comply, that I would just calmly accept my fate . . . And it was suddenly very ironic that all of my efforts to fit into Japanese society—to bow at the right times, to say the right things, to work hard, to become a member of the company family with a company pin—all of this might have provided my secret ticket out! Unknowingly, the police had given me a chance. I had to take it! I knew that with the clarity of a cold, clear winter day. And then I hoped . . .

But there was no time for hope.

Sixty-six and a half minutes later, back at my room in Sanjo, I rifled through my bags of clothes and belongings. In my knapsack, I found my plane ticket—thank God I had the foresight to get an open-ended return. I stepped out into the hall and lifted the receiver from the bulbous pink phone, a 1970's remnant. I dialed the Tokyo number for United Airlines on my ticket sleeve. "Reservations," came the metallic female voice. It almost sounded computerized.

I put as much urgency into my voice as I could muster without seeming insane, without yelling. "Yes! This is an emergency, a family emergency! I have a ticket with a variable return to Los Angeles. I have to leave immediately!" I held my breath while the operator checked my name on the computer, clicking keys on a computer terminal. But she didn't say anything for a while. Then the line went dead. Was I just on hold? My arms shook. I had to calm down. I had to relax. Where was the operator? Another click. A series of beeps . . .

"I'm sorry, sir, we can't find your name in our system. Did you purchase the ticket through a Japanese office?"

"No, I bought it in America."

"One moment."

But it was more than a moment. It was seven or eight minutes. It was an eternity of gasping and grasping and clicking. Finally, there was another beep as the attendant returned to the line. "Sir, what time can you be at the airport?"

I smiled. I felt the moisture in my eyes—but I wasn't crying, right? No . . . It was just an irritation. "I'll be there in two hours."

I scanned my room with a fluttering gaze, the frantic sweep of a man abandoning his home to fire. I only needed two things that were irreplaceable: my portable electric piano and my passport. And maybe a carry-on bag to make it look official. Like I wasn't a war-torn escaping prisoner, a convict on the lam. I counted all my money, even the rest of my "emergency fund" tucked under the insoles of my shoes. Only 11,000 yen, about ninety dollars. Not enough to take a taxi all the way to Narita Airport, but enough to get there by bus. Maybe the taxi drivers had all been put on the look-out for me, so the bus might be better anyways. Of course, my fleeing the scene would be interpreted as an admission of guilt for breaking the sign— so what? I didn't care. They had already found me guilty. I just had to leave.

Could I even get out of Japan? Had they already tracked me and put a hold on my passport at the airport? It had only been a few hours since I left the police station—Were they red-flagging my pass-port number right now? How long would that take? All the police had to do was talk to my boss or one of the secretaries, and they could get the passport number . . . But maybe everyone was still out of the office because of the smell—the pesticide itself might save me. Maybe not. I had to get on that plane as soon as possible.

Did I leave anything important at the office? One sport coat— but I didn't need that. Let them throw it out, toss it away with the memories of my employment. Surely, they would see me as a bad seed, a turncoat foreigner, untrustworthy at heart. But in the end, they had to excuse me. They had to grant clemency to my name. I was never expected to fit in.

The hall phone rang, a searing buzz of a ring. Instinctively I went to pick up the phone. I took the heavy receiver in my hand—and knew just then that I shouldn't have answered. But it was too late. Without saying a word, I pressed the phone to my ear. Then I gave in and uttered a single word, "Hullo."

There was a stream of rapid Japanese from a demanding male voice. "*Kori wa Tokyo Keisatsu desu. Watashitachiha gaikoko hito kyoju-sha o sagashitimasu.*" This is Tokyo police. We are looking for a foreign resident—Then I heard my name.

"I don't speak Japanese," I said, and hung up the phone. Just like that.

The police were already searching for me. They had found out where I lived . . . Had they called the taxi companies to get my location information from this morning? Did the detective decide that the officer made a mistake letting me out? Were they coming to Sanjo right now to take me back to jail?

Somewhere in the distance, a police siren sounded, and my arms went weak. I hurried back to my room to finish packing. What else did I need? I had to clear my mind. What else should I take? A pen, maybe. My wallet. Watch. Glasses . . . I ran down the stairs and dashed out the door.

Outside it was raining. The drops were soothing at first, then turned cold and oily. I grabbed a newspaper from a trash bin, checked to make sure there was no spittle or urine on it, and held the paper above my head as I headed to Ikebukuro Plaza Hotel, toward the Airport bus that would take me home. I didn't have to give my name to buy a bus ticket. I would keep my head down when I got on the bus and turn away from the driver—so he couldn't see who was taking a seat.

Along the sidewalk in front of the liquor store, the soil in the banzai tree pots was muddy and foamy. A tiny little frog, no bigger than a penny, crawled to the rim of a pot and waited—throat trembling, chest beating. Then it dove off onto the sidewalk. In a few furious jumps, springing seventy times its body length with each, the frog made its frantic way between two buildings and disappeared.

When I was much younger, in third grade, a friend and I had crept under a bridge where there was a drainage pipe and thousands of tiny frogs like these. We had collected a whole pail of the little creatures, hundreds of them, brought them home, and dumped all of the frogs into the bathtub. Then we left to watch television. But when we returned, all of the frogs had escaped—vanished entirely from the bathroom. They were nowhere to be found. And the doors and windows had been closed. None of the frogs were under the sink or behind the toilet. None were in the towel rack or on the windowsill. And the stopper was in the bathtub drain. Where did the frogs go? They had made a *miraculous* escape, an ascension into thin air. They must have hated their new home, confined by the rigid glistening white walls of the tub. So they departed. Without a trace.

I walked faster, swinging my legs as far as possible without actually running. I couldn't run—or else I might be spotted. My knee hurt like hell. The wound had opened. It was bleeding again. I could feel the blood dripping down my calf. My arm ached from holding the newspaper over my head, so I threw the paper down and let myself get wet, let the rain refresh me—cleansing, dousing, re-baptizing . . . I slipped and almost fell in some grease on the pavement. But I recovered and stared down at the wet toes of my shoes as I walked. The dampness crept up my socks.

Then I saw it—a squashed body! A tiny lifeless form with red and yellow internal organs exposed. It was the popped remains of a little frog on the sidewalk. I didn't stop.

At the hotel, I bought my bus ticket and waited outside under an awning for twenty minutes until the next bus arrived. I stood next to a potted maple tree, out of sight. I shivered. My forehead burned. But I couldn't wait in the warm hotel lobby—I had to avoid any unnecessary contact or surveillance cameras. So I stayed outside, like a soldier standing watch. There was a rack of free Japanese magazines. I saw my company's magazine, Tokyo Time. But I didn't want that one. I took another and held it in front of my face.

At long last, the bus arrived. It was a gleaming silver with huge wheels and double-bladed wipers scraping at the windshield. I was first in line at the door—I kept my head down. Then I took a seat at exactly the mid-point of the bus, which seemed the most inconspicuous place. I wouldn't get caught now, right? How could they have traced me in the streets? Would there be a detailed emigration check at the airport? I had to leave very quickly. Maybe there would only be light traffic, and the bus could travel fast . . . I had to disappear. If I made it on the plane, in a few more hours and a couple hundred miles, I would be in international territory, on an American-owned airline. Then they couldn't get me, right?

My heart was beating rapidly. I had to relax and look calm. I unzipped the piano case slightly and slid in my hand to run my fingers over the keys, to think about happy hours of music . . . Out of my peripheral vision, I caught a man's glance—a Japanese passenger across the aisle with a triangular face and cold stare. Quickly, I zipped up the case and gazed straight ahead. I sat perfectly still.

The bus was out of the city now, passing through a marsh with reeds and trees. After fifteen minutes, we headed over a tall bridge. I slid open the bus window as far as it would go. A gust of rain splattered on my arm, and the cold, wet air slapped at my face. I took a deep breath and looked down into the street far below: There were

hundreds of pedestrians scurrying back and forth. An ocean of umbrellas. If you squinted, they were sea organisms, bryozoans, ink dots
. . .

I shut the window and sank back into the dampness of my seat. The slick vinyl of the seat cushion stuck to my thighs like glue. I barely moved a muscle for thirty or forty minutes at least, until I rolled my neck, so it didn't get too stiff to move. That was okay, right? That wouldn't attract any extra attention. All Japanese rolled their necks.

Abruptly, the bus stopped. It screeched to a halt in the middle of a wide street. Five or six uniformed airport policemen stood lining the sidewalk. My throat tightened, and my chest constricted—I breathed through my nose. The policemen boarded the bus, blocking the door. They stalked up the center aisle. *"Passuporto! Ryoken!"* they demanded, in clipped voices. "**EVERYONE OUTSIDE!**"

I didn't want to be first. I hated to go out at all. I wanted to let the sick weight in my abdomen drag me to the floor, through the bus chassis, and deep down into a hole in the earth . . . I let a good many passengers go ahead of me and finally, unsteadily, pulled myself up. What would the Japanese newspapers say? What the headlines would read? "**Escaping American Caught On Bus**" or "**Caught! Foreign Criminal On The Run**!" But then I felt oddly calm and resigned. There was nothing more I could do now. I had done my best.

The police officers had set up tables outside a precinct office. They told the bus passengers to line up. I had to choose a line right away, or I would stand out. I chose one—and stood behind the most attractive female passenger. She wore a pink raincoat and matching pink boots. At the table, she was quickly released and sent back to the bus. Then it was my turn. I stepped up to the table and held out my passport before the guard could say anything. But he still demanded, *"PASSUPORTO!"* His black eyes seared through me. I stared back, gathered my reserve. If I was going to get arrested and go to prison, dammit, I would do it right. With a burst of final glory, standing tall and proud. *Grace under pressure* . . . Slowly, I pulled the passport from my pocket. I was squinting now. My irises burned.

The officer opened my passport and glared at it. He stared at it for a long time. Then he slapped the passport shut and handed it back. I was free to go! Or so it seemed. I tried not to smile. Maybe the airport police were an entirely separate division. Maybe they didn't receive my name yet . . . Maybe their stupid fax machine was broken . . . I could only hope.

But at least, for now, I could continue on the bus to the airport. It wasn't much longer. In ten more minutes, I was at the Narita Airport bus depot, with long lines of buses, side-by-side. And soon, I was out in the rain again, limping toward one of the heavy chrome doors of the airline terminal, taking a deep breath. I stood still for a moment and closed my eyes—one last rest before the end.

I bought no gum or candy for the plane ride. I bought no magazines. I didn't even use the restroom. I went straight to the desk and showed my ticket. "Where is your luggage?" the airline attendant asked.

"Oh, just carry-on," I said, and heard the loudness of my breathing.

The girl frowned and, with two fingers, pointed the direction to the Departures terminal. "Your plane is already boarding at gate five," she said, as if somehow I should have known this.

I hurried toward the gate. At the emigration desk, the clerk scrutinized my passport, grunting and tilting his head, sighing as if he had never seen such a document. He flipped the pages back and forth, ogling my visa stamp, peering at the entrance date, looking up something in a thick book—he was taking too long! The plane would leave! Slowly, he typed some numbers into a computer terminal. More eternal waiting while the man gazed as if mesmerized by the computer screen. For some odd reason, he didn't need to blink.

At last, the computer let out an electronic gong, a musical approbation. I exhaled as the guard waved me through the metal detectors. But then suddenly he was shouting at me, stomping up next to me, touching my shoulder—*"Matte!"* Wait!

My chest pounded like a jackhammer.

"YOU MAY NOT ENTER BOARDING AREA. YOU MUST COME THIS WAY." A sick heaviness grew in the pit of my stomach as I followed the sloping shoulders of the guard back through the metal detector, back over to the desk, back to the computer . . . *"PASSUPORTO!"* he demanded again.

I considered running—a quick sprint through the doors—a wild dash out the emergency exit . . . But obediently, I handed back the passport. My arm was stiff. My fingers were numb. My head was a thick concrete block.

Will you be returning to Japan?" the guard asked, staring down at my visa.

"NO." I spoke too quickly though. "—I don't think so," I added.

Then the guard pummeled my passport with a big red stamp the size of a mallet, and handed the passport back, cover bent. I was free again, at least free to board the plane. But it would be only a few more minutes until I would be in the air, liberated . . .

I found my seat on the plane and buckled in tightly. I folded my hands and leaned back, watching the other passengers search for their seat numbers amidst endless shuffling and luggage storage. Finally, everyone found their places, and I allowed myself a small breath of relief—only a little one, though. It was still premature. I just wanted the plane to get in the air, to get the hell off the ground.

Two Japanese stewardesses walked by, and I was told to fasten my seat belt, even though it was already fastened. I said nothing. Behind me, Japanese businessmen were speaking loudly and laughing— something about whiskey and business. I forced myself to ignore them, to think of a sandy beach at sunset. That was a good technique, right? To think of beautiful things. To seek these things out . . . Then, with a shiver, I remembered the lyrics from a very old Japanese folk song:

> *Life is fleeting*
> *Follow your passions*
> *While your lips have color*
> *Before your desires fade*
> *There is no such thing as Tomorrow . . .*

These words had fit in so well with my Japanese dream, my justification to simply leave America and go to live in Japan. Now, just as well—and possibly even better—they justified my return.

But why was the plane taking so long? Why were we just sitting on the runway? This wasn't normal. The airport security couldn't be checking on me now, could they? Had the office re-opened to answer the phone and give the police my passport and visa number? Were the police holding up the plane? What would I do if officers boarded the plane looking for me? Should I make a run for the emergency exit, pop the door, and burst out the inflatable exit slide? That would get international attention! Maybe someone in the U.S. would help me then. Or maybe it would just increase my Japanese jail time . . . Tough decision.

Sharp pains stabbed at my knee, but I couldn't ask for Tylenol—that might cause a scene. Someone might see my bleeding leg. I had to keep a low profile. I had to force myself not to think about bad scenarios . . . Maybe, just maybe, I would be okay.

Finally, joyously, miraculously—the gift of ages—the jet engines were whining and torquing. The plane began to move, and, slowly, we picked up speed until we were shooting along the runway . . . And then the plane lifted into the air. I smiled. I gripped the armrests as hard as I could. We were up in the sky now, under the cloud cover. Below us were little toy houses and cars and tiny trees. I didn't want to look anymore. I closed my eyes, kept them shut. I didn't know for how long. Ten minutes? Twenty minutes? I waited until the plane had leveled out, until everything was gentle and horizontal.

I ignored the passing clank of drink carts and forced myself not to listen to the grate of landing gear stowing up inside the wing. I waited, meditating in the reddish darkness behind my eyelids until the danger was past; until we were far away from Tokyo—in international air.

The captain's voice, in English, came on to say something about cruising altitude, fair skies, and fortuitous trade winds. I blinked once, twice, three times, at the sun flickering through the windows. It warmed the damp spots on my shirt. I felt the pressure of my piano wedged against my ankles under the seat in front of me. And because it seemed like a good idea, I zipped open the case, pulled out the keyboard, and played a few notes with the volume very low. I felt better now. The soft electronic tones were soothing, and the plastic keys were smooth and familiar under my fingers. I pulled out the piano and began to play a tune.

Like a vision, a hallucination, a blonde stewardess was standing beside me. Her long legs almost touched my shoulder. Her hand lay on top of the seat, a few inches from my cheek. "You're having fun, aren't you?" she said, with a Pepsodent smile.

"Now I am."

"What kind of instrument is that?" She leaned closer.

I played a series of triplets.

"Ooh," she shivered.

"It's the kind of instrument you play in an airplane to lure over passing stewardesses. Is it *stewardesses* or *stewardi?*"

She didn't answer but kept looking down at the keyboard in my lap. I ran a hand across it, stroking the keys as if demonstrating a prize.

"That's a nice piano," she said. "Cool . . ."

"You can try it if you want."

"No, I don't play." She shook her head nervously, as if I had asked her to play strip poker.

"Just try," I coaxed, holding up the piano. "Just touch a key . . ."

She looked doubtful, bit her lip, and leaned back.

I smiled. "You have to try, or you won't know. Here, just play these notes . . ." I pointed to the first three keys of a C-minor scale.

And then she couldn't resist. With a look of great concentration, she leaned over and pressed a red fingernail upon a key. I could smell her faint perfume. But she didn't straighten up right away. She played a few more notes, sliding her fingers in the grooves between the black and white notes, rubbing them, testing them.

"Sit down," I offered. "I'll teach you a duet—Oh, you're on duty. I forgot."

"No," she said quickly. "I'm just getting a ride back. I'm off duty."

I didn't need a neon sign. "Here," I said, and patted the empty seat next to me.

Obediently she squeezed into the row and sat down, folding her skirt so it didn't rise too far up her thighs.

"Okay, this is how it works," I explained patiently, easily. "I give you three notes. You can play them in any order you want. You can make up any combination. It doesn't matter that it hasn't been played before. It just has to sound good to you. And these notes always sound good."

She nodded, and I set my hand over hers to show her the keys. With my left hand, I kept a bass line going, and she giggled. Her laughter itself was trinkling music, far more melodic than the electronic piano tones. We played four bars of a quick tune. I looked again at my stewardess, at her pretty eyes and golden hair. Behind her, out the window, the clouds formed a blanket, glinting orange and pinks in the setting sun.

"Okay," I said. "Let's try it again now. From the beginning . . ."

ABOUT THE AUTHOR

R. Sebastian Bennett was born in New York City and grew up in California. He attended Columbia University, the University of Southern California, and the University of Louisiana – Lafayette, where he was awarded a Doctoral Regents Fellowship.

Bennett worked as an Advertising Representative in Tokyo in the late 1980's. Later, he founded the literary journal, THE SOUTHERN ANTHOLOGY, and taught Fiction Writing at UCLA, University of Louisiana, and Muskingum University, where he directed the Creative Writing Program. Bennett's work is widely published in magazines, including *The Brooklyn Review*, *Columbia Journal*, *Fiction International*, *Los Angeles Review*, *New World Writing*, *Paris Transcontinental-*Sorbonne (FRANCE), *The Bombay Review* and *Modern Literature* (INDIA), *The Galway Review* (IRELAND), *Alécart* (ROMANIA), and *Equus* (ENGLAND), *and many others*.

Learn more at rsebastianbennett.com.